This Place is Magic

Also by Irene Te

THIS SONG IS OURS

THIS PLACE IS MAGIC

Irene Te

RABBIT YEAR PRESS
HOUSTON

This one's for Ayana — I spade you

1

By the time Eunjae found the door, his brothers were already piling into a van outside their hotel. A plain black van with windows like portholes reflecting the abyss of deep space. No one could see inside its dim interior, where it was widely assumed that all were accounted for: their manager, a stylist, three members of the global K-pop juggernaut known as Apollo. But, as the travelers would realize shortly after reaching the airport, one person was missing. That person was Eunjae.

Eunjae didn't care about any of this, though. Not then. Dusk had fallen in strokes of blue violet that seeped across the sky and down the sides of buildings. The city seemed different, now — softer, kinder. In the glow of the streetlights, he noticed things he'd somehow missed in the glaring illumination of day. The number of people walking hand in hand, for example, and a popsicle tumbled to the sidewalk, bleeding out on the concrete in a glorious shade of magenta. He had a disposable camera and an unfounded certainty that the others were somewhere just around the next bend. Eunjae was beyond all his usual concerns.

Besides, he'd found the door.

It was an orange door set with four panes of stained glass. The paint was almost a perfect match for the fancy orange and almond gelato he'd chosen for dessert, which had to be a good omen.

In Eunjae's favorite book, there was a door that looked a lot like this one. Long before he left Australia for Korea, and even before his existence became a blur of voice lessons and dance classes, he'd been searching for that door. A gateway to magic.

Some part of Eunjae had continued to believe that such a threshold existed, that it could be found if he only remained faithful to his quest. It was a part of him that had been sleeping for a decade or more. Now, coming upon that door on a balmy summer evening, Eunjae suddenly felt wide awake.

He hadn't felt that way in a long time. The quest returned to him, tart and vibrant as a burst of citrus, and Eunjae wondered where his copy of *The Brass Key* had gone.

That battered mass market paperback used to be his most constant companion. He could see it in his mind's eye even as light hewed through the stained glass, casting a miniature aurora onto his clothes. When was the last time he held the book in his hands? There was never any time, and when he had the time, there wasn't energy to spare. He made a mental note to look for it anyway, once he got back to Seoul. The door in the story would still be there, waiting for him to turn the knob and step through.

In the meantime, the door he'd discovered in real life had flown open. Eunjae breathed in a gust of sugar-scented air, warm despite the roaring AC, tinged with top notes of fried dough. And on the threshold, staring expectantly at him, was a girl brandishing the most gigantic waffle Eunjae had ever seen.

This place is magic, he thought to himself then. It wouldn't be the last time.

The girl in the doorway smiled at Eunjae. "Coming in? You'll never guess, but we've got waffles."

She pointed to the sign mounted above the orange door. He took a step back, craning his neck to read. Hanging slightly crooked, it featured two words in looping electric blue script: WANNA WAFFLE. Not a question, but a fact. For emphasis, the period at the end was styled to look like a waffle, perfectly round and graced with a pat of butter.

"It's Waffle Wednesday for another twenty-ish minutes. Here, I've got that." She propped the door open with her foot and Eunjae went inside. Why not? They didn't need to be back at the hotel until 8:00. At least, that's what Eunjae remembered from their manager's speech that morning. In any case, wasn't the hotel just a few blocks away? Surely he didn't have to rush anywhere just yet. Surely he could stop to see what was behind this door.

"Waffle Wednesday," he mused, tugging his mask more securely over the bottom half of his face. Turning to the girl who had welcomed him, Eunjae asked the first question that rolled into his head, quickly translating it from Korean to English. "What's Waffle Wednesday?"

2

"**O**h, well. If you want the full marketing speech, I'll have to go get my brother. Long story short, it's free waffles for two hours every Wednesday night." The girl offered Eunjae the waffle she'd been carrying around. "Our signature waffle," she clarified. "As many as you want before time's up. Everything else on the menu is discounted, too."

Eunjae realized at this moment that his new acquaintance was not at all dressed like the other employees behind the counter. For one thing, her orange apron was layered on top of a blazer patterned in bright red poppies. The red and orange clashed with such exuberant cheer that it had the air of something deliberate. And there were the tiny flowers somehow suspended amid the strands of her dark hair, which fell in waves over both shoulders. Who was she? The owner, maybe? Someone who wandered in from a movie set?

He took the waffle and allowed himself to be settled at a table in the corner, far from any windows or the main entrance. Before she swiveled to answer a question from another customer, Eunjae caught sight of the name *Emma* embroidered on the orange apron. And underneath this, another name in Hangeul: *Han Jiyeon*.

Despite having eaten dinner plus dessert less than an hour ago, Eunjae went to work on that signature waffle with a vengeance. No one was around to stop him. The waffle was delicious, in part because he wasn't supposed to eat it. His manager would be aghast, but she wasn't here, and stepping through the orange door had roused some long dormant spirit of rebellion. It was Waffle Wednesday and Eunjae was going to enjoy this waffle, which had the perfect combination of slightly crisp edges and fluffy texture. Just the barest hint of lemon came through, bright as a drop of sunlight. More magic.

Perhaps ten minutes before Waffle Wednesday came to a close, Eunjae got up to order another free waffle at the counter. He still had a bit of cash in his pocket from splitting that gelato with Jungwoo earlier, so he added a scoop of vanilla ice cream too. He might not be back in this area for a while, if ever. He might as well.

It was Jiyeon who brought it over, along with a glass of water. She sat down in the empty chair across from Eunjae, opened her mouth as if to make small talk, then suddenly paused to study his face. The mask dangled from his right ear. He'd taken it off to eat.

Eunjae's heart clawed right out of his ribcage and up into his throat. Had she guessed already?

He took this opportunity to stuff a giant bite of signature waffle into his mouth. He was determined to chew forever. As long as it took for her scrutiny to break, for something else to snag her attention. Eunjae wasn't about to give his identity away, not when he'd gone the whole trip without being recognized. If only it was possible to devour his second helping with the face mask still on. Would that be weird?

That would be extremely weird, scolded a voice in his head. *Don't you dare do that. Be normal!* Eunjae shuddered reflexively even though this rebuke was a fabrication of his mind. Did the voice of his conscience have to sound so much like his eldest brother?

Really, it wasn't fair. In cartoons they had pudgy angels and miniature devils perched on their shoulders, whispering advice in characters' ears. Eunjae got to have an echo of Jeon Jaehwan that lived inside his head and occasionally berated him just like he did at dance practice.

What would the most terrifying of his brothers say right now? How would Jaehwan handle this question?

I wouldn't have wandered off in the first place, supplied the invisible Jaehwan in tones of deep disappointment. *You could get caught. You know what would happen then.*

Eunjae lowered his head a little. At least his hair was longer now, and it had been mostly restored to its original color at last, no longer dyed deep purple all over. Maybe this would help him avoid being recognized right away. The borrowed bucket hat further obscured Eunjae's looks from immediate view. He chewed some more. Then, deciding it would be suspicious otherwise, he made himself glance up at Jiyeon and shrug.

She tapped a fingernail on the plastic tumbler she'd set down in front of him. "Hmm."

Invisible Jaehwan waved his arms wildly. *Misdirection, misdirection, misdirection!* "Is it Emma," asked Eunjae, "or Jiyeon? Both?"

"You can read that? I wish I could. My brother did the apron order and I had to trust that this actually spelled out my name." She smiled at him. "It's both, I suppose. Depends on who I'm talking to or where I am. But here at the shop, it's just Jiyeon."

Eunjae nodded. He understood what it was like to have two names.

"Let's see," Jiyeon said, then. "You look like your name might be…

Ryan."

"Ryan? Really?" He had to laugh. "Why?"

"I can't explain. You just have the aura of a Ryan. Super nice Ryan Kim who's in town for his sister's wedding and plays tennis on Sundays."

"Tennis."

"Yeah. Doubles, with your cousin. He's a sore loser but you love him anyway. And you live in... San Bernardino. That's a little over an hour from here." Jiyeon squinted at him in an exaggerated manner. "You wear glasses while reading. You'll read anything, but only one book at a time. Your mom still buys you an ice cream cake for every birthday. And after this, you'll stay up way too late with your sister even though you're both supposed to be up early for a big family breakfast."

"Why are we staying up so late?"

"Talking. She's getting married in a few days. She'll be feeling nostalgic. Trust me, my sister was the same way." Here, Jiyeon glanced over Eunjae's shoulder, waving at a customer on their way out. "You know what else, Ryan Kim? She'll want to look at all the old photo albums. It'll be fun. You haven't seen those in forever."

Eunjae leaned back in his chair, considering. "But will I cry at the wedding?"

"A little. What kind of monster doesn't cry at noona's wedding?"

"You're right."

"About which part?"

"All of it. You know everything about me. There's nothing more to tell."

Jiyeon flashed him another dimpled smile. She seemed about to say something else, but then another person in an orange apron lumbered out of the kitchen. An older man, squarely into his late sixties but built like some of the bodyguards Eunjae had met and worked with on countless occasions. He had the bearing of a warlord in full armor and the smudge of batter on his stubbled cheek did nothing to detract from that impression. With a grin, this formidable personage reached over to bang on a gong that sat near the register.

"All done! No more Waffle Wednesday! Thank you!"

3

E unjae set his fork down on the plate, wondering if this announcement meant the place was closing for the night. He didn't have a chance to ask Jiyeon, though. As if summoned by the gong, a younger, similarly built fellow popped his head through the swinging kitchen doors. He'd looped the orange apron around his neck like a towel. "Dad, what the heck," he bawled out. "You do this every night!"

Across from Eunjae, Jiyeon snorted.

"What? It's done! How else are they supposed to know?"

"Because they can tell time?"

Jiyeon rose from her chair. "My brother," she whispered to Eunjae. Louder, she said, "Okay, Denny. Let it go. We've still got customers."

"They can't hear me. It's fine." Denny entered the room like a tectonic disturbance. Barrel-chested, wearing jeans that may or may not have been ironed, he displaced the very atmosphere with his presence. Scowling, he pointed at the gong. "That," he hissed at his father, "is for display purposes only."

"This is what you're worried about? You think I'll break the stupid gong?" The older man muttered something under his breath. Then he caught sight of Eunjae, who was transfixed by this tableau and still had a forgotten forkful of waffle in transit to his mouth.

"You!" the man exclaimed, beaming so widely that his whole face was transformed. "Where have I seen you before?"

This was a difficult question to answer, and not just because Eunjae couldn't afford to be honest. Apollo was an international phenomenon. He and his brothers had starred in their own Netflix documentary, endorsed a staggering number of brands both individually and collectively, and had sold out two global arena tours in the past five years alone. There was at least one bus in Bangkok with their faces on it, plus three hotels in Tokyo with Apollo-themed luxury suites. For their last single with all nine members present, Apollo had performed on multiple American talk shows. Record-breaking, critically acclaimed, they were known as one of the most successful K-pop acts of the past decade.

Case in point, this man could've seen him anywhere. Maybe even some kid's lunch box.

Thinking about all of this left Eunjae feeling so fatigued that he wanted to curl up on the spot and take a thousand-year nap. That kind of thing happened frequently in the world of *The Brass Key*. It ought to be socially acceptable in the real world, too.

Thankfully, Denny saved him from having to respond. "And don't announce that Waffle Wednesday is over!" he scolded his father, carrying on as if he'd never been interrupted. "I told you, we start the Closing Countdown five minutes before special pricing ends. It goes up on the TV like those New Year's Eve countdowns. I even showed you!"

"I couldn't make it play!"

"Then why didn't you ask Yeonnie? She's right there!"

A belligerent huff. "I'm not speaking to your sister about anything. Not until she says sorry."

Jiyeon took a deep breath, then exhaled slowly through her nose. She marched over to the counter and jabbed a finger at the kitchen door. "In there. Both of you, let's go."

"You know, Han Jiyeon," her father fired back in rapid Korean, "those were our hopes and dreams. And you stomped on them! Bam! How could you? We didn't raise you that way!"

"I thought you weren't speaking to her," mumbled Denny.

An older woman bustled out next, wiping damp hands on the apron tied around her waist. Her t-shirt had the word PEMBERLEY printed across the front in big block letters. "What are you fighting about in front of everybody? So tacky!" Then she grinned at some customers in scrubs a few tables down from Eunjae. "Oh, those guys from the hospital are back. Nice guys! Bring them some smoothies, tell them to come back with more friends."

Eunjae assumed this newest character to take the stage must be Jiyeon and Denny's mother. They'd both inherited that wavy hair and the dimple in her left cheek, although Mr. Han took sole credit for their height.

"Dad's sulking about the Arthur Hong Betrayal again," Denny said. Eunjae could hear the capital letters. He couldn't see Jiyeon's face, but it was like her whole body frowned in response.

"Oh, Arthur Hong!" groaned Mrs. Han. "Arthur, that good boy! That good, sweet boy!" She came out to join the others, bringing Jiyeon no closer to her goal of getting everyone back into the kitchen. "I'm still mad too. I thought it was all happy again, you and him. Maybe you're too picky, huh? Too much like me."

"Yeah, probably. Let's talk about this after closing, though."

"We should talk about it! We should talk about lots of things! You never come home, you never bring Arthur —"

"Uh-huh. Yes, I know. I'm awful."

"Not awful, Yeonnie. You are not awful to me." Mrs. Han patted her on the cheek. And then, just when it seemed the matter was resolved, she whispered, "But I miss Arthur!"

"I've seen him before," Mr. Han continued insisting to no one in particular. He motioned at Eunjae, who had to expend a great deal of willpower just to remain seated. His body's rote response was to slither under the table and disappear from view. "Jeannie-ah, where have I seen this one before? Tell me. You have a young brain, remembers everything."

The teenager working the register replied much too quickly for Eunjae's taste. "That's easy. He looks just like Ari from Apollo —"

"Aren't you supposed to be closing out?" Denny interrupted, indicating the cash Jeannie held in one hand. "You forgot how to do it again, didn't you?"

"I didn't forget," she wailed back. "I can't forget something I never learned. Don't listen to Uncle. My brain is young and it holds nothing."

Jiyeon was still locked in a whispered exchange with Mrs. Han. Denny launched into a lecture about why leaving the drawer hanging open was a surefire way to invite bandits onto the premises, and why was she counting all the smaller bills first? Leaving the others to their respective arguments, Mr. Han maneuvered around the counter, crossing to the window so he could flip the sign from OPEN to CLOSED.

"Okay," he said, grinning at Eunjae. "Now, don't tell me your name. I'll guess. I can do it. You want more food? No, no, don't worry about the time. You stay right there."

Mrs. Han appeared at his elbow. "Only one waffle? You don't like them?" Without waiting for an answer, she caught Denny's attention with a snap of her fingers. "Woosung-ah, go get some more food. We have batter left over."

Denny leveled a stare in Eunjae's direction. "Is he paying for it?"

"So rude! It's on the house. I'm the boss, do as I say."

"You play sports?" Mr. Han inquired, still focused solely on Eunjae. "Been on the news? Oh! Those commercials, maybe. Yes, that could be it. Yeonnie," he bellowed, "what's the commercial I like, with the ice skating and the big panda bears?"

"I'll tell you," Jiyeon said evenly, "if you help me with something in the kitchen first."

Eunjae felt her hand come to rest on his shoulder. "I'm *so* sorry," he heard her murmur in his ear. "Stay as long as you like. No one's rushing you out. Though if you wanted to run as fast as you can, I wouldn't blame you." And then she was off, rousting various family members into the kitchen even as customers began trickling out through the orange door. Before acquiescing to his daughter's demands, Mr. Han turned around to address Eunjae one more time.

"If you're lonely," he said, brows knitted together, "come visit us here, yeah? We'll save a spot for you. This same spot. No questions. Just come in, doesn't matter when."

Jiyeon eyed her father askance, smiling even as she led him away. "See, that was nice. You should've opened with that instead of shouting at him."

We'll save a spot for you. What had brought that on?

They had their backs turned, but Eunjae bowed to them both anyway.

4

J iyeon returned a few minutes later. Lagging behind despite telling himself three times that he needed to go, Eunjae was still sitting at his table, cradling the empty water glass. He didn't intend to eavesdrop. Jeannie made it too easy, though. There was a quality to her voice that recalled his three younger brothers: earnest, plaintive, a little whiny. Like a radio frequency signaling, "Pay attention to me."

"I've really missed you," Jeannie pouted at Jiyeon, unwrapping a piece of candy and popping it into her mouth. "I was glad you moved back, but you're only here in the mornings while I'm in class and I get stuck with Denny-boss from like, sunup to sundown. And he says TikTok is a scourge on humanity or whatever, so he won't let me use it while I'm here. Not even when it's super slow in the afternoons."

Jiyeon laughed. "Jeannie, your shift is six hours long. That's more like afternoon to sundown."

"But it feels like forever. And one time, I was going on a date right after work, and Denny scared the bejesus out of that guy! He was like, 'WHAT IS YOUR DRIVING RECORD, YOUNG MAN.' And he waved some tongs at him! And I'll die alone now! And I don't get why this keeps happening to me!"

"Our Woosung. I'll yell at him next time, just call me."

Jeannie crunched down on the candy, her long, braided ponytail swinging like a pendulum as she bustled around behind the counter. "Hey, Mom and Auntie Clary want to know if you've got anything available soon. Graduation's in two weeks."

"Gosh," sighed Jiyeon. "When did you and Evan get so old? And they want to come in at the same time, don't they? I'll see what I've got." She grabbed a pen from a cup perched next to the gong and scrawled a reminder on the back of her left hand.

"Speaking of graduation, I want my hair like how you did Riley's, okay? You know, with the bun. And the twirly bits."

"The twirly bits."

"I found the post again and took a screenshot," Jeannie said. "I'm glad you never deleted any of those. I was really worried that you would."

"Hmm." Jiyeon lifted a stack of receipts waiting on the counter, tucking them into an envelope. "I'll be right over there if you need help with the register."

"Don't tell Denny if I mess it up. He'll make me another infographic. Or an instruction manual."

"He won't hear anything from me," Jiyeon assured her. Then she went around checking on the remaining customers, stopping to chat for a little while at every table.

Eunjae finally finished his second waffle. He wondered why the ladies wanted to know Jiyeon's availability, and what the Arthur Hong Betrayal had entailed. Who was Arthur Hong? Why was it a Betrayal, capital B? And he had other questions as well, all of them orbiting in the general Wanna Waffle galaxy, but then he got a look at the time. Waffle Wednesday was over, yes, and so was Eunjae's stint as an aimless private citizen.

The others had probably made it back to the hotel without him. They'd all be concerned about where he'd gone on his own.

As a rule, Eunjae and his brothers weren't allowed to go anywhere on their own — not truly alone, not without at least one manager or someone from security hovering on the periphery — even now, nine years after their debut. They still went sightseeing in groups, ate together, shopped together. All but one member of Apollo lived in the Emerald Entertainment dorms, no more than a quick trip in the elevator or down the hall at any given time. Jungwoo and Max might be in the car already, waiting, and Eunjae was sitting here gawking at the clock on the wall. He had to get going.

It pained him to think of rushing right through that orange door without offering it the reverence it deserved. It had indeed led him into another world, a remnant of something magical. The people were warm, in this place. They argued and laughed and fed everyone who walked in. Since they hadn't guessed who he was, Eunjae had been free to pretend he belonged with them, just for a short while. It was a comfort he'd desperately needed.

Eunjae knew he had to go. The spell was sure to break soon and he didn't think he could bear to watch it happening. He also knew that he had a plane to catch. It was long past time to get moving, to start making tracks back to his actual existence, but it was hard to do it. And once he forced himself to cross that threshold, Eunjae would sag once more beneath the mantle of his other self.

When did it become so heavy, to keep being that person? Why couldn't Eunjae be stronger, more resilient?

"Ryan." He almost dropped his fork in surprise. It was Jiyeon, pausing at his table with the pitcher full of water and a questioning look on her face. She pointed to his drink. "Want a refill? Maybe one more waffle for the road?"

He held out the glass. She filled it to the brim, ice cubes clinking. The bonus waffle was tempting, but between himself, Jungwoo, and Max, Eunjae would need to bring about twenty more, so he turned it down. Still, Jiyeon smiled at him so warmly that he felt bold enough to ask at least one of the questions running through his mind.

"You said that you go by Emma or Jiyeon depending on who you're talking to, or where you are."

"Uh-huh."

"Which name do you use when it's just you, and no one else is around?"

Jiyeon set the pitcher down, fingers still wrapped around the handle. "Hmm."

"Sorry," Eunjae rushed to say. "Weird question."

"Oh, no. Not weird. Interesting. I don't think anyone's ever asked me that one before."

"Don't feel like you have to answer. I just wondered."

"I've never thought about it much, until now. But I suppose when it's just me, in my own head, it's Jiyeon. Emma's more like... a sweater I can take off. And when I need it again, I put it back on. Make sense?"

"Yeah. That makes sense."

Eunjae envied her certainty, and the implied ease with which she could shed one name and assume the other. He didn't consider his own names to be interchangeable. Each one belonged to a distinctly different version of himself, separate and contradictory, incapable of co-existing. If he was Ari, he couldn't be Eunjae. While he was Eunjae, he wasn't Ari.

As if she could hear what he was thinking, Jiyeon mused, "There was a time when I was Emma, just Emma, and Jiyeon was harder to reach. I sort of forgot how to be her. But she was always there, and I just needed to learn who she was again."

Eunjae went very still. She couldn't have known it at the time, but her words were points of light in a darkness that often felt absolute.

"Do you think you've learned it? Everything you'd forgotten?"

"Still working on that. But it's okay to keep working on it, I think." Jiyeon took up the pitcher again. "Those were some deep thoughts, Ryan Kim."

"You're right. I should've offered you a penny for them. Or two. Or ten."

"Ten whole pennies? I'm set for life."

"Big money."

Laughing, she replied, "I meant that you've got some big thoughts, not me."

"Ah, well," he replied, laughing with her. "Didn't sleep much last night. I'm probably losing it, but thanks for humoring me anyway."

"I'm the one who started sounding like a self-help guru. You were mostly humoring me."

Distressed noises began emanating from the area behind the register. Jiyeon glanced over, then patted Eunjae on the arm and said, "I'd better go help. Are you on your way out?"

"Yeah. I'm supposed to be on a plane soon."

"Be safe, wherever you're headed. Here, I'll walk you to the door. I have thirty seconds or so before Jeannie starts hitting the register with a spatula."

"That's... a straightforward approach."

"If only it worked."

And so Eunjae was still laughing as he left.

Jiyeon held the door open for him again. They traded goodbyes. Then he started walking, and although he waved to her once, he didn't allow himself to look back again.

Eunjae would never know the rest of this story. He would never be Ryan Kim who had a sister he'd shed tears for, whose mother remembered ice cream cake on his birthday. The people he'd met this evening would fade into footnotes in his memories in the same way he'd fade for them, their lives touching only for a moment.

He believed Mr. Han, when he said they'd save a spot for him. And he'd been avoiding being seen for days, but when Jiyeon was sitting across from him, spinning a tale about a life he'd never live, Eunjae had felt the flicker of a wish stirring in his heart: to be known.

Really, truly known.

Jooney Chun (Host) - Well folks, not sure if you've seen it yet 'cause the post went up on official channels less than 30 minutes ago, but it looks like they've finally announced what's next for Apollo now that their fearless leader has enlisted.

Freddie Dang (Co-Host/Producer) - Jooney, you know your mom doesn't get on Instagram except to check on like, two accounts. And one of them hasn't posted since the week before Christmas — a tragedy for both of us, by the way, 'cause we love her — so just spit it out already.

Jooney - I was going for suspense! Wait, does

she even follow our account? Ma, you follow @ommagoshpod on Insta, right?

Maisie Chun (Co-Host) - (*ignores him*) Talks too much. Always like that, even when he was little. His teachers always telling me, "Oh Mrs. Chun, your boy, he just talks all day, blah blah, nobody gets work done." One time Jooney got in bad trouble for talking in the middle of a test, he was in first grade. He took $3.00 and some dimes out of my purse. Tried to give it to his teacher!

Freddie - (*snorting*) What, so like a bribe? Jooney was bribing teachers back then?

Jooney - If you guys were on the fence about hosting a podcast with your mom, I hope this episode is helping you figure out your lives. And I wasn't bribing her! I was apologizing!

Freddie - Okay. It was apology money. Like when a country loses the war and they have to pay the winners or whatever.

Maisie - But did he ever apologize for stealing mom's money? No.

Jooney - (*clears throat*) Okay, anyway! Anyway, Apollo's official Instagram just posted a teaser announcing a unit debut next month. I happened to see it right before we came down to record and I'm glad I did because this is big news, guys. The last time Apollo debuted a unit was in 2021 with members Kazu and Kei. We'll link to that in the show notes for you.

Maisie - Oh, Apollo. I like them. They seem like good boys.

Jooney - They've been very busy boys, even after sending Jaehwan to basic training back in April. Just saw Kazu on the cover of *Vogue Korea* and Jesse was announced as a brand ambassador for Givenchy last week. Several of the guys have regular gigs on variety shows and as radio hosts this season. And now we're getting a unit EP from three Apollo members: Jungwoo, Ari, and Max. They're calling it A/M/J. Emerald... does not get creative with the unit names. (*laughs*)

Freddie - Right, like wasn't the last unit just K/K for Kazu and Kei? But yeah. (*wistful sigh*) Max, my problematic fav.

Maisie - Which one is Max? Tall boy? Aussie?

Jooney - No, Ma. You're thinking of Ari.

Freddie - Max is the one who had to apologize in January after what he said on Eric Nam's podcast.

Maisie - Oh, I don't care about him. I like the tall boy. The one who dressed up like a lion on *Mask Singer*.

Jooney - Technically 50% of Apollo qualifies as "the tall boy." They are a freakishly tall group. Also my mom's memory for what happened on Korean TV like three years ago — uncanny. For those of you who don't remember or don't keep up with music game shows where people sing in crazy costumes,

Apollo's Ari almost won *King of Mask Singer* back in 2020. He actually did better than his fellow member, Namgyu, who is the group's main vocalist.

Freddie - I think there's a whole series on YouTube called *The A in Ari is for Angel*. It's just clips of him being ridiculously nice. I was watching some other idols talking on a variety show about how Ari is famous for finding things people lost in the dressing rooms at music shows.

Maisie - See? Nice boy. Get that one on the show, Jooney. No, all of them. How many in Apollo? Nine? We can fit them all in the studio, easy.

Jooney - Oh yeah, I'll just casually get one of the biggest groups in the industry to guest star on this podcast. Totally happening, Ma.

Freddie - I heard Apollo was supposed to have like, twelve or thirteen members. But Jaehwan threatened to quit, so they cut it down to nine. Or did he threaten to murder someone? Either way, it's on brand.

Jooney - Apollo has the scariest leader in all of K-pop. I'll stand by that. But anyway, I'm very interested to see this unit, considering the three members participating. With Apollo being a self-produced group, they've always been really hands on with their music. I assume most of this unit's tracks, if not all, will be written and produced by Jungwoo. This is no secret, but I think the guy's brilliant. On top of that, Ari's got one of the most distinctive voices in K-pop currently. And then there's Max.

Freddie - Apollo's got a strong rap line, gotta give Max a lot of credit there. Even though he's, you know, a gremlin. (*clears throat*) A hot gremlin.

Jooney - Okay, what?

Freddie - You can give me that look all you want, but this is the hill I'm dying on.

Jooney - (*laughing*) Maybe call a gremlin watch, then, 'cause I did hear those three were stateside this weekend. Filming a music video? Doing some magazine shoots? I'd guess LA or San Diego. Help me out here, Sunshines. The fans always know what's going on. Drop some Apollo intel in the comments.

Maisie - Lion boy was in San Diego? Jooney, you didn't drive me there? San Diego so close by! LA even closer! (*begins scolding Jooney in Korean*)

Jooney - Uhhh.

Freddie - Really quick, let's hear from one of our sponsors!

5

The hotel should've been just a block or two away. Eunjae recalled a short walk to the restaurant where they'd eaten dinner, and the equally short walk between the restaurant and Wanna Waffle. But had it been short? Or had he actually been following a much more meandering path all along, entranced by the scenery and giddy with freedom?

Because the fact of the matter was this: Eunjae couldn't find the hotel. And he couldn't use his phone to navigate, because his phone was nowhere to be found. It must be in his duffel bag, or lying forgotten on the bed in his hotel room. He wasn't sure when his one link to the others had snapped, but without his phone, Eunjae realized that he was about ten different kinds of helpless.

They must be losing their minds at the airport. Maybe they were already on the plane. Eunjae wasn't wearing a watch and the last glance at the clock had been when Waffle Wednesday came to an end at... what time was that?

In his mind, the specter of Jaehwan paced back and forth, lecturing about the follies of relying too much on a smartphone to function on a daily basis. At least Eunjae wasn't short on funds. He had the card this evening, since the other two were hopeless at keeping track of such things, and it was still tucked securely in his wallet.

He'd backtracked to the waffle place mainly because it was easy to retrace his steps back to that orange door. Oddly enough, he knew the way. Eunjae hadn't been recognized while he was there. That made Wanna Waffle the safest harbor for now. He could borrow a phone there, maybe.

He paid better attention this time around. The shopping center was comprised of two buildings positioned at a right angle to each other, forming two sides of a rough square. A sign facing the busy boulevard read *The Village at Lemon Grove*. Wanna Waffle's side of the parking lot had emptied out, but the karaoke bar on the opposite end was pretty packed. None of the other establishments had such a unique entrance.

The larger windows were dark, shades drawn all the way down, but through the stained glass was a dim glow that told Eunjae he wasn't too late. He knocked. A minute slipped by, and then two. Another knock couldn't hurt. Eunjae raised his fist again, then dropped it when someone approached from the other side. Someone wearing red.

"I have no idea why I came here," Eunjae heard through the door. Jiyeon had her back turned to him again, but the tense line of her shoulders was visible through the glass panels.

"Because it's my birthday!"

"I offered to take you out for dinner. That's what we should've done."

"You guys are fighting about the stupidest thing in the history of all stupid things. Buying me dinner at the Cheesecake Factory was not gonna make it better."

"The Cheesecake Factory? Denny."

"I love that place. Don't start."

"Nothing in there even makes sense except for the cheesecake," argued Jiyeon. "The five hundred menu items, the decor —"

"The decor," Denny argued back, "is Venetian."

"What? How is it Venetian, like what even counts as a Venetian aesthetic?" Jiyeon threw her hands up almost before she'd finished the sentence. "Actually, no. I'm not sticking around any longer. I'm sorry your birthday turned out like this. I love you, but this was a mess and I regret it. I'll try again in another month, I guess. Maybe they'll be over it by then."

She stepped backward into the door, pushing it open without turning around. Eunjae was forced to lurch away, off the stoop and onto the sidewalk. Denny's face appeared over Jiyeon's shoulder. His eyes went wide, almost as wide as a signature waffle.

In an instant, he'd shunted his sister behind him and blocked the doorway, seemingly growing another three inches taller as he glared at Eunjae.

"Can I help you?"

6

"If this is another wacko from the Internet, I'm calling a full Code Blue, no holds barred, special forces and SWAT team —"

"Denny, stop." Jiyeon shoved past her brother, moonlight turning the tiny flowers in her hair into silver stars. To Eunjae, she said, "It's the mystery man. Did you forget something, Ryan Kim? I can double check with Jeannie. She might have found it before she left."

"Mystery man? You're talking to some new man already, Han Jiyeon?"

The siblings exchanged looks as their father stomped onto the scene, Mrs. Han following close behind. He made an abrupt switch from Korean to English. "You broke up with Arthur Junior one month ago, now it's a new man?"

"Does Arthur Junior know our parents are obsessed with him?" muttered Denny.

"And who is Ryan Kim? I've never met a boy named Ryan Kim. Is he from church?"

Eunjae's gaze darted back and forth between the various family members before landing, finally, on Jiyeon's apologetic smile. He smiled back. At least, he tried. Truth be told, he felt much too queasy to manage it very well. The mask prevented anyone from seeing this pathetic attempt, which was a small mercy. He dropped into the lowest bow he could execute without tipping over and commenced an apology of his own. A deluxe apology, Max would call it.

Max would be the authority on that subject, what with all the apologies Eunjae had helped him draft over the years. His younger brother really needed to quit running his mouth so freely on public broadcasts.

Eunjae had never generated enough of a scandal to warrant such an elegant apology on his own behalf. In fact, he'd failed to drum up any scandals whatsoever. He practiced composing apologies nonetheless. His eldest brothers, Jaehwan and Kazu, had given many a speech about how they were bound to disappoint their legions of fans at some point down the line. Maybe they'd be seen chatting too long with the members of a girl group backstage at a music show. Maybe they'd cause an uproar over an Instagram post. Or maybe there would be dating rumors dutifully reported by the tabloid press, true or false. It was best to master the art of saying sorry. Eunjae saw the sense in that.

His apology that evening was apparently so epic in nature and composition that it left all four members of the Han family speechless. Eunjae remained as he was, bent at the waist with the bucket hat fallen to the ground at his feet. "I apologize for my inadequacy," he reiterated in Korean, in case they missed it the first time. And then he translated it back to English, just for good measure.

Jiyeon recovered first. "It's okay," she said faintly. "You got lost and you don't have your phone. Nothing to be sorry about." This last sentence shook her out of the stupor. She took a few steps forward, pausing to collect the bucket hat and hold it out to Eunjae. "I'm here. Whatever you need, I'll help you."

Fans loved to extol the virtues of Eunjae's smile. They liked to say that it was the kindest, the warmest, the most reassuring smile they'd ever seen. And why wouldn't they? This girl had never smiled at them. They didn't know any better.

Eunjae stopped staring, accepted the hat, and jammed it back onto his head. "Sorry. Thank you. I'm just... I'm really grateful. I think I've missed my flight, but if I could just call our —" He stumbled, coming close to saying manager. That wasn't going to work if Nami had gotten on the plane with the others, so he should think of something else. "If I could just call someone, that would be a good place to start."

"Of course. Here you go." Jiyeon dipped a hand into her bag and produced a phone. She unlocked the screen before passing it to Eunjae. "You know the number, right?"

Eunjae did not, in fact, know the number. It wasn't that he hadn't bothered to memorize any of his brothers' numbers, since he did know one of these by heart: Jaehwan's number, because he was leader, and because he made the whole group memorize that string of digits ages ago. Then they'd been bombarded with pop quizzes for weeks afterward. If Eunjae knew anything, it was Jaehwan's phone number.

This was the sort of emergency that Jaehwan had been preparing them for, by searing those digits into their brains, but it would be no use to call him now. Apollo's leader was completing mandatory military service, having enlisted back in April. Jaehwan would want to help Eunjae — and probably also flay him alive — but there would be very little he could do about it.

Besides, Eunjae didn't want to bother him with this. There had to be a solution that didn't involve alarming Jaehwan while he had so much else to be worried about. And didn't he deserve a two-year break from parenting eight other group members?

While the cogs were turning furiously in Eunjae's head, Jiyeon had been waiting for him to admit that he didn't know which numbers to dial. She said, "It's not a big deal if you don't remember. The only numbers I've got memorized are mine and my sister's."

Denny emitted a squawk of pure indignation.

"Woosung-ah, I'm joking."

"Ha! Ha, ha, ha!"

Eunjae hung his head and returned her phone. "I'm so sorry," he said again. "I hate to waste your time like this."

Jiyeon's brother marched up and resumed acting as a living barricade. "Listen up, my guy. I know your name isn't really Ryan Kim."

"Why do you have zero sense of humor, Denny?"

"Why do you have inside jokes with complete strangers, noona?" Denny volleyed back, scowling at Eunjae all the while. Noona. So Jiyeon was Denny's older sister. "What's your real name? We'll help you out 'cause we're upstanding citizens, pillars of the community and etcetera, but you owe us that much."

And he did, of course. He did owe them that much, if not more. But Eunjae absolutely could not give these people his real name. If anything would break the spell and seal his fate, it was his name. Obviously no one in the family was an Apollo fan; this was the only reason he'd lasted so long without getting caught. Still, it would take just one Google search to obliterate his hopes of remaining undetected until he sorted this out.

Eunjae vacillated on how to respond. He knew he should rattle off a fake name, but not a single believable option came to mind. The best he could come up with in the moment was, "Um."

Jiyeon peered at him from behind the looming figure of her brother, brow furrowed. Was it concern or suspicion that Eunjae saw in her eyes? She tried to push past Denny again, but he halted her progress with an outstretched arm. "Seriously, man. Who are you?"

"He doesn't know!"

Their father's declaration resounded in the parking lot. Over by the karaoke bar, a group of teenagers heard him and turned their heads toward the sound, then vanished into the building, giggling.

Mr. Han nudged both of his children aside and came to stand in front of Eunjae, prompting him to master an urge to bolt. It was like facing down a giant. Two giants, what with Denny being there too. The pair of them had been sheared off the same mountainous crag.

"He doesn't remember his name," repeated Mr. Han, sounding oddly triumphant. "It all makes sense to me, now."

7

"Dad, come on. Nothing about this guy makes sense. I'm going inside to run a freaking background check."

Jiyeon poked Denny in the arm. "Since when can you just casually run a background check on someone? Who do you even think you are?"

"I have resources, okay?"

But Mr. Han shook his head at Denny and Jiyeon with great vehemence. "No. This boy, he's more than lost. Just look at him, look into his eyes."

Here, he took Eunjae by the shoulders and angled him so that the murky glow of the nearest streetlight could illuminate his face.

"I thought he looked familiar, but I was wrong. Something about him just reminded me of that drama we used to watch on Thursdays and Fridays. You know the one, Lizzie."

"Aigoo!" gasped Mrs. Han. "The one with the chaebol who lost his memory!"

Jiyeon closed her eyes, pinching the bridge of her nose. "So... every Korean drama ever made?"

"No, no." Mrs. Han clapped her hands together. "*I Loved You.* That's what it was called. The hero, he grew up never knowing he was the son of a rich CEO because he got kidnapped as a child."

Mr. Han joined in with some enthusiastic nodding. "Uh-huh. So the kidnappers are stupid and lose him on Jeju Island. The kid hits his head, pow! Forgets everything about being a chaebol heir. He's raised by a nice family with a son the same age."

"Very nice. Not rich, though. Just normal. Almost poor."

"Almost poor?"

Mrs. Han latched onto her son's arm and gave it a firm shake. "You know what I'm saying, Han Woosung!"

"They go to school together and he's best friends with these four other boys," Mr. Han recounted. "Everything is great. So happy."

"But then," the parents exclaimed, practically in sync, "the hero and his fake brother fall in love with the same girl!"

"So," said Denny, arms crossed, "still like every Korean drama ever made?"

"This one was different," hissed Mr. Han. "Anyway! Bad guys start looking for him again. He has to hide or they'll kill him, boom, to get revenge on his real family. The hero runs away, leaves everybody behind. Probably just like this guy you found!"

Mrs. Han clapped her hands. Everything about her was suddenly electric with excitement. "You're right, Joey," she told her husband. "Mystery Ryan, he has the same... what do you kids call it, Yeonnie? Same vibes?"

"Of course I'm right," huffed Mr. Han. "This boy — he has amnesia."

Silence fell. On Mrs. Han's part, it was a sympathetic silence. She clearly felt compassion for Eunjae's plight but was also thrilled to be living in a drama episode. Denny, meanwhile, had descended into the kind of false calm that denotes the eye of a hurricane.

Eunjae couldn't know this, of course, but the expression on his face was a perfect fit for the Han parents' amnesia theory. No one had ever looked more like a blank, bewildered slate.

"This is crazy," Denny said, digging a phone out of his back pocket. "I'm calling the cops."

At this, Jiyeon elbowed her way over to Eunjae. Ignoring the uproar as her parents and brother clashed over what was to be done next, she took him by the sleeve and led him a few steps away, keeping her voice low so the others wouldn't hear.

"Are you in trouble?" Jiyeon asked, releasing him. She caught his gaze and held it. "Is that why you won't tell us who you are?"

The paralysis broke just enough for Eunjae to shake his head. "I'm not," he stammered. "I mean, yes, I'm definitely in trouble. It's not that kind of trouble, though. I promise."

For a long moment, neither of them spoke. Eunjae did his best to radiate sincerity. At last, Jiyeon gave him a brief, decisive nod. "I believe you. What do you want to do?"

Looking back, Eunjae would find himself thinking about the way Jiyeon hadn't asked what the specific trouble was, or why there was trouble in the first place. Instead, she'd simply asked what he wanted to do.

When did anyone ever ask what Eunjae wanted to do? It was overwhelming to be asked, honestly. Part of that was because he'd sensed right away that she wasn't inquiring about the mess he'd made — the flight he'd missed, the people he should inform, the name he wouldn't divulge. Jiyeon seemed to understand what Eunjae had still not allowed himself to admit. She saw that he didn't really want to rectify the situation. What he wanted was to stay.

8

What if he did stay? What then? This was an impossible notion, and yet Eunjae couldn't dislodge it from his heart once it found purchase there.

If he stayed, if he didn't run to the airport now and get himself on the next plane to Seoul, his agency would eventually launch a manhunt in the streets of Jiyeon's neighborhood. Someone, or several someones, would travel to the United States and haul him back to reality. He'd worry his brothers half to death. The news outlets would have a field day. And the fans? He didn't even want to imagine that part of the equation.

Eunjae would cause so many problems for so many people, by staying here. So why did he want to do it?

Because I'm tired. Because all I ever want to do is run, lately. Because I don't even know why I'm doing it anymore.

Because I don't want to be that person anymore.

But was that accurate, really? Eunjae did want to be the person who made music for a living. Most of all, he did want to be the person with eight brothers, always joking and fighting by turns. He'd done so much of his growing up with the other members of Apollo. How could he even think of leaving them? They'd promised to keep going for as long as they could. They'd sworn to stay together.

For a moment, as he thought of his brothers, Eunjae almost managed to tell her no. But then he caught sight of the orange door again, and he remembered another promise he'd made a long, long time ago. A promise to himself.

"If the magic ever calls me, I'll listen," he used to whisper, buried under the covers with *The Brass Key* under his pillow, or reading it by flashlight in his closet. From Friday evening until late on Sunday afternoon, Eunjae learned to make himself scarce in the huge, echoing house in Brisbane. As his mother threw dinner parties for her work friends, the actors and understudies and people from her modeling days, he would pretend that every door upstairs was the way to another world.

If he found the right one, Eunjae could escape before it came time to be appraised by the guests. Unfortunately, he never did. "Sit here," his mother would croon when he came down, "and sing that song again. The one you were singing with Vivian yesterday." She'd straighten his collar or frown at a smudge on his cheek. "We never knew he was so talented. We can't let it go to waste."

He would sing because it was what she wanted, but it never felt the way it did when he sang with Miss Vivi. Then, it was like joy transmuted into sound. Then, it was like truly being himself, everything that he was, hiding nothing.

While his mother's friends listened to him singing, Eunjae ran from one door to another in his head. As they took his face into their cold, dry hands and peered at the shape of his eyes, the lilt of his mouth, Eunjae would hope for the magic to find him. He'd let their words wash over him like water. *Feed him less, try this diet, keep the boy out of the sun. Have him learn an instrument. Have him learn to dance. He needs voice lessons. He needs to stop being so shy.*

We'll make something of him yet. Just wait and see.

That's what the magic was, Eunjae decided long ago: a place where you were already something, and whatever you were, that was enough.

Back then, Eunjae had often worried that he wouldn't recognize the magic when it finally appeared; that it would call his name and he would be too timid to answer. Worse, he would find the door limned in light and never have the nerve to cross over. Well, now the magic might be happening. Now, when he had nothing much left to give and everything to lose. Would he be a coward? Would he let himself down for the thousandth time?

A chorus of sirens blared in the distance. Disjointed bursts of music filtered down from the high rise across the street. Eunjae locked eyes with Jiyeon in the half-dark, feeling as if he'd spent a lifetime contemplating her question.

"I want to stay," he told her. "Not for long — nothing like that. If it's okay, that is. I understand if it's not."

"Of course it's okay." Without letting another second slip by, she turned around to interrupt the family squabble. "Alright, quit fighting and listen to me."

"You may remain in this realm for one night and one day," said the Doorkeep, holding up a single taloned finger. Her curving claw seemed sharp enough to slice straight through the sky, peeling back the layers of dusk and afternoon and mid-day until morning showed through.

Theo looked at Knob. Knob looked at Theo. Lock danced around them both, jingling like a dozen pockets full of coins.

"Mortal child, make your choice."

"Tell us now! Use your voice!"

"You found the door, you turned the key."

"Go or stay? Which will it be?"

The Doorkeep waited. Theo couldn't imagine her rushing anywhere, even if her roots and one elbow hadn't fused with the door frame over the long centuries standing guard. He sensed that she never hurried through anything, whether it was a choice to be made or a thought to ponder. Theo appreciated that she seemed so patient.

"What happens if I'm here longer than one night and one

day?" he asked.

"You will begin to pay the price."

"But what is the price?"

"That," said the Doorkeep, "is not something anyone can predict. Not even the Glass Lady can say."

Theo felt as if his mouth simply brimmed with questions. All the questions his parents were always too exasperated to answer, the questions that made him so much more difficult than other children. He wanted to know about the Glass Lady, and about others like him who had come through the door in the past. Theo wanted to ask what their prices had been, if they'd been forced to pay. But maybe the others had been good. Maybe they didn't break the rules, ever.

Yes, the more he thought about it, the more Theo felt certain that the other visitors to this place had all been much better at following rules than he ever was. They probably didn't even consider staying longer than one night and one day, despite the loveliness of the trees and the soft blue velvet of the sky.

Knob tapped his foot on the lush, green grass. Lock had found a twig. She twirled it in her tiny hands.

"Stay or go? Stay or go?"

"The price to pay? No one knows."

Theo turned back to glance at his own world, bright and hazy with heat, asphalt still baking even as the summer sun dipped low in the sky. Tomorrow was the Midsummer Solstice, Aunt Hattie had told him. The longest day of the year. He wondered if that would count, here. If making his decision now might give him a little bit more time. Because of course Theo was going to take the chance. What if he never found this door again?

On the other side of this door, he could be another person. A better Theo. The true version of himself.

He squared his shoulders and took a deep breath. "I want to stay," he told the Doorkeep.

And the Doorkeep bowed, filling the air with the creak of branches heavy with fruit, crickets chirping, the trilling of a lone nightingale. All the sounds of evening came together to become her voice as she spoke.

"Be welcome then, mortal child. For one night and one day, all the wonders of these lands are yours to behold."

9

E unjae stood in a corner of the kitchen at Wanna Waffle, trying to stay out of the way while Denny Han slammed blue plastic trays into orderly stacks on the counter. Every resounding crash made him leap partway out of his skin. It didn't help that he was still waiting to be struck by lightning. He'd made a decision to stay here and would surely suffer the consequences soon.

There would be hell to pay. Even so, Eunjae didn't regret what he'd done. At least, not yet. This lack of regret was the most surprising thing about his situation. He'd expected to feel more of it.

In the main dining room, Mr. and Mrs. Han were having a spirited conversation about the ending of *I Loved You*. From what Eunjae could gather, it had been tragic. There was something about a smashed lifeboat, and something else about a carousel. Had he been coerced into watching this drama with Jungwoo? He couldn't remember. There had been so many dramas. Jungwoo was always looking for songwriting inspiration.

Thinking of his brother brought on a brief bout of dizziness. Was Jungwoo angry with him? Was he imagining the worst?

Finished with the trays, Denny went around unplugging waffle irons, yanking the cords out of the wall with such force that Eunjae feared for the building's structural integrity. "Do you seriously believe this guy has amnesia? Like you're really buying what our wacko parents are selling?"

Now it was Jiyeon who slammed the refrigerator shut with a bang. She glared at her brother and said, "I believe he needs our help, Den. That's all I really need to know."

"But he can't actually have amnesia. No one is coming after him. This is not a sixteen-episode drama, it's just life." Denny waved a fistful of spatulas at Eunjae. "So how'd you find my sister, huh? Location tags? Tracking her IP address? This is exactly why it's a bad idea to have a digital footprint, noona. I've told you a hundred times to delete everything. Any pea-brained stalker out there can find you just by downloading an app."

"Ryan," said Jiyeon, "if you're stalking me, now's the time to confess."

Eunjae shook his head furiously. Denny was not swayed. "I'm gonna figure you out, buddy. You can't hide the truth from me. I am all about the truth. The truth is my crusade."

"I thought getting people to proofread public signs was your crusade."

"A man can have more than one crusade!"

Jiyeon had moved into the pantry that took up the back corner of the kitchen. "What if he's just a person who needs a place to stay? What if we just helped him as best as we can? We don't know the whole story, but he hasn't done us any harm."

Denny trailed her into the cramped space like a chastened puppy. "I don't mind helping," Eunjae heard him insist. "I just don't get why he has to be so weird about this. What if he's on drugs? What if he's a serial killer who specializes in small-business owners? We can't adopt everyone who walks into the shop with floppy hair and big, empty eyes. We can't just say they have amnesia and call it a day."

A significant pause. "You think he has big, empty eyes? The floppy hair, sure. But you have no evidence for the eyes. You haven't even looked."

"But *you've* looked?"

"Be mad all you want. I can at least back up my claims with evidence."

Denny made an exasperated noise, then emerged from the pantry and came barreling over. Eunjae stood very, very still and tried to accept that this might be the end for him. Maybe he could still make a break for it, though. Denny was a colossus made flesh, but Eunjae had tyrannical older brothers who made everybody run wind sprints as a warm-up before performances. He figured he had a reasonable chance of escaping before he could be bludgeoned with a wooden spatula.

But Denny only scrutinized Eunjae's allegedly big, empty eyes before making yet another exasperated noise. "Okay, you win that one. They're not empty. I guess there's a brain behind them. However, his eyes are purple. PURPLE!" He tossed his bouquet of spatulas into the wide, industrial sink. To Eunjae, he barked, "Why are your eyes purple, Mystery Ryan? Explain."

"Um, they're colored contacts."

"Huh? Who even uses colored contacts?"

People like me who forget their normal contacts and have to borrow spares from the stylist, Eunjae answered silently. Apollo's stylists always had a wide array of unusual colors to choose from. They might come in handy on a shoot, especially if numerous closeups were involved.

"I'm telling you, Yeonnie. Something weird is going on. Like, this guy might be a method actor, or a unicorn, or one of those freaking K-pop people. Normal people wear normal contacts. Eye-colored. Not purple."

"Eye-colored?"

"You know what I mean!"

Eunjae took a deep breath. "Actually," he said to Denny, tugging the mask off his face, "I am one of those K-pop people. You're right."

This pronouncement was met with one of the most intense stares he'd ever endured in his life. And then Denny threw back his head and laughed, a thunderous sound that somehow made Eunjae want to laugh along with him even as he went boneless with relief.

"Okay. Nice joke, well played. You can stay for now, Mystery Man. Ryan. Whatever your name is." He stuck his head out the kitchen door and commenced hollering for his parents to hurry up. "Let's go home!"

10

About fifteen minutes later, Eunjae climbed out of the Hans' bright red Camaro feeling half exhilarated and half seasick. Despite becoming roughly 5% less hostile since the colored contacts reveal in the kitchen, Denny had still banned Eunjae from riding with his sister. He'd practically buckled him into the seat behind Mrs. Han before hopping into Jiyeon's car himself.

The short trip swept by in a blur. Mrs. Han, while a careful driver, was also very well acquainted with her gas pedal. As for Mr. Han, he spent the ride assuring Eunjae that he was welcome in their home for as long as he needed, and that they would all work together to see about dispelling his amnesia. Why, anything could trigger the return of those missing memories. And until Eunjae remembered who he was, he would of course be safe with them. "No one will find you," Mr. Han bellowed. "They'll have to go through me first."

"That's right!" said Mrs. Han. "Joey worked security, you know. Retired now. Best in the business!"

Mr. Han twisted in his seat, eyes narrowed. "You got enemies, Ryan Kim?"

Eunjae thought about it. Solemnly he replied, "Yes."

"Ha! I knew it. Well, don't worry. You're in good hands."

"At least he remembers that much, yeah? Not like that boy in *I Loved You*. Better to know the bad guys might come after you, then you can be prepared. Set traps. That kind of thing."

You couldn't set a trap if your life depended on it, whispered the voice of Invisible Jaehwan. *I'd better be the first one you call*. Eunjae shivered involuntarily.

When he wasn't listing examples of drama plots involving amnesia, Mr. Han was reminding his wife that going five or ten miles above the posted speed limit was perfectly acceptable. Mrs. Han would nod and agree, already going around fifteen miles over and beaming all the while. Within this woman's petite frame burned the soul of a Formula One racer. Eunjae oscillated between dizziness and admiration. That had to be a superpower, being able to take every corner like it was a hairpin turn. It was better when he stopped trying to read the signs that kept blasting past his window at warp speed. Thrilling, even.

Upon arrival, Mr. and Mrs. Han led the way to a small, two-story apartment complex. Eunjae followed them on wobbly legs. The whole building was painted in shades of forest green — the wooden stairs, the railings, all the siding and trim. Trees extended their branches over the sidewalk and reached for the second floor balconies, burgeoning with flowers. Everywhere he looked, there was something growing, blooming, bursting with life: crowded window boxes, herbs frothing out of jars, a row of tomato plants in tin coffee cans. Someone's bougainvillea scattered drifts of papery fuchsia blossoms across a parking lot the size of a postage stamp.

There was a light in all the windows but one. He heard wind chimes stirring in the soft breeze, at least two different sets of them judging by the timbre and pitch. A sign beneath the largest of the flowering trees read *Ivy Lane Apartments*.

Eunjae felt for the disposable camera in the bag slung across his chest. It was much too dark to take a decent picture, so he had to make do with memorizing as much of the scene as possible. Something to save for later, to warm himself when the world felt cold.

Mrs. Han backtracked for the sole purpose of resting a guiding hand on Eunjae's back, moving him along as if he might get lost again between the car and their front door.

"Home!" she announced. "Come, come. Yeonnie parks on the street. You can wait for her inside."

The camera follows Ari, dressed in nondescript blue sweatpants and a matching sweatshirt. His hair, grown out for the music video, is a light shade of brown and just barely brushes his shoulders. He leads the way down a corridor with plush maroon carpet, the pile so high that it swallows the sound of his footsteps. The walls are lined with closed doors.

"The first time we heard Ari sing," says the voiceover narration, a female voice speaking in subtitled Korean, "he was fourteen years old. He came to the auditions in Sydney."

The scene cuts to two women sitting side by side in matching green upholstered chairs: Sun Soyeon and Choi Haewon, founders of Apollo's agency, Emerald Entertainment.

"We knew right away that we wanted Ari," Haewon continues, "but later we couldn't decide if he should be a soloist or if he should debut with a group."

Soyeon laughs, covering her mouth with an elegant,

beautifully manicured hand. "It was one of the worst arguments we ever had, actually."

"You know, I think people assume we never fight because we've been seen by the public as best friends for most of our lives at this point."

Here, clips of the two women scroll slowly across the screen, showing scenes from their time as members of Jewell in the late 90s. Known as a first-generation girl group, Jewell is often listed among other forerunners of the Hallyu wave. They arrived on the scene during a massive surge in the global popularity of South Korean entertainment, including K-pop and Korean dramas.

"We fought over Ari, though," says Soyeon, laughing again. "Oh, we went back and forth for ages. I kept saying, Haewon-ah, he can't debut alone. We can't do that to him. His mother told us before the audition that that he was very, very shy. She actually thought he might try to sing badly, sabotage his own audition so he could go home and hide."

"Unnie kept telling me he'd be lonely on stage," Haewon explains, referring to Soyeon as her older sister, "but I hated to think of that voice being overshadowed by anybody else's. Although there were stronger vocalists among our trainees on a technical level, Ari's voice still managed to shine in its own unique way. What a waste, if the world never heard this boy sing. That's what I was thinking. I wanted to just pick him up and put him on a plane to Seoul right away."

Now the episode switches back to Ari at the hotel in New York, where the film crew records him sharing the contents of his suitcase. We glimpse clothing neatly rolled to minimize the wrinkles, a worn paperback book with a door on the cover, and not one but two different cameras. He pretends to take a picture, aiming a Nikon at three people jostling for space on the room's other bed. (Fans have since identified these people as Max, Kei, and Jesse; known as Sunshines, members of Apollo's fandom are legendary for their remarkable ability to identify members with only the barest glimpses of kneecaps and elbows as reference.)

Soyeon is heard commenting, "Ari has such a memorable voice. Memorable is what you want, in this business. Especially in a group, you want that strong vocal color. And there's something about it that just makes you feel..."

"Lighter. Like your feet can't touch the ground. That's for a happy song, like the lyrics are about falling in love, whatever. That joy is yours. And when the song is sad, he just breaks your heart. It's like the pain belongs to you, too."

"He has a voice that tells a story," says Soyeon.

The women look at each other, then nod again, almost in perfect synchrony. Slightly grainy footage fills the screen: Ari's audition in Sydney, dated August 2011. He sings the iconic chorus of Taeyang's *Wedding Dress*, an international sensation released in 2009.

"To tell you the truth, I couldn't understand Soyeon's determination to put him in a group until we saw him again in Seoul. We used to watch the trainees every Friday when they did their weekly performances."

"That time, Ari had been matched with some boys who'd been with us longer — Jaehwan, Kazu, and Jungwoo."

"It was crazy to me, but somehow, his voice had an even brighter sound when he was part of a group. Soyeon was right."

"But we asked him, you know," Soyeon puts in. "Before we finalized the lineup for Apollo, we offered Ari the choice. We felt like that was fair. Did he want a career as a soloist, which we'd support just as much, or did he want to debut with the others?"

"I would love it if Ari would finally listen to me and agree to do a solo EP, but I'm glad he's part of Apollo. I do think he chose very well back then."

Soyeon smiles. "He chose to stay with his brothers."

11

"Let the guest have your room, Denny."

"What? Why?"

Mr. Han zoomed around the living room, snapping blinds shut. "Because you don't have windows facing the street," he replied. "We can't let any bad guys see him, and if he's in your room he can jump out on the patio in case of an attack."

"There isn't going to be an attack!"

"How do you know?"

"Oh my god. The same way I know the sky is blue?"

"I don't need to take anyone's room," Eunjae said in a rush. He pointed to the couch. It was overstuffed, sage green, and patterned in tremendous yellow and white roses. "I can just sleep here. And anyway, I really don't sleep much."

Jiyeon tossed her keys on the dining table and set off down a shadowed hall, flicking lights on as she went. "Come on. We can figure out the room situation later."

As he followed a few paces behind her, Eunjae couldn't help noticing the decor. Framed landscapes of pastoral meadows shared space with family photos on the walls. Every now and then he'd glimpse a painting of some battle involving rearing stallions and flashing sabers, or hunting scenes filled with foxes and forests. And in a niche that might have once been a closet with open shelving, Eunjae came upon a mind-boggling profusion of Jane Austen merchandise.

The books were there, of course. At least two or three editions of each one. Some copies bristled with sticky note flags in a rainbow of colors. Squashed in beside them were DVDs and even some VHS tapes, the cardboard covers beginning to fade with time. It appeared that a few of these had been adopted from a now defunct video rental store.

There was more. Eunjae spotted a set of porcelain plates featuring hand painted English gardens, manor houses, and Austen quotations in curling script. Coffee mugs bearing similar or identical quotations huddled beside wine goblets festooned with portraits of Mr. Darcy, as played by various actors. Eunjae could tell that one particular Darcy was the favorite because his face also graced several other items, including coasters and a music box.

He was leaning in to examine a framed photo of a sour-faced little boy dressed in period attire when Jiyeon appeared beside him. "Ah, the Austen shrine," she said, straightening a trio of faux mile markers. These were carved with the words Pemberley, Kellynch Hall, and Northanger Abbey. According to the signs, all were approximately one mile away from this location. "Mom's a little bit obsessed."

Eunjae pointed to a worn and weathered paperback of *Emma*. "Found you. And I guess Lizzie is short for Elizabeth?" He vaguely remembered a character named Elizabeth from the time he saw *Pride & Prejudice* with Jungwoo. They'd watched it one night because Jungwoo was in a historical romance phase. He called it research for his songwriting efforts. Eunjae had slept through most of the movie, wiped out from hours of choreography drill.

"Yeah," said Jiyeon. "And our older sister is Jane. Well, Janie. Denny narrowly missed being named Darcy. He only ended up being Dennis instead because our dad threw a tantrum and named him after his best friend."

"Darcy Han. It has a ring to it."

Jiyeon laughed. "Never tell him that."

"Why Jane Austen?"

"Hmm, well. When she first came to America, Mom really wanted to speak better English. To her logic, the best way to learn English, like proper English, was to study how they talk in England. She tried the Brontë sisters first and thought they were too depressing. All that wuthering and the crazy wives in attics. 'Eh! I can get that from Korean shows!' This Austen lady was pretty funny, though, once you figured out what she was saying."

"She's right. You really can get all of that from Korean shows."

"The one thing she complains about when it comes to Austen is that twenty different people are named Charles. Like, per book."

Eunjae could feel Jiyeon watching him even as she said this, studying his face in profile. He turned his head to look at her. Quietly she asked, "If you tell me your name, will I know too much about you?"

He closed his eyes for just a moment. "Yes." His name was the key to everything. It would give away the game. And yet, how was it fair for Jiyeon to have given him so much while he offered her next to nothing?

He had two names. At the very least, he could trade her one of them, pay back her trust in him by trusting her in return.

"Eunjae," he said, the syllables so strange to pronounce after all the years of only using that name in his head. "My name is Eunjae."

Now, Eunjae knew that revealing his name could go a few different ways. He'd made too much of a snap decision to consider more than a few possible scenarios, but none of these involved Jiyeon frantically clapping a hand over his mouth and hustling him into a dark room. To say that it took him by surprise would be an understatement.

She shut the door behind them. There was a click as she locked it for good measure. Eunjae's imagination began cranking out visions of Jiyeon's male relatives chasing him into the street with baseball bats. He pictured her mother hurling Mr. Darcy wine goblets like projectile missiles and fumbled for the doorknob, fearing for his life.

Jiyeon's warm fingers curled around his wrist, preventing escape. She hit the light switch with her other hand. Eunjae winced at the ensuing brightness.

"Why did you tell me your name?" she demanded. "Now I know too much."

Eunjae blinked at her. "You didn't want to know it? It seemed like you did."

"Yes? No?"

He unlocked the door in the name of self-preservation. "I wanted you to know it, though," he said. "Really, it's okay."

Her expression softened for a moment. "Hopefully no one else heard. Please tell me it's a fake name, at least."

"It isn't. I'm sorry. But I have more than one name, just like you."

"I'm not sure I can handle this responsibility. What if I'm captured and interrogated?"

Eunjae smiled. "You could refer them to Ryan Kim in San Bernardino."

"That won't work. They might go after his mom next."

"Good call. She seems like a nice lady."

"See? Exactly. I'm in a bind, here." She reached around him, turned the knob, and tugged the door open. From the living room came snatches of cooking show narration and Denny's noisy commentary. For the second time that evening, Eunjae almost crumpled to the floor out of sheer relief. He went to go sit at the desk before his knees could buckle.

Jiyeon tossed her tote bag onto the bed and plopped down beside it. Sighing, she began removing the tiny red flowers from her hair, setting them in a pile on the nightstand. "I don't know who you're hiding from or why," she said, "but the less I know, the better. Keep your secrets, Ryan Kim."

12

Generally speaking, Eunjae had little experience with keeping his own secrets. He'd kept plenty for his brothers over the years. Small secrets like shoes borrowed and never returned, and the big secrets bound up with Jungwoo's latest fated — or star-crossed — romance. But Eunjae didn't have many secrets, personally. This was one of the few.

"That wouldn't bother you? Not knowing much about me?" His hesitation came from a genuine place. In addition to rarely having secrets worth keeping, Eunjae was accustomed to people wanting to know every tiny detail about him.

A flower fell apart in Jiyeon's fingers, disintegrating into individual petals. She frowned. "Me, specifically? No. The world could stand to be a little more mysterious. And I guess I'll know who you are, sooner or later. Amnesia can be reversed. I learned that from Korean dramas and Joey Han."

A little more mysterious. Entire websites were dedicated to the minutiae of Eunjae's life. Search engines had long since indexed his birthday, his favorite food, even the name of the Montessori school he'd attended at the age of five. Receiving permission to maintain an air of mystery was nothing short of refreshing.

"But it does bother me that someone is probably worrying about you, wondering where you've gone. You have at least one person who would worry about you, right?"

"More than one," admitted Eunjae. And now remorse crested over him like a wave, blotting out the light. But he still didn't regret what he'd done, so did that make him the most selfish person on the planet?

Jiyeon stopped tugging at a flower that had gotten tangled in the strands framing her face. She reached into the tote bag for her phone, executing what seemed to Eunjae like an unusually long chain of swipes and passcode entries. When she finally got up to press the phone into his hand, he saw that it had been reverted to factory settings. Perplexed, Eunjae held it flat on his palm, looking down at the setup screen as it politely waited for him to select his preferred language.

"All yours." Jiyeon closed his fingers over the phone before he could drop the thing entirely. "If you don't know phone numbers, maybe you can email. Either way, try and let someone know you're safe."

"But I can't just take your phone."

"I can spare it. See? I have another one."

Eunjae's consternation only intensified as Jiyeon showed him her second phone, a relic that flipped open to a no-frills, pixelated display. He wanted to ask if she'd raided an early 2000s time capsule. Instead, he tried not to laugh. This attempt ended in failure.

"Oh, sure. Laugh all you want. But I do have a functional phone, so you can have this one without feeling bad about it."

"Won't it still be linked to your number?"

Jiyeon shook her head. "No one has that number except family. It's almost brand new, especially since I barely use it. Denny got it for me after my old phone, um, fell. Into the Pacific Ocean."

"The Pacific Ocean."

"Uh-huh. I prefer the other one. It can't run any apps and it's better for me, that way. It makes everything... quieter."

Quieter. Well, he could see the appeal there. Eunjae squinted at the screen. "So... you can call and text? That's it, right?"

Soberly, Jiyeon replied, "No, there's more. I can also play unlimited games of Snake."

"You've got it all then," Eunjae choked out.

"Everything I need and nothing that I don't." A little too brightly, she added, "I'll go see if I can find you some clothes. Denny's got plenty in his closet. You're about the same height so it should work out. Use the phone, okay? I'll shut the door. Take your time."

And then she was gone, leaving Eunjae to face the next hurdle on his own. This was unfortunate, because he could've used all the moral support he could get.

At least the phone's setup process provided him with an excuse to procrastinate a little longer. As he plodded through the steps, Eunjae took the opportunity to look around. He so seldom found himself in another person's room. His brothers didn't count. The members of Apollo considered the walls between dorm rooms to be porous membranes. They went in and out of one another's spaces at will.

Eunjae paced around, giving in to curiosity. Relics from past school days were still tacked to the corkboard: the tassel from her graduation cap, photos of a younger Jiyeon posing with friends in front of the Haunted Mansion at Disneyland, a rainbow of laminated hall passes labeled with the names of at least ten different clubs and organizations.

Eunjae thought he might have enjoyed being part of a club or two in high school. Yearbook, maybe. He liked taking pictures. Trainees had busy schedules, though, and at Emerald they worked with private tutors rather than attending school.

The phone was still updating software. He left it on the desk, almost tripping over a cardboard box containing an ancient, bulbous CD player and a ring light on a flexible stand. Multiple ring lights, actually, snarled with the cable of a microphone. Then he almost tripped again when he sighted the row of stuffed animals on the dresser. One of these was a lion wearing a red bow around its neck.

Every member of Apollo had been assigned an emoji by the fans. These had become synonymous with their public-facing identities. The terrifying Jaehwan was symbolized by a hammer, while the sunflower was chosen for Jesse, and so on. Even in the years before his costumed stint on *Mask Singer*, Eunjae's emoji had been the lion. It came from his stage name, Ari, which meant 'lion' in Hebrew. Chosen by his mother, it was a family name inherited from her grandfather.

This lion on Jiyeon's dresser wasn't Apollo merchandise, thankfully; their stuff was always in pastel blues and yellows, in keeping with the group's official colors. Even so, a spooked Eunjae turned the lion so that it faced the wall.

His tour concluded at a bookcase crammed with travel guides. The shadowbox propped up on its middle shelf showcased a collection of souvenir keychains, all printed with the name JANE. Jiyeon's older sister, the one whose phone number she still had memorized. The other twin bed must have belonged to her. Eunjae shared his own dorm with Jungwoo, the brother closest to him in age. Seeing that pair of beds inspired some feelings of homesickness as a result.

What was Jungwoo doing now? He wouldn't be shocked that Eunjae didn't have his number memorized. They'd never had any need for that. The two of them were rarely apart for longer than a week at a stretch. Even on their last mini vacation, a gift from the agency after record high sales, Eunjae had chosen to spend part of the holiday in Busan with Jungwoo and his family.

The phone trilled out a triumphant melody once setup was complete. Before his courage could disintegrate, Eunjae tapped in Jaehwan's number. He saved it to the list of contacts. Then he spent the following thirty minutes typing, deleting, retyping, and meticulously editing an explanation of his behavior. He put it all into three long paragraphs and tacked another apology onto the end, just to be thorough.

It was harrowing work, and he wasn't even fielding Jaehwan's replies yet. When Jiyeon knocked on the door around 11:00, nearly two hours after Eunjae punched the Send button on that message, he had fallen asleep at her desk.

Her arms were laden with borrowed clothing, enough for at least a few days. Jiyeon set the bundle down on Janie's empty bed and went to very gently rest a hand on his back.

"Hey," she whispered, shaking him a little. Eunjae mumbled an incoherent response. He opened his eyes, saw her there, and closed both eyes again.

He would have no memory of how he got from the desk to the bed; such was Eunjae's exhaustion that he barely registered the words he spoke to Jiyeon before she left him there for the night.

"Do you know who I am yet?" he'd murmured. The pillow under his head smelled faintly of her shampoo.

Jiyeon plugged the phone into the charger and put it next to the pile of red flowers she'd plucked from her hair. "No," she murmured back. "Not yet."

Ari: Anyway, I missed the flight. I'm safe, though. I found a place to stay. I won't be gone long. I'm sorry, but don't worry about me. I just felt like this was something I had to do.

Jaehwan: What??????

Jaehwan: What do you mean, you missed the flight?? You're still in the US??

Jaehwan: How did this even happen?? How could they make it all the way to the damn airport without noticing you were gone??

Jaehwan: And why didn't you add that idiot Kazuhiko to this chat??? I have to do everything around here and I'm not even AROUND

[**KAZU** *has been added to this group message*]

Kazu: Wait

Kazu: Wait what

Kazu: ARI

Kazu: ARI WHERE THE HELL ARE YOU

Kazu: ARI YOU DON'T KNOW MY NUMBER

Jaehwan: How did you lose one of the children!!! Better question!!!

Kazu: I didn't lose him! Jungwoo did!

Jaehwan: I see

Jaehwan: Your response is to blame one of the other children

Jaehwan: Nothing should surprise me anymore but here we are

Kazu: Ari this is nuts

Kazu: Are you ok? Do you need anything?

Kazu: Do you have money?

Jaehwan: Why? Are you offering to send him some?

Kazu: Yes! If he needs it!

Jaehwan: If the others find out you play favorites like this

Kazu: I don't play favorites, my favorite is whichever one of these morons isn't giving me a hard time at that given moment so if you think about it, the favorite is NOT Ari right now

Kazu: Ari just be careful

Jaehwan: They'll be back for him soon

Jaehwan: Probably landed @ Incheon and sent someone right to the ticket counter for the next flight out

Jaehwan: That's if Nami didn't stay behind

Jaehwan: My god, wake up and reply before I reach through the phone and strangle you myself!!!

Kazu: He's asleep, I bet

Kazu: But you know what

Kazu: I'm proud of him

Jaehwan: You were supposed to be watching, Zu

Jaehwan: You're supposed to be leader while I'm gone

Kazu: It's fine

Kazu: He said he's safe, and back then, remember what we said?

Jaehwan: As if I could forget

Kazu: There you go then

Kazu: We're here for you

Kazu: Hwannie will get over it, give him some time

Kazu: Be happy, Ari

Jaehwan: Don't be happy!!!

Jaehwan: Be smart!!! Make yourself hard to find!!!

Jaehwan: Now that you've done this stupid thing, you might as well do it right

Jaehwan: And by the way, you owe me $$$, Zu

Jaehwan: My god, wake up and reply before I reach through the phone and strangle you myself!!!

Kazu: He's asleep, I bet

Kazu: But you know what

Kazu: I'm proud of him

Jaehwan: You were supposed to be watching, Zu

Jaehwan: You're supposed to be leader while I'm gone

Kazu: It's fine

Kazu: He said he's safe, and back then, remember what we said?

Jaehwan: As if I could forget

Kazu: There you go then

Kazu: We're here for you

Kazu: Hwannie will get over it, give him some time

Kazu: Be happy, Ari

Jaehwan: Don't be happy!!!

Jaehwan: Be smart!!! Make yourself hard to find!!!

Jaehwan: Now that you've done this stupid thing, you might as well do it right

Jaehwan: And by the way, you owe me $$$, Zu

Jaehwan: You know what else we said?

Jaehwan: That this would happen on YOUR watch

Kazu: … … …

13

The first thing Eunjae saw when he woke up was Jiyeon's phone on its charger, the lock screen showing a chain of notification icons and a time that made no sense at all. How could it be past noon? He did the math in his head, calculating the number of hours he'd been asleep. The last time he slept anywhere near that long was right after Apollo returned from their second world tour. He'd been too sick to get out of bed.

Eunjae sat up. He'd passed out on top of the covers, bowled over by a combination of stress and lingering jet lag. He retained no memory of how he got from the desk to Jiyeon's old twin bed, but someone had draped a blanket over him, fluffy and emblazoned with what had to be an Austen quote. Eunjae wondered which book it came from. And then he remembered that he'd sent a text to Jaehwan, who might have replied by now. He snatched the phone off the nightstand.

His brother had indeed replied. Not just Jaehwan, but Kazu as well. This meant both of Eunjae's oldest brothers were now apprised of the situation. He found himself curled up on the mattress, eyes burning with unshed tears. Reading his brothers' words was almost enough to make Eunjae feel as if they were sitting on either side of him. There was

Kazu's hand on his shoulder, his big laugh that could fill a room with sunlight. And here was Jaehwan scolding him in person. In all his days, Eunjae never guessed that he'd miss those scoldings so terribly.

Be happy, Ari. He read that line again, and then all the other lines twice over. In some ways, they'd responded just as he'd thought they might. In others, they'd surprised him.

Jaehwan was right about making himself hard to find. Eunjae hadn't thought of that at all. He also hadn't made any decisions about how long to stay, but returning to Seoul still felt as inevitable as sunrise.

He should go back, but he didn't want to.

Just then, there was a brisk knock at the bedroom door. "Mystery Ryan. You up?"

"I said check if he's sleeping still, not shout at him!"

"Who's shouting now? You're louder than I am!"

Eunjae hurried to inform them he was awake. Denny fixed him with an appraising stare. It was like submitting to an x-ray that revealed character flaws rather than broken bones. Squirming a little, Eunjae came to the realization that he had yet to shower or change. He'd been more exhausted than he thought.

"Finally," boomed Denny. "I was getting tired of Dad texting me that you might have been murdered in your bed by assassins. Like they could breach the perimeter! Ridiculous."

"Han Woosung! I never said he was a dead person! He just *sleeps* like a dead person." Mr. Han presented Eunjae with a towel. "Ryan Kim, you're so tired, huh? What's your job? Graveyard nurse? Late night comedian?"

"Graveyard nurse?" muttered Denny.

"You know what I'm saying!"

"Ah," said Eunjae, trying to decide if he should remove the bucket hat or leave it on and avoid displaying the abominable state of his hair. "Something like that."

Denny hooked a finger in his shirt collar and hustled him into the hallway. "Yeah, okay. Liar. Come on, you need to get cleaned up. You look like bad news. I can't put you to work like this, we're a family-friendly brunch spot. Where's all the stuff Yeonnie stole from my closet? You're lucky I kept all my clothes from high school. I was scrawnier then."

Shortly thereafter, Eunjae was in a bathroom two doors down, clutching the towel and some plastic bottles containing shampoo and conditioner. Jiyeon's, possibly left here in case she ever stayed the night at her parents' place. Eunjae could tell because the scent was the same as the pillow he'd fallen asleep on the previous night. He was trying to get a better grip on these items when Denny began pelting him with articles of clothing: a royal blue t-shirt stamped with the Wanna Waffle logo, jeans, underwear and socks and a belt. Last came an orange apron that sailed through the air and landed on Eunjae's head.

Denny shooed him into the shower. "Go, go. You've got ten minutes. The worst of the lunch rush is over, but Mom will need us back for that retirement party coming in at 2:00."

Eunjae lifted the apron away from his face. "This is for me? Really?"

"Who else would it be for? We've all got one already. Kindly note that there's no name on it because you continue to withhold vital information. Such as who you actually are and how many felonies are on your record."

They were giving him a job. Eunjae could hardly believe it. Mr. Han's explanation of how to work the fussy shower knob went in one ear and right back out the other.

"Geez, why are you smiling like that? This family attracts nothing but weirdos. Get going!" Denny stomped away, scratching his head. About halfway down the hall, he whipped around to point at Eunjae. "And you'd better come out of there looking wholesome. *Wholesome,* you hear me?"

14

"You don't look very wholesome," pronounced Mrs. Han. She pushed another plate of waffles at Eunjae. "Too handsome. Who do you look like, Secret Ryan? Mommy? Daddy? Which one?"

Eunjae sat back against his battered wooden chair. "Mum," he answered. "Mostly."

"I knew it. Same thing at our house. My kids, they got all those good looks from me."

They sat across from one another at a folding card table tucked into a corner of the Wanna Waffle kitchen, where Eunjae had been duly transported by Denny and Mr. Han in an SUV roughly the size of a Spanish galleon. It was a far less exciting ride with Denny at the wheel, as he proved to be the opposite of a hellion while driving, but Eunjae was grateful. He couldn't have eaten all this food if the car ride had made him nauseous.

The Hans seemed intent on feeding him a week's worth of breakfasts. Waffle after waffle came sliding onto Eunjae's plate, plus bacon and eggs, sausage and hash browns. A grumbling Denny had refilled his coffee the instant Eunjae finished it. Mr. Han popped up with orange juice two minutes later.

Eunjae ate everything they put in front of him. After coming to believe that he'd grown used to the omnipresent gnawing sensation of hunger, he discovered that it had only been the tip of the iceberg that whole time; he was ravenous. Eunjae had either never been this hungry, or he'd been quietly hungry for far too long.

Food wasn't something to be thoughtless about, in the world he'd temporarily escaped. Portions were doled out to precise measurements. Treats were few and far between. He and his brothers weren't made to subsist only on bowls of lettuce or one slice of watermelon per meal, nothing like that. But calories were certainly counted, everyone's intake closely watched, and Eunjae hit the treadmills and weight benches at the agency's gym according to a strict schedule.

Someone was always watching him. What he ate, what he wore, how he moved. If he smiled or if he didn't. Not here, though.

Unless you counted Mrs. Han monitoring his progress through all the waffles and scrambled eggs, but that wasn't the same thing. For starters, she wanted Eunjae to eat, observing every mouthful with a grin that betrayed gleeful satisfaction. And when he tried to protest, saying he'd been brought there to work, she flipped another waffle out of the iron and set it in front of him. "This is your work right now. You want to get fired? I can do that. I'm the owner. Not Denny, not Joey. Don't you forget!"

So Eunjae ate, and it was easy enough to do because food had never tasted better. This place really was magic.

"How long has Wanna Waffle been here?"

"Ah, not too long," replied Mrs. Han, offering more maple syrup. "We've had it eleven years, now. It was my big brother's shop at first. He was always opening a new business. Donuts here, boba there. You name it, that dummy tried to sell it. When he got tired of making no money, he decided to go back home to Korea. A fancy coffee place, that's what this guy wanted to do next. So we bought all of this from him. Everything, even the waffle recipe."

"Hey!" barked Denny from the other side of the kitchen. "That's classified!"

"Nobody's teaching a class about how to make the waffles," his mother barked back at him. She returned to Eunjae with the rest of the story. "I always wanted a place that was mine. You know, we pay rent at the apartment. And we pay on time, every single month. Did that even when it was hard. We've lived there a long time. Not ours, though. Not on paper. But this shop, it has my name on it."

Mrs. Han stretched her arms out wide. "Yes, this is mine. Something I can leave to Janie and Yeonnie and Denny when I'm gone. They can keep making waffles forever. Or they can sell it, use the money for something else. Whatever they want. They can pick. That's special, to me."

"That is special."

"Oh my, don't smile like that! The way you listen, it makes people want to talk and talk and talk. What will I tell you next?" She made a show of clutching at her chest as if to prevent all her secrets from flying away. Eunjae obligingly covered his ears.

She laughed, but he was doing it in earnest. A few years back, he'd been cajoled into serving as a reluctant guest emcee on *Music Bank*. While waiting backstage, Eunjae's co-host had spent ten straight minutes sobbing into his shoulder about a bad breakup. Strings of tragic text messages were quoted word for word, line by line. Suddenly, he knew way too much about this young man. They'd never even spoken before that day. The stylists took one look at Eunjae's tear-stained shirt and called for a last minute wardrobe change in a panic. His brothers teased him for weeks, pretending to weep into his shoulder at every opportunity.

"I'm bringing you to poker night at the senior club," Mrs. Han said, patting Eunjae's hand. "The ladies will tell you all their cards. Then I'll win." This prompted Denny to grouse that they were paying $50 a year for his mother's membership to a gambling den. The complaint was ignored.

"Is there a bookstore nearby?" Eunjae thought to ask, sometime after the slabs of toast slathered in strawberry jam but before the bread pudding Denny described as 'experimental.' He thought he might have enough cash left for a paperback of *The Brass Key*. If nothing else, he could flip through the pages, re-read the parts he liked best. Would the book resonate as deeply now that he'd found the magic and crossed to the other side of that door?

Mrs. Han pursed her lips, thinking. "Hmm. Don't think so, but I can drive you. Maybe tomorrow. You stay 'til tomorrow, yes?" Without pausing to let him answer, she added, "Good."

"You don't need to drive me there. You've done so much already."

She patted his hand. "You're a sweet boy, Ryan Kim. Always have amnesia, okay? Stay here with us. Wherever you came from, they don't feed you there." Her eyes were suspiciously bright. She pulled a hankie from her apron pocket, swiveled in her seat, and blew her nose. "Allergies, allergies! All done? Feel better?"

Eunjae surveyed the empty plates and drained glasses, the dregs of his coffee and the hopeful smile on Mrs. Han's face. He nodded. "Much better."

The way her smile could blossom in an instant, like a full spring season flowering in timelapse — that was something else she'd passed on to her children.

"If you like to walk," she said, while Eunjae helped to clear the dishes, "Yeonnie can bring you to the library, let you use her card. Not far from the house. And it's free! You stay 'til then, yeah?" Mrs. Han reached up to pat him on the cheek. "Good."

15

Eunjae spent the rest of the time stationed at the sink. This was fine because he'd always liked washing dishes. It was an ideal mindless task, perfect for slipping away into a daydream or puzzling through a problem without sacrificing productivity. And thank goodness he knew his way around a sink — Denny had him scrubbing for most of the afternoon.

"Everyone starts at the bottom here, even amnesiacs. If you prove yourself worthy, I'll give you something less lame to do."

Eunjae harbored no resentment over this setup. He tackled all the dishes at a steady pace, still enjoying it even though his head wasn't as far up in the clouds as usual. There was too much to look at, to wonder about. If he drifted too far away from the present moment, he might miss something. The kitchen was full of stories. Constantly humming with activity, its surfaces bore a patina of age and steady use. Someone had scratched a tiny heart in the corner of Mrs. Han's stainless steel prep table. A child's drawings were tacked up in the pantry, the paper faded and curling with time. Eunjae realized that the artwork depicted prototype Wanna Waffle logos. All were signed with the initials DWH in bold, unswerving strokes.

Around 4:00, a girl swept into the kitchen and collected her orange apron. It was Jeannie, the same teenager from the night before. She came to a halt next to Eunjae, eyeing him with great interest.

"Denny-boss," she hollered, glossy ponytail swinging. "New hire? Since when?"

"Since whenever I felt like it, Vho. Where's Evan?"

"Still on the way. Traffic was bad and he had orientation for his part-time thing at the aquarium." Jeannie studied Eunjae as she tied the apron strings into a sloppy bow around her waist. "Hey, this is the guy from last night! I knew I'd seen him before."

"Yeah, on a wanted poster." Denny beckoned to Eunjae, car keys jangling in his hand. "Let's go, Lying Ryan. The reinforcements are here and we've got errands to run."

"Oh," said Eunjae, turning the faucet off. He dried his hands on the faded blue gingham dishtowel he'd tossed over his shoulder. "Where are we going?"

"I'm glad you asked. First we're doing something about the creepy purple eyes. There will be no more sleeping with those contacts still on your eyeballs." Denny pulled a face. "Ugh."

"But I don't have my prescription with me. And what about the insurance?" Did he even have insurance? Eunjae had no idea. He had no idea about anything, it seemed. It occurred to him that almost every part of his life was arranged by someone else. What he did know was that he shouldn't use the company credit card. That was obvious even without Invisible Jaehwan hissing a warning in his ear.

Denny waved these concerns away. "Don't worry, I've got a guy for this. Last minute, rush job optometry with no questions asked. Owes me a favor anyway. We catered his daughter's birthday waffle brunch after less than twenty-four hours' notice. I bet he does this for free."

The following two and a half hours were a nonstop whirlwind of activity. While waiting around in the lobby, the elderly receptionist regaled him with the full, unabridged story of how she lost the love of her life to a rival who stepped on her debutante gown. She sniffled loudly through most of the account. The rollercoaster of emotions left Eunjae somewhat winded, but he did come away with a new pair of glasses to tide him over until contacts were ready. Now he watched from the passenger-side window while the sun slowly set on his first full day as a fugitive. It had gone by too fast. Tomorrow, he'd make sure to wake up long before noon.

Tomorrow. Was he really staying here 'til tomorrow? Did he have the audacity?

Eunjae wrestled with these thoughts as Denny parked the Camaro. At first he didn't even notice that they weren't back at Wanna Waffle. This was a different shopping center, fronted by a mostly deserted parking lot and containing, among other establishments, a salon called The Final Cut.

His window rolled down, courtesy of Denny, and then Jiyeon was standing right outside the car.

"Good timing," she said to her brother, with a smile for Eunjae thrown in. He smiled back, lifting his hand in greeting just a few beats too late.

Denny drummed his fingers on the steering wheel. "You sure about this, Yeonnie?"

"It'll be fine. Everyone's gone already. Olivia's monthly VIP stylist dinner, you know."

"Where'd she take them this time? I'll call ahead, make sure they get her order wrong."

"Woosung-ah."

"What?"

The breeze picked up, setting the skirts of Jiyeon's green dress whipping around her ankles. A floral pattern of petals and leaves danced along the hem, picked out in watery blues and violets. She tipped her head to the side and said, "So, Ryan Kim. We've had complaints from the management that your hair is floppy. How about a free haircut?"

Eunjae was late to process that, too. In truth, the sight of Jiyeon in that last, lingering bit of daylight had caught him unawares. The waning sunshine revealed details he'd previously missed: the pale gleam of a scar that skimmed her collarbone, a chipped nail, the subtle undertones of red rippling through her dark hair.

These were things he was never meant to see. These were people he was never meant to meet, let alone get to know. If he hadn't missed his flight, Eunjae would be in Seoul right now. He shouldn't be here as the light changed, as another day came to a close.

Eunjae was glad to be here. It felt like thievery. It felt miraculous.

As he climbed out of the car, Denny honked the horn twice. "There will be zero romantic moments while you're cutting his hair," he announced to his sister. "No funny business, Yeonnie."

Jiyeon looked back over her shoulder. "Oh, I see. You've cast me as the villain here. I'm the one to watch."

"I mean, yeah. Look at him. Not exactly the most seductive crayon in the box."

"Which colors," asked Jiyeon, "are the seductive ones, by your standards?"

"You know what I'm getting at!"

"I promise not to make things weird while cutting his hair, Denny."

But Denny made as if he might get out of the car and follow

them inside, after all. "You're not taking this seriously," he complained. Pointing at Eunjae, he added, "This one is spoken for. Let's just put it that way."

"Are you?" Jiyeon inquired, turning to Eunjae. The breeze had yet to die down, teasing strands of her hair from its elaborate braid. A length of jade green ribbon had been woven through the plaits.

"No," replied Eunjae. He was able to answer that one quickly because it was such an easy question. Of course he wasn't spoken for. Imagine the general furor if the fans thought he was dating someone! But he shoved both hands in his pockets, subconsciously worried that any and all sudden movements might be interpreted as seduction.

Denny put the car in reverse. "He's spoken for. By Interpol. Because he's some kind of fugitive trying to dodge international law. They're probably looking for him as we speak, so don't get attached." Suddenly, he put the car back into park again. "And the phone! Did you think I wouldn't notice the phone? Now you adopt mopey strangers and give them phones? This is worse than the time Mom and Dad adopted that weirdo cellist from church —"

"Her host family had an emergency out of town and couldn't pick her up from the airport. She stayed for one weekend. I don't think that counts as an adoption."

"Yeah, 'cause it counts as a classic con. I'm shocked you didn't give her a phone, too."

"Ryan needed one," said Jiyeon, "and I had two, so why not?"

"That garbage piece of plastic doesn't count as a phone! And what are you gonna do when they stop supporting a 4G network around here? I'm losing my mind all over again."

"It can handle calls and texts just fine. There's nothing else I need it to do. Not anymore."

Something unreadable passed between them. Denny looked away first.

Not long after, Eunjae and Jiyeon stood together in the parking lot, having finally mollified her brother into leaving. "Let's head inside before Interpol detects your presence," she said.

"Probably for the best," agreed Eunjae.

The boys are awash in a sea of puppies.

Most are openly elated by this situation. Jesse lies sprawled on the floor in a state of rapture, puppies treading on his face. Not too far from him, Nicky and Namgyu are busy comparing two puppies they've scooped up and claimed as their own. Each insists his puppy is cuter and more intelligent. Kei informs them in a dreary monotone that the puppies are definitely cuter and more intelligent than they are.

"The puppy interview," gushes Kazu, grinning at the camera. He's lounging on a pile of cherry red cushions in a shirt with one too many buttons undone. The comments section is full of jokes about Apollo's eldest member baring his chest the instant he's not on South Korean mainstream channels. He jostles Jaehwan, who is seated beside him. "We've been waiting to do the puppy interview forever."

Clearing his throat, Jaehwan says, "Shine bright, it's Apollo!" The other eight members echo their leader's words. It's the group's official greeting, used for every introduction since their debut.

"Today we're answering some questions while playing with puppies." Jaehwan's smile radiates serenity even as he cuts a pointed glare in Nick's direction; that was supposed to be his line. Realizing his mistake, Nicky laughs nervously. The fans assigned Jaehwan the hammer emoji three weeks after Apollo's first EP dropped in 2014 and it has never ceased to be an accurate representation of his leadership style.

There is a round of brief introductions. In addition to stating his name, Kei announces himself as a cat person. This triggers a chorus of lighthearted booing from everyone around him. When everyone's had their turn, Jaehwan gestures at a producer off-screen. "Don't bother with subtitles. We brought our own translators. If they don't work, they don't eat."

The video splits into three panels, each showing one of Apollo's fluent English speakers: Ari, Max, and Jesse. Max is paying absolutely no attention whatsoever. He appears determined to teach Apollo choreography to some puppies who keep trying to toddle into Kei's lap. As for Jesse, he hasn't moved at all since the last time we saw him.

With his brothers otherwise occupied, Ari becomes official translator by default. From the comments, we glean that this is the fate which usually befalls him. Fans find it extra funny because Ari is well known to be quieter and more reserved than the other members.

The interview questions have been submitted by Apollo's fans. These are printed on cards which Ari pulls out of a basket and reads aloud. "Do you guys ever fight? What happens if you do?" He looks up, laughing. "I can answer that one. We fight all the time."

Referring to Jaehwan by the respectful honorific for an older brother, Kei says, "Hyung makes us hold hands when we're fighting."

"I read about it in a magazine. Holding hands makes it harder to stay mad."

"Because it makes it harder to punch each other," Namgyu elaborates, beaming.

Ari pulls the next question, still laughing. "What's your go-to pickup line?"

Several members express confusion, so Ari explains the question in Korean. Jungwoo is the first to respond. The camera zooms in on Apollo's resident songwriter, composer, and producer as he says, with a completely straight face, "Your beauty has earned me many enemies."

The group devolves into instant uproar. Max stands up and proclaims, "Those are song lyrics! And they aren't even ours! Cheater! Cheater, cheater, cheater!"

Jaehwan raises his voice above the din. His smile never falters. In fact, it only becomes more beautiful and more mesmerizing as the chaos unfolds around him. Firmly he declares, "No pickup lines. We belong to our fans. Next!"

But the camera zooms in on Kazu, who scoffs, "Pickup lines. Sunshines, are you saying I need those? I thought I could get by on my looks." Animated sparkles twinkle around his face, which is indeed so pleasing to the eye that it ought to be illegal. Kei lobs a cushion at him, unimpressed.

"Ari-yah," calls Jaehwan. "*Next question.*"

Goaded by the power of his older brother's glare, Ari rushes to oblige. "Favorite fanmade sign you've seen at concerts and events?"

"Oh!" Nicky exclaims. "The one that just said DADDY. That's it. Like, is that for all of us? Just one of us?"

A shower of thinking emojis floods the screen. Namgyu holds up his puppy and squeals, "Daddy!"

"I mean, that sign isn't for me. I know that for sure. I'm more of a hot uncle."

"Shut up, Nicky."

Jesse groans from his spot on the floor. "You're the worst!"

"Favorite Apollo memes?"

This one prompts some discussion. It's finally enough to get Jesse to roll to a sitting position in the middle of the debate, puppies wriggling in his arms. "Okay, so it's not a meme," he says in English, "but the stories fans write about us on, like, Tumblr and stuff..."

Kei nods vehemently. "The fanfiction. Yes."

"Wait, what?" demands Jungwoo, intrigued. "They write stories about us? Like what kind of stories?"

"Nobody's writing about you, Jungwoo," says Max. He's pelted with rubber chew toys as a result. Each missile is returned with twice the force.

"They write about everybody. I saved some of it on my account. But man, the stuff they write about Ari." Jesse widens his eyes at the camera. "You guys are *thirsty.*"

Nicky covers Jesse's eyes. "No, my son! Your innocence!"

"Do the managers know you made that account?" Jaehwan inquires. Jesse flails his arms dramatically and shouts that Max and Kei have accounts too. The accused plead 'not guilty' with the fervor of men sentenced to the guillotine at sunrise. Meanwhile, Ari hides behind the basket of question cards. Jungwoo leans against him, laughing himself hoarse.

Kazu feeds treats to any puppy who wanders by. "But what are they saying about him? Hit me. I'm old enough for this content."

"I thought Ari's fans were the most chill," supplies Kei, "but then he had that scene with Hazel Lim in the *Trickster* music video."

"Aww! That scene was so romantic! Mine was just sad."

"Namgyu really does get all the sad parts."

Jungwoo stops laughing. "That scene barely lasted ten seconds!"

Even as he voices this complaint, Nicky is in the background attempting to make a Tumblr account on his phone. Kazu suggests potential usernames. Judging from the looks he's getting, these suggestions are universally terrible. Jesse and Kei are clapping as Max re-enacts the music video for *Trickster*, an Apollo song released in 2022. He assumes the role of Ari while a puppy takes the place of Hazel Lim, the young actress who starred in the video and has since become wildly popular. Chaos descends once more.

There is a burst of animated puppy paws and then the interview cuts to Ari pulling a new card. Everyone has been made to sit in a semi-circle around him as if this is story time at a preschool. Fans in the comments overwhelmingly note the grim satisfaction on Jaehwan's face.

"In an alternate universe where you never debuted with

Apollo," Ari reads, "what would you be doing with your life?"

"Proud father of three!" Namgyu chimes in.

"Proud father of four!" Nicky one-ups him.

"Living peacefully, nowhere near any of these people."

"You love us, Keiichi."

More members speak up, naming alternate fates ranging from delightfully mundane to highly improbable. The only one to show even the slightest bit of hesitation is Ari, who maintains that he isn't sure what he'd be doing. He gives the camera a shy, sheepish smile. "Just... being normal, I guess?"

"Hyung, are you saying you'd just be some random guy?"

Jungwoo slings an arm around him. "Ari always wanted to sing. He'd be on stage in every parallel universe, same as me. Right?"

And although the smile gutters like a candle flame, Ari turns to Jungwoo and replies, "Right."

16

Eunjae followed Jiyeon into the salon, where almost all the lights were dimmed, the other five stations deserted. Each space bore a stylist's name in custom neon signage. She led him to the one marked *Emma*. Her sign appeared to be newer, slightly different in lettering style than the others.

Eunjae was no stranger to salons; he and his brothers had to have spent a century in hair and makeup by now, nine years since their debut. He'd seldom seen a place so immaculate. Magazines were fanned out on a glass-topped table, ordered by color. Products for sale had been meticulously shelved in rainbow order, and the chairs in the waiting area were upholstered in blinding white leather, no scuffs or signs of wear.

The stations were just as tidy. Various certificates took pride of place at each one. Most of them looked to be of an official nature, diplomas and credentials. But Eunjae also noticed that the other stylists had lavish floral arrangements on display, along with ribbons, stuffed animals, and even trophies, as if they'd medaled in some kind of salon Olympics. On nearly every mirror, a message had been scrawled in dry erase marker, saccharine and loaded with cheer: *So jealous of your lucky clients, babe! You're making the world so beautiful! Top stylist for the third week in a row!*

It became painfully obvious that Jiyeon's station was the only one without a single ribbon, trophy, or plaque beyond the requisite credentials. No words of praise were scrawled across the mirror. She had no flowers, no stuffed animals. It made her workspace seem strangely bleak and clinical when compared to the warmth he associated with her presence. If not for the big, neon *Emma* emblazoned above it, he might have theorized that she was borrowing someone else's spot temporarily.

"Hurry up," she chided Eunjae, drawing a comb out of her apron pocket. "I've been waiting to do this since I met you."

"You've been waiting to cut my hair...?"

Their eyes met in the mirror. "Oh my gosh, yes," Jiyeon replied, with feeling. "Did you think you could hide this situation under a hat?"

"Maybe...?"

Jiyeon ran a hand through his hair, grimacing. "So much damage. What have you been doing to it? Switching colors every two weeks? Are you trying to bleach it 'til you go bald?"

Her stern expression brought out the opposite sentiment in Eunjae. He cracked a smile and then a laugh, relaxing into the chair and forgetting everything he'd been worrying about. "You really want to know?"

"Not only do I want to know, I need to know. This is depressing and I'm gonna fix it. Otherwise it's on my conscience." She held up her right hand. "Hairstylist's oath."

"Okay. So last month it was still purple on the ends. A really dark purple, almost black. And before that, it was silver." Apollo had released an EP in Japan that dominated the Oricon charts for weeks.

Jiyeon regarded him with something like despair. "Silver."

"And it was long, too. A lot longer than this."

"I feel like I've seen this anime before."

"I think everybody has," said Eunjae.

"Hmm. I'll regret asking, but what came before the silver?"

Eunjae had to roll back his memories to early January, when Apollo was promoting an album and its title track, *Never Too Late*. "Oh, my hair was normal then." They'd let him go back to the natural color on tour because it suited the concept for the music video anyway.

Jiyeon lowered the chair, pumping the pedal with one foot. "What do you mean by normal? And just know that if you tell me it went from dark to silver, and then from silver to dark again, I'll have to go into that break room over there and cry for an hour or two."

"Don't cry," he hastened to tell her. "The normal color is brown." A lighter brown, shot through with hints of gold that intensified under summer sunshine. Eunjae didn't have to describe it in great detail because Jiyeon seemed to know exactly what he was talking about.

"The kind of hair with highlights built in? The kind that clients are constantly paying me to recreate?" She shook her head. "They should arrest the people who told you to bleach such a gorgeous color."

"We could send an anonymous tip to Interpol," joked Eunjae, absently. The sound of his mother's voice echoed back to him through years and across long miles. Every memory left him feeling bruised.

In childhood, compliments on Eunjae's looks were usually met with a lamentation about his hair — the way it hadn't managed to be black as ink, like his father's, nor the sunny blonde of his mother's. Instead, it was something of both. A drab and uninspiring brown, Leila would say. Caught between the two and failing to manage the brilliance of either, not nearly striking enough for her tastes.

"He came so close to having it all," she'd joke with friends and strangers alike, a sharp glint in her eyes even as she smiled. "Either color would've been perfect. Oh, well. Hair can be dyed, right? With his face and that voice, he might just make it anyway."

His younger brother was born with the same hair. Eunjae was twelve, listening to Leila complaining about this to his father, Simon, who neither agreed nor disagreed. And in his heart, Eunjae had discovered a deep seam of anger that he'd always been able to bury, before.

He was still trying to clear his head when the phone went off. Eunjae hadn't remembered to silence it or change out the default ringtone. As a result, the explosion of sound scared both Eunjae and Jiyeon half to death. He yanked the phone out of his back pocket, accidentally swiping the screen in the wrong direction as he did so. Now he'd answered instead of hanging up. Too late, Eunjae realized it was a Korean number, and not one of the two he'd saved to contacts.

He brought the phone to his ear but couldn't bring himself to utter a single word. And then, coming through on a terrible connection, he heard his name being spoken. His other name.

"Ari? Hey, Ari, come on. It's me."

That was a voice he knew very well. It belonged to Jungwoo.

17

Eunjae bolted out of the chair. He rushed outside, gesturing to Jiyeon that he needed to take the call.

"Jungwoo, I'm here. The signal's pretty bad."

There was a sharp intake of breath, and then a few disjointed sentences before Eunjae managed to find a spot where the connection was better. "— happened? Where did you go? I thought you were right behind us!"

"I was," said Eunjae, "but then I stopped because I saw this door like the one in my book. I've told you about it before. I'm sorry."

"Never mind that. Never mind any of it. I'm the one who's sorry." Here, Jungwoo's voice wavered, although perhaps not from any weakness in the cell signal. "I should've seen it. It's like everyone knew you were miserable except me. I never even pictured you doing something this drastic, not in my whole life."

Jungwoo was interrupted by a jarring thud and then the rustle of someone scooping the phone off the ground. Muffled at first, but getting louder and clearer by the second, another person joined the conversation. Eunjae knew right away that it was Max, the most cantankerous of his three younger brothers.

"You're the shittiest friend. I don't get why they sent you the number and not me. At least I noticed Ari was about to crack." Bringing his mouth to the receiver, Max said, "Hyung, you couldn't take me with you when you ran away? What the hell, man?"

Eunjae winced, partly because being addressed as an older brother was somewhat jarring after going a full day and night without hearing it. "I'm sorry, Max. Can you give the phone back for a minute, though? I need to talk to Jungwoo a little longer."

"No way. We all got chewed out for this, okay? CEO Yoon put everybody on lockdown. No leaving the dorms, no leaving hotel rooms, no social media, nada. And why are you always apologizing?"

During Apollo's trainee days, before they made their debut as a group, Mr. Yoon had been an occasional specter in the corridors of Emerald Entertainment's massive complex in Seoul. The agency's founders, Choi Haewon and Sun Soyeon, played a more active part in day-to-day operations back then. They used to drop into the practice rooms regularly, conferring with producers while artists were recording and even catering lunches or dinners for everyone at least once a month.

Now, Eunjae struggled to recall the last time he'd seen the founders in person. Yoon seemed to handle everything. And once he took over, things had changed. Their schedules became more hectic. Nights stretched longer even as sleep became a commodity none of them could ever seem to get their hands on. The number of social media posts and livestreams went up incrementally until it felt like every hour of every day had been earmarked for the creation of content to be fed to their fans. But Apollo's star burned brighter and brighter, so it was all supposed to be worth it.

On the phone, Max continued to rant. "Everything sucks right now because of you," he clinched. "So if I wanna make you feel bad, I will."

"I'm sorry," Eunjae said again. He allowed himself to be pulverized by the belated remorse, certain that he deserved it.

"Don't worry about Max," said Jungwoo, having reclaimed the phone for the moment. "He just hasn't bounced back yet. Jaehwan-hyung sent a ten-page text to the group chat and then he copy-pasted that same text to everybody's number individually."

Max wrestled the phone away again. "Quit saying sorry! I don't care that you're sorry! Hyung, the individual texts were *personalized*. We got the standard text, plus special Jaehwan death threats tailored just for us."

This made Eunjae wince again. Jaehwan had such a flair for incendiary text messages.

"He said I have to write song lyrics with Jungwoo for six straight hours 'cause I didn't tell anyone you seemed sad. Do you know how fucking depressing that is? He only writes breakup songs now! *Though our love has shattered, I won't forget the view.* He wrote that the other night! I saw it in his journal!"

Jungwoo could be heard protesting in the background. Max only talked louder to drown him out. "I can't believe the army is teaching him how to fire guns and drive tanks. We're all dead. You'd better be more than sorry. Sorry isn't enough!"

"Max, I'm serious. Let go of the phone and let me talk to him."

"I'm talking to him! Go away!" Max exhaled a shuddering breath. "You'd better be happy," he all but shouted into the phone. "You'd better be fucking happy and you'd better not come back!"

Eunjae leaned against the wall, listening to Max's furious sobs. *I am happy,* he wanted to shout in reply. *I've been happier in the past twelve hours than I have been for the past twelve months.* But how could he tell them that?

He was sorry, and yet he wasn't.

"You there? Ari?"

"Yeah," he replied. "I'm still here."

Jungwoo said, in a rush, "Look, just tell me where you are. I'll come get you tonight and then this can all be fixed. We'll meet with the bigwigs. You can ask to go on hiatus after the unit promos, or if you're really not up to it, we could shorten promo to one week instead of three. You're tired, that's all. We can work it out with them, okay? Just come back, Ari. Come home."

Eunjae froze. "Tonight? What do you mean?" How could they get to him so quickly?

"We didn't leave," said Jungwoo. "When we realized you were missing, Nami-noona said she'd turn back and look for you. I stayed too. They're sending two more people out, last we heard."

"Nami-noona tried to make me get on the plane," added Max, still sniffling a little, "but I ran for it. It was hilarious. Too bad you went rogue and missed that part."

"You guys didn't need to stay. I should be the company's problem, not yours. I didn't mean for that to happen, hyung."

It got so quiet that he almost thought the connection failed. But then Jungwoo responded, clearly stung. "I wasn't leaving without you. I could never do that."

His unspoken words crackled on the line like a live wire: *I could never leave without you, but you left without me.*

From Ari's most recent livestream on the Star-Connect app, dated May 26, 2023

Ari sits on the floor inside an Emerald Entertainment practice room. The company's logo is partially visible behind him, outlined in green light. He holds the phone with one hand, using the other to wave at the fans who have tuned in to watch. Messages scroll rapidly across the screen. These range from incoherent, all-caps screaming to declarations of eternal love. Ari's eyes track the lines. He's trying to read as many messages as he can.

>> Oppa, have you eaten?

>> omg look at him

>> I'll be at the next fanmeeting! So excited!

>> AAAAAAAHHHHHH

There is a slight delay to Ari's responses, of course, what with the flood of sentences and the speed at which they blink in and out of sight. "I've eaten, yes," he answers dutifully. "What about you? Oh, you're coming to see us. Wave to me, okay?"

>> ari, u look so tired tho

>> Can you sing something? Anything

>> Oppa, it's my birthday!

He smiles. "Your birthday? And you're spending it with me?"

This prompts a flurry of heart emojis, birthday cake stickers, GIFs of balloons and presents tied with giant bows. Someone squeals that they want to spend every birthday with Ari because he's the sweetest. Dozens of fans are quick to agree. The chat fills with links to YouTube videos like citations at the end of a research paper:

Just Apollo's Ari Being an Angel for 10 Minutes Straight

Ari Helping Rookies Figure Out Their Lives - Best Moments

Ari Comforts Crying Fan @ Apollo Fanmeet (SUBBED)

One fan contributes the URL for a video entitled *Ari (Apollo) - Top 5 Wardrobe Malfunctions*. Ari sees this and laughs.

>> Why are you so nice, oppa?
Sometimes I think you're too nice.
You'll get hurt.

"Why am I so nice?" Ari frowns at the screen. His frowning face elicits just as many lovelorn sighs as his smiling face. "Honestly, I'm not nice all the time. I just try to understand people as best as I can. Everybody's got a story."

>> Lol I wish he'd understand that he
needs to marry me

>> u know he wasn't nice back when
Jungwoo ate his snacks on the bus!!

>> omg his face when that happened

>> RIP jungwoo

>> Still the nicest! Thank u Ari's
mom for raising him RIGHT

Once Ari catches up to this message, his frown becomes

more pronounced. "I didn't learn that from my mum, actually. It was someone else, someone really important to me. She was always saying that kindness comes back to you. Maybe not right away, and maybe not in the way you might expect, but it will. So you should just keep putting it out there."

This is quite the monologue from the typically taciturn Ari. His fans melt. He doesn't notice, though. Ari allows the comments to scroll, lost in a memory. When he returns to the here and now, multiple people have asked for specifics. Who gave him that advice? Doesn't he get along with his mother very well? It's true that she's never been seen at any of Apollo's concerts or events. And if it's a she, is it an aunt, a cousin, a grandmother? (Not a girlfriend, surely. Ari wouldn't do that to them.)

They're always hungry for more of him, every piece that they can inspect and devour and claim. Whatever he feels, whatever he's doing, someone in the world is interested. And in a way, it means never being lonely, never suffering neglect. But in other ways, it means being lonely all the time. It means he can do nothing without first considering how it will be dissected, interpreted, consumed.

```
>> Oppa I just wanted to tell you
   that I passed my exam from last week,
   thank you for cheering me on!!!!!
```

Ari scrolls back to that one. He remembers the girl from his last livestream, fretting about a test she should really be studying for. Her username stands out to him because she's often here, watching his streams on the app. "Hey, that's great," he replies to her. "You can rest now. I'm glad."

>> You rest too, oppa!!!

Ari gives her a thumbs up. "Someone sent me a letter with a picture of their dog dressed up like a lion. A service dog. You said she came with you to one of our Seoul concerts. Are you here?"

>> Ya! That's my friend!!! She's here!!!!

>> ari it was me, omg i cant believe u read my letter

"I try to read them all but it takes me forever," he admits. "I'm sorry I can't reply. There's a lot of letters. How's the dog doing? Is she feeling better?"

>> she's okay! her leg is still healing! thank u for asking abt her

Footsteps ring out against the practice room floor. Jungwoo plops down next to Ari, chugging an energy drink tinted neon blue. He playfully pretends to edge his groupmate out of the frame. "Sunshines! My Sunshines!" he calls out, and the chat explodes with greetings in return. The warm welcome drowns out the round of griping from fans who only wanted to see Ari tonight. There's always a few of those.

>> AAAAAAAHHHHHH

>> Jungwoo oppa, did you eat yet?

>> oppa those energy drinks are poison, pls go get some water

>> My otp together again!!!!!!!

Jungwoo flicks through the chat history, responding to some comments on Ari's behalf. Now that his brother has effectively taken over the livestream, Ari seems content to fade into the background.

"You guys had to remind him I ate his snacks," laments Jungwoo. "It's not like I didn't buy him more snacks later on! I'm not a monster." He scrolls through the chat some more. "See, your livestreams are always so cozy. When it's my turn to go live, I get nothing but —"

>> oppa is it true that u wrote *love me leave me* for hazel lim

>> Which songs on the album are about
your ex gf????

>> pls jungwoo who hurt you?

>> love triangle… ari jungwoo hazel
GO

>> Get out, that's disgusting

>> Jungwoo's dating Ruby or Mi-yeon
from Athena but the agency paid off
the tabloids again

"This! This happens every time!" Jungwoo gets to his feet and pretends to flounce off in a huff. "I can't believe you guys," he says to the fans, feigning insult. "I wrote all those songs for you! Yes, you! And you, and you, and you!"

"We belong to our fans," Ari pipes up.

"We do belong to our fans! Goodbye!" Jungwoo points at the camera. "And you, the one with the unicorn profile pic — if you want to marry Ari then you have to marry the rest of us too. We're like, a package deal. Right, Ari?"

Ari shrugs, laughing. "Right."

NOTE: *Fans refer to Jungwoo using the rose emoji because of the costume he wore to Emerald Entertainment's Halloween party in 2016. He showed up as a certain masked hero from a classic anime franchise about magical girls in sailor suits.*

18

Just come back, Ari. Come home.

Home. But the life that Jungwoo wanted him to resume — did it really count as home?

Back at the Hans' apartment, Eunjae polished off another chocolate chip cookie and tried to evaluate how much of a trail he'd left behind. He hadn't gone about this with anything resembling strategy.

He looked around at the people seated at the dining table. Midway through dinner, Mr. and Mrs. Han had fallen back into a circular argument about whether the ending of *I Loved You* qualified as tragic or hopeful in nature. Denny, arms crossed, was in a separate circular argument with Jiyeon about whether or not Eunjae's hair had been properly rehabilitated of its floppiness.

"Den, for the last time, the floppiness is part of the charm."

"The goal wasn't to make him charming! The goal was to make him wholesome!"

"So the only way to make Ryan look more wholesome was to give him an ugly haircut?"

Denny pointed at her. "Yes!"

"But earlier, didn't you say he was the least seductive crayon in the box? I seem to remember." Jiyeon looked over at Eunjae. "He said that, didn't he?"

Eunjae nodded, then popped another bite of cookie in his mouth. Denny glared at him. Perhaps neutrality was the wiser course, but he liked the haircut. Loyalty was the least he could give in lieu of actual payment, which she refused to accept every time he tried to offer.

"So," Jiyeon continued, having scented blood, "by that logic, we can safely say that Ryan Kim was already pretty wholesome in appearance. He didn't need a haircut to reach peak wholesomeness. The haircut was just a bonus. Now he's wholesome with a side of charming."

Jiyeon put another cookie on her brother's empty plate. "Just think about how useful that will be. Do you know any aunties or grannies who don't like that combination? You'll have a line out the door and around the block."

"Oh, lots of money. You wanted a new fridge, yeah?" Mrs. Han tapped a fork against her water glass. "Mystery Ryan, ticket to brand new fridge!"

"The haircut was a good idea," boomed Mr. Han. "The more we change how he looks, the harder it'll be for his enemies to find him. He's got enemies, you know. He told me."

"Oh, I bet he's got enemies," muttered Denny. But he took the cookie from Jiyeon and dumped it on Eunjae's plate instead. "Here, have some more. It's obvious they had you locked up in some basement." With that, he gathered up his plate and carried it to the sink, mumbling something about Vitamin D supplements.

Eunjae got up right away. "I'll wash the dishes."

"No, no. Sit down, eat your cookie."

"Lizzie is right," said Mr. Han. He smiled slyly at Eunjae, conjuring visions of what Denny would look like in the far future. "We owe you, Ryan Kim. Now Yeonnie comes by every night again like before."

"Someone has to make sure you people are letting him watch something other than super depressing episodes of *I Loved You*," Jiyeon replied. "But really, eat the cookie, Ryan."

Eunjae ate the cookie and pondered his dilemma. His brothers liked to tease, calling him a lion, but he understood quite well that he wasn't the most lionhearted person around. More often than not, he relented to outside pressure, surrendered in arguments, whipped out his white flag in a fight. Among his brothers, he was the designated peacemaker. Or, as Max preferred to call him while in a mood, the family doormat.

Eunjae just liked for everyone to get along. If this required him to serve as a bridge for the others to cross so they might meet in the middle, then so be it. And as for himself, Eunjae almost never demanded that anybody meet him in the middle. He caused no trouble. He made no waves. And he'd survived, but it was clear to him now that these tactics would not win him any chance at living. Because he hadn't been living, not truly. Not for a long time.

If I hadn't met these people, if I hadn't found the magic, I'd leave for Korea without a fight. I'd head home and never know the rest of this story.

But he'd found them. Eunjae was here, and he still wanted to stay. There was still so much to do, so much he wanted to know. Another person he so desperately wished to be — or maybe just to discover, at least. Maybe it wasn't too late to figure it out.

He sent a text to Jungwoo's number. *I need more time. Please try to understand.* There was more he wanted to say, but he'd hurt his brother enough and he was already asking for so much. It seemed egregious to ask for more.

What felt like an eternity later, as Eunjae stood at the sink washing dishes, the phone chimed with Jungwoo's reply: *Okay.*

Instantly, he felt better. But even with Jungwoo agreeing to keep his secret, the company was bound to find him. The only question was when.

If Eunjae played his cards right — what few cards he possessed — this didn't need to happen right away. There would be no dodging his fate; he couldn't simply vanish off the face of the planet, no matter how many times Max helpfully texted that Eunjae should fake his own death. But it was possible to buy himself some time.

"Misdirection," he said to himself, not realizing he'd spoken this thought out loud. Denny looked up from the grocery list he was tapping into his phone.

"Yeah, I know you're misdirecting all of us, my guy. That's not news."

Eunjae stopped scrubbing at the remains of chocolate chip cookie dough in Mr. Han's favorite red mixing bowl. He grabbed a bar stool and sat down next to Denny at the narrow kitchen island.

"I need to ask you something."

Denny lifted an eyebrow at least a quarter of the way up to the ceiling. "Okay, weirdo. Go for it, I guess."

"Thank you. I was wondering —"

"Wait, you want to know why we don't just use the dishwasher, don't you? Fair question. It's a perfectly operational dishwasher, almost brand new. Which is exactly why we can't use it."

Derailed from his purpose, Eunjae glanced over at the dishwasher, then back at Denny. "Hold on. What?"

"The dishwasher is for special occasions only. Birthdays, holidays, that kind of thing. Too good for everyday use. You'd have to be catering a banquet for the British royal family before Lizzie Han will let you use it." He added something else to his grocery list. "Or, you know, the Spanish royals. The Dutch. Pick your favorite colonizers."

"Oh. I guess that makes sense."

"No, it doesn't," said Denny, laughing. "Damn, do you ever disagree with anybody?"

Eunjae thought about it. "No. Not really. At least, not out loud."

Denny laughed some more. "Well, you should. You might even be good at it."

Again, Eunjae felt that laugh all around him, boisterous and joyful as a game of tag. Although the conversation with Jungwoo remained an open wound, he ended up laughing too. And then he remembered he was supposed to be asking for help.

"I was wondering," Eunjae tried again, "if you could help me buy a plane ticket."

Denny narrowed his eyes. He set his phone down on the countertop, hitting Eunjae with the full force of his scrutiny. "What did you say?"

"A plane ticket."

Sit up straight! ordered Invisible Jaehwan. *This is not the posture of a winner!*

Eunjae hurriedly corrected his posture. "I need to buy one. But I have to figure out how to do it without anyone tracing the card to my actual location."

"You want to buy a plane ticket and leave? You've finally had enough of our hospitality?" He cracked a knuckle, then another. "You don't care that Yeonnie will be sad to see you go?"

"She'd be sad? About me? Really?"

"Answer the original question! Why do you suddenly need to buy a plane ticket?" But before Eunjae could respond, Denny's face lit up with comprehension. "Nah, that's not it. You don't want to leave. You want them to *think* you left. And you don't want them to know you're *here*. In this apartment. Eating my food and wearing my clothes."

"Yeah," said Eunjae, nodding urgently. "I think this will get me at least a few more days. I just need... a little more time." He bowed. "And thank you for the food and the clothes."

"You're welcome. I'll invoice you later. Who's *them* in this situation?"

"I can't tell you. I'm sorry."

"Trick question," gloated Denny. "It's Interpol. I knew that already. And how can you be sure this card of yours will work? It might have been canceled, or it could trigger an alert when it's used in a different country."

"They wouldn't have canceled it. That card is the only way I can pay for anything unless I use cash, so they'll be waiting to see if I use it."

"Right." Denny stretched the word from one syllable to at least four. He crossed his arms, reverting to what Eunjae had come to think of as his habitual forbidding expression. "And you thought I'd be the best one to ask about this because...?"

Eunjae sat up even straighter, a feat he hadn't originally considered possible. "Because you have resources," he replied, serious as the printed program for a funeral. A funeral which might very well be his own, if Denny Han suddenly felt like punting him into the nearest asteroid belt.

The ensuing silence lasted just long enough for Eunjae's life to flash before his eyes. And then Denny grinned at him, all dimples and teeth.

"Correct. So are you flying economy or coach?"

19

"Do I want to know what you and my brother were scheming about in the kitchen last night?"

Eunjae stood at a crosswalk next to Jiyeon, holding a massive umbrella over their heads. The trek back from the library had morphed into a waterlogged gauntlet, made perhaps a little too exciting by the threat of getting splashed as cars went by. He adjusted his grip on the umbrella and replied, "Probably not."

"Hmm."

"The thinking noise. I'm in for it now."

She laughed. "Don't bother offering me a penny for my thoughts. I don't want your pennies. I don't care if you have ten whole pennies, even. I've decided I'll just avoid thinking about all the trouble you and Den could get into. Got it? I have no thoughts about it. Zero."

The pedestrian light turned green. Eunjae turned out the lefthand pocket of his borrowed rain jacket as they crossed, emphasizing its emptiness. "Couldn't afford your thoughts anyway. I'm broke. I could pay you with a song, I guess."

Jiyeon glanced over at him. "You can sing? Really?"

"I've been told I'm not bad at it," said Eunjae.

"This sounds like dangerous information. Something the enemy can torture out of me when I'm caught."

"You seem so sure you'd get caught."

"How many dramas do you think I've seen? Of course I'd get caught."

Hearing a car coming up behind them, Eunjae maneuvered himself between Jiyeon and the street, nudging her to the middle of the sidewalk. There was an inevitable wave of gray water from the gutter as the car sailed by. It sloshed all over Eunjae's shoes, which were his own pair and not Denny's, at least.

Jiyeon's eyes flashed gratitude even as she admonished him. "Don't be such a hero, Ryan Kim. Those are some nice shoes. Or they were, anyway."

"You're dressed for work," Eunjae pointed out. "Better me than you."

"Ah, well," she replied, lifting one shoulder in a halfhearted shrug. Under the raincoat, sprays of sunny yellow blossoms edged the collar of her blouse and the cuffs of each sleeve.

"Not excited?"

"Nope."

They reached another crosswalk. On the opposite side of the street, the wet wooden railings of Ivy Lane Apartments had darkened to an even deeper green. Eunjae's phone buzzed several times in quick succession. He ignored it, knowing it was probably Max texting FAKE! YOUR! OWN! DEATH!

Jiyeon sighed. Staring straight ahead, she said, "I'm waiting for you to be surprised that I don't like my job. Or disappointed. I'm just so good at it, after all. And I'm lucky to have a job, period. I should be happy. I get paid to do something I love." She spoke as though reading from a teleprompter, delivering lines written by others. Did she believe in what she was saying?

He opened his mouth to answer with the first thing that came to him, then thought better of it. As they crossed the street, Eunjae sped up a little, just enough to be a few steps ahead. The umbrella boasted such an enormous span that he could walk backwards, talking to her face to face, without either of them getting rained on.

"So, not Ryan," said Eunjae, "but someone else — someone you don't know and can't be tortured for knowing. Let's say his name is Eunjae. Can I tell you what he thinks of that?"

She smiled at this. "Is he an amnesiac, a wanted fugitive, or all of the above?"

"None of those," he assured her. "He's just some guy from Brisbane."

"Oh, good. Okay, go."

"Eunjae's really good at his job, too. That doesn't mean he always likes it. And it doesn't mean that he should like it and be happy doing it, just because everyone expects him to."

It felt as if the umbrella sealed them off from the rest of the world, although Eunjae knew this was just his imagination. "He used to believe that," he told her, "but he doesn't anymore. And you don't have to believe that about yourself, either."

They picked their way down the sidewalk, the concrete slick with rain and sodden flower petals. Jiyeon looped an arm through his, saying nothing and everything all at once: that she was thankful, that she was sorry, that she knew just what he meant.

Out loud, she said, "Eunjae seems very wise."

"He has his moments."

"I don't know him personally, as established," Jiyeon added, "but

I wouldn't mind knowing him. If you could pass it along."

"Can't. That would just go straight to his head."

Laughing, she said, "I see. Well, they do go on and on about how it's important to stay humble."

At the apartment complex, many residents had carried their potted plants onto balconies or set them on the walkways, taking advantage of the rainfall. Eunjae skirted around the tomato vines in their bright red coffee cans. "Do you ever think about quitting?" he asked Jiyeon. "Would you be happier if you did?"

"Sure, I think about it all the time. But I need to be working, you know? Bills and groceries and all that. Saving up, too." The wind picked up, battering the umbrella, and she wrapped her fingers around the handle to help him hold on to it. "As for being happier if I quit, I don't know. I feel like I might not be. I love what I do when I'm actually allowed to do it. The rest, I love a lot less."

"Yeah," he said quietly. "I understand that."

"Plus, what else would I do? This is what I know. I have this weirdly specific set of skills. Where else would they fit in? What could I do with them, if not this?"

The rain poured harder than ever in those last few yards they had left. They were forced to make a run for it. Eunjae angled the umbrella so Jiyeon might avoid getting drenched while she opened the door with her key. All the while, he reflected on how terrifying it was, but also oddly comforting, to hear his own thoughts coming from someone else. To ask the questions that he'd been asking himself so often lately, and be trusted with another person's honest answers.

Feeling less alone, for a change — that was magic, too.

20

Denny materialized on the threshold between the Hans' living room and their back porch, making such a disruptive entrance that the crickets briefly stopped chirping. He swept the glass door aside with the air of a behemoth rolling a boulder for sport. His stance matched the exact energy of an ancient, judgmental monolith casting its shadow across vast, windswept plains.

Eunjae sat bolt upright in his metal patio chair. Balanced on the porch rail, Jiyeon stifled a laugh.

"It's been fifteen hours," barked Denny. "Go time."

"Right. I pulled it up already, just need to hit the order button."

"So do it, then. God."

"Woosung-ah," called Jiyeon, hopping down from the rail. She went to poke Denny in the cheek. Even without the heeled boots she'd worn to work, she stood only a few inches shorter. "You sound a little jealous. Wanna come sit with the big kids?"

"Ryan doesn't count as one of the big kids." He pitched a water bottle at Eunjae, who caught it with a yelp. "Stay hydrated! And she's older than you, make sure you're showing proper respect. No slacking off just because I wasn't here to supervise."

"I'm barely older than him. It's like six-ish months. Ryan's birthday is in July."

"You know his birthday now? I told you not to get attached!"

"Hmm. I'm not allowed to know his birthday, but you are?"

"I needed to know it," hissed Denny, "to run a background check. Duh."

Eunjae set the water bottle on the table, right next to Denny's laptop. He scrolled through the grocery order he'd assembled half an hour ago, before Jiyeon got back from the salon and came to see what he was up to. He'd moved to another tab as soon as she stepped onto the porch, minimizing an email from one of his brothers and a PDF attachment covered in columns of microscopic print.

It was better if she didn't see. The PDF probably counted as information she didn't want tortured out of her. Also, Eunjae didn't know how to explain his browsing history or why he was ordering random junk food through an Australian grocery chain.

He'd picked the store ten minutes' drive from his father's empty house in Brisbane. He knew it would be empty because Simon Song traveled for work at least three or four days a week. Probably more than that, actually, now that he had nothing to come home to except the floral arrangement left by the cleaners. Eunjae's mother had moved to Sydney after the divorce. Not long after that, she'd enrolled eleven-year-old Ezra at Blackridge Academy, an exclusive international boarding school in Singapore.

Eunjae hit the checkout button and used his company card to pay. Emerald's watchdogs should've seen the plane ticket purchase hours and hours ago; if they were monitoring him as closely as he thought, this transaction would be noted as well. Thanks to something Denny called a VPN, checking the IP address would only tell his pursuers that Eunjae was in Australia.

He was banking on one crucial thing: the agency would never admit that they'd lost him. Not at this stage. They would want to retrieve Eunjae without anyone guessing that he'd slipped through their fingers in the first place. Thus, there would be no asking the airport to view CCTV footage, no canvassing door to door within a ten mile radius of the hotel where he'd stayed. Those were extreme measures that risked media coverage. They would try to get at him by other means until he pushed them too far.

So, for now, Eunjae could count on them to watch this credit card. Whoever had been sent to find him would be under strict orders not to draw attention. That limited how thoroughly they could search. He thought of this as his main advantage.

His other advantage was how little the company's representatives seemed to know about him. Eunjae would never run away to his childhood home. Nor would he ever voluntarily take shelter with either of his parents. Any of his brothers could've told them: that house no longer symbolized home to Eunjae in any sense of the word. His parents didn't count as shelter.

The website accepted his card without complaint. Eunjae exited the tab and then closed the laptop, braced once again for the karmic payback slap he'd surely earned by now. But there was no clap of thunder except Denny's voice.

"That's the book he wanted? Are you kidding?"

"I suppose it really is true," Jiyeon mused. "You're either a *Brass Key* kid or you're a *Molly Merriweather* kid, and there's no middle ground."

Eunjae stared at them both. "Hold on," he said. "You've read it, too? You've read *The Brass Key*?"

"Sure we have," answered Jiyeon.

"And we hated it," added Denny.

Crestfallen, Eunjae said, "Oh. Okay."

"We didn't hate it. You suck, Den. Go back inside." Jiyeon dropped into the patio chair opposite Eunjae's. She offered him the same apologetic smile from Wednesday night, only this time it held a touch of mirth.

"While you were reading that series, we were reading *Molly Merriweather*. Those books came out around the same time. I remember all the kids at school were obsessed with one or the other."

Eunjae had never heard of Molly Merriweather, a confession which offended Denny to the core. "Well, Molly's amazing," he declared. "Her mom was basically Indiana Jones, only smarter and not wearing an ugly hat. And Molly had like twenty different pets." Denny began counting these off on his fingers. "There was a squirrel, three penguins, a chinchilla... oh, the Komodo dragon. How'd I forget him?"

Jiyeon explained, "Instead of going through a magical door, Molly ends up transported to different worlds when she touches certain objects. Or sometimes it's the same world, but she's thrown into a different time period. Her mom is an archaeologist so she comes across a lot of artifacts. They travel all over."

"It was about the evils of colonialism and the societal prison of traditional gender roles," said Denny, as he left them on the porch. He was now a man on a mission. "I'm gonna find those books and make you read them."

"I think I would've really liked that series when I was a kid," Eunjae admitted to Jiyeon, once her brother had gone. "I only had the books my nanny brought me, though. She's the one who gave me *The Brass Key*. Later, she tracked down the rest of the series at garage sales and the flea market. She wanted me to have them at home so I could read whenever I wanted, even if my parents didn't have time to bring me to the library. Or if they didn't want to."

Home. When Eunjae was little, the house in Brisbane felt the way a home should feel, but only when Miss Vivi was there. She lived with them in a shoebox of a room that always smelled like perfume and the posy of flowers she kept on the altar by her narrow bed. A framed print of the Virgin Mary occupied this altar, and a wooden rosary with beads worn smooth by Miss Vivi's fingers.

She was always singing. The house swelled with music throughout the day. Eunjae learned dozens of songs with her, from Disney movies and the radio. He studied the ballads that played during Miss Vivi's treasured drama programs, in English and Korean, Japanese and Tagalog. Whatever she was watching, whatever she was singing, he would sing it with her. He remembered going through a phase when he was very young, stubbornly believing that it was fine to communicate only through snatches and snippets of song lyrics, or by humming melodies instead of pronouncing words. Miss Vivi always knew what he was trying to tell her.

But she didn't live with them on the weekends. From Friday night until Sunday afternoon, she returned to her sister's house in town, leaving Eunjae with his face pressed to the panes of the downstairs windows. Unmoored without Miss Vivi, he fled into the pages of his books.

"Do you still keep in touch with her?" asked Jiyeon. "Your nanny."

"No. My parents... fired her. I was thirteen, almost fourteen. After they sent her away, I didn't know how to reach her. I think she tried to write to me a few times but Mum was still mad and got rid of the letters. When I moved to Korea, I only knew that her name was Vivian. Miss

Vivi."

He hadn't talked about her for so long. Why did it still hurt so much?

"So they wouldn't buy you books, and they didn't want to bring you to the library. They gave you a nanny to love you and raise you because they weren't around, and then they took her away." Something fierce glittered in her brown eyes.

He looked down at his shoes. "Pretty much."

Jiyeon pushed the water bottle in his direction. Gently, she said, "I'm sorry. You don't have to talk about it anymore. But... wherever she is right now, I bet she still loves you."

"I still love her, too."

Eunjae uncapped the bottle, grateful to drink and have an excuse not to talk. He'd drained almost half when his phone went off, rattling on the black metal tabletop like something possessed. Jungwoo's name popped up, along with the words INCOMING VIDEO CALL.

Jiyeon saw the notification and vacated her chair right away, rushing to give him some privacy. Even so, six of Eunjae's nine brothers still managed to catch a fleeting glimpse of her as she left the porch. Nothing substantial, just the back of Jiyeon's pale blue blouse and a fall of long, dark hair, but that was more than enough.

Immediately, Jesse shrieked, "You're with a *girl?*"

21

"Is this one of those... what do you call it, Nicky? A midlife crisis?"

"Hong Namgyu, why are you stupid?"

"Ari's not old enough for a midlife crisis," said Kei, imbuing his voice with levels of patience you'd typically reserve for toddlers and kittens. "It's more like a quarter life crisis."

"I'm not having a quarter life crisis," Eunjae argued, in vain. Not even Jungwoo paid him any attention. He was still focused on the spot over Eunjae's shoulder where Jiyeon had been just a few seconds ago, before she pulled the glass door shut behind her.

Kazu yawned. "It's really goddamn early here," he complained, joining the call from his hotel room in Paris. He went every year for the Vuitton show, since he was an ambassador for the brand. "What's going on now, kid? Hurry up so I can sleep for another hour."

"God, can you put some clothes on?"

"Yeah, why's Zuzu always naked?" Jesse demanded.

"Naked? I have pants on! And underwear!"

"Oh, wait," said Kei, rolling his eyes. "Let me just give you an award for that."

Namgyu gave a wistful sigh. "Aww! I wish we could all have awards for putting our clothes on. Life would be so much happier."

"Jungwoo-yah, where's Max?"

"Taking a nap. He said he already told Ari what to do and there's nothing else to discuss."

"He wants you to fake your own death, doesn't he?"

Eunjae nodded at Nick, who nodded sagely back.

"Ari-hyung," Jesse wailed again, "you're over there with a *girl* though? Like, you abandoned us for *romance*?"

Namgyu's smile wobbled. Nicky watched Eunjae's face on the screen and so did Jungwoo. Kazu just snorted.

"Oh, well. If that's the special announcement then I'm going back to sleep. Good luck, Romeo."

"Wait," said Eunjae to all six of them. "I need your help."

"How are we supposed to help you, hyung? We're all in jail."

"Kazu's not in jail."

"Kazu's not in this jail," said Kei, darkly, "but he's still in jail."

"I bet jail is worse when you can see the Eiffel Tower from your window. And he had to go with Doyoung."

This cued a collective groan about their least favorite manager. But then Jesse cried out, "What do you even need us for? You have a *girl* now."

"Jesse, whine about that one more time and I'm not buying you anything you wanted from Paris."

"What? But I'm out of the really good cold cream!"

"Who still uses cold cream?"

"My granny! I love her!"

"Why can't you moisturize like a normal person?"

"I have unique skin care needs! You wouldn't understand!"

Eunjae telegraphed some desperate hand signals to Jungwoo, who obligingly used his host privileges to mute everyone. Able to hear himself think at last, Eunjae said, "The founders — does anyone know how to reach them?"

The screen became a checkerboard of frowning faces and furrowed brows. Nicky replied, "I doubt anyone knows how to find them except Mr. Yoon. Remember when we were filming for Netflix? We didn't even see the founders then."

"Don't they have offices on one of the top floors at Emerald?"

Kei clicked a button that somehow filled his backdrop with giant letters spelling the word NO. "That's just a rumor. I mean, who's even been up there? Unless..." He switched to Japanese. "Grandpa, what about you? You've been alive for like a hundred years. Share your knowledge."

"First of all, shut up," Kazu shot back, also in Japanese, "and second of all, no. Whenever the big bosses wanted to see us back then, they just came to wherever we were. Nowadays they send all their orders through Yoon."

Eunjae blew out a frustrated breath. "Surely they have company email addresses at least. How can there be no way to contact them?"

"But why do you even want to contact them?" asked Jungwoo. The steadiness of his gaze felt like a drill piercing Eunjae's skull. "You just needed to get away for a while. That's not something they'd bother to tell Haewon and Soyeon."

"There's nothing wrong with needing a break, Ari. You're not the first and you won't be the last. They can't really be too mad at you." Namgyu tugged on a loose thread unraveling from the cuff of his sweater. "I think we're allowed to take breaks sometimes...?"

"It's the running-away-and-hiding part that they're mad about. And what I'm mad about is that Ari-hyung is out there living an actual rom-com while I'm stuck here, wasting away —"

"Jesse, I swear —"

Eunjae hastened to end the call before any death threats could be delivered. "Okay, okay. Don't fight." He propped the phone against his half empty water bottle and bowed at the screen. "And I'm sorry for causing so much trouble for everyone, I really am."

Jungwoo waved his apology away. He offered Eunjae a wan smile. "Stay safe and get some rest, Ari. You can just buy us dinner when this is over."

"Yeah! Oh my gosh, dinner! Real dinner!"

"I'm so tired of eating everything out of a bowl!"

"Ari won't make us split everything five ways like Zuzu."

"I don't see what's wrong with trying to save money. Take a hot second to count how many mouths I have to feed."

"Shut up, hyung! You sleep on a bunch of gold bars!"

"It's so unfair, you have sooooo much money —"

Eunjae watched his brothers sign off one by one until only Kazu was left. "Don't go yet," his brother said, wrangling his inky, shoulder length hair into a low ponytail which, of course, looked both effortless and elegant at the same time. Bedhead, but luxe.

"Did you get to see your family? I know you mentioned they'd be in Paris the same week."

"Hell no. I'm here with Doyoung, remember? You know how he is. Of course the one manager we all hate is the one who will never quit. He wouldn't let me leave the hotel except for Vuitton events the whole time I was here. Yoon's orders, he'd say. That guy's so far up Yoon's ass that he hasn't seen the sun in about three years." Kazu went rummaging around in his luggage for a shirt. "And if you're wondering, my aunt has threatened to buy out his contract with Emerald so she can fire him herself."

"I was wondering," admitted Eunjae, which made Kazu chuckle. "I'm sorry, Zu. We hardly ever get to be with family and I ruined that for you."

"Don't worry about that. I talk to them every day. Worry about this instead: Yoon's getting pretty pissed that they haven't found you. I heard Doyoung on the phone earlier when he thought I was asleep."

"Ah."

"You got the email I sent?"

"Yeah." Eunjae sighed. "Your contract says the same thing mine does."

Kazu nodded at this. "I figured as much. We're all under the same terms."

"There's this one part that really bothers me, but maybe I'm reading it wrong. And surely Jungwoo's would be different. All the music he's written... and what about the rap lyrics? Nicky writes his own and so does Max, as of last year. I need to talk to the founders. This just doesn't make sense."

Checking that Doyoung wasn't lurking behind him, Kazu said, "Ari, don't trust them to play fair. Don't expect them to listen to us. Not Yoon, not the founders, not anybody. This is their game, not ours. I know you want to settle this without a fight, but that might not be possible. It's just not the same anymore, at Emerald. In the beginning, when it was me and Hwannie here and most of you hadn't even been recruited yet, I'd never have thought it could be like this."

"They care about us, don't they? They used to. I thought they did."

Kazu shook his head, at a loss. "I guess we'll find out soon enough."

**Transcript from the K-pop news podcast *Omma Gosh!*
Season 4, Episode 37 (September 2022)**

Jooney Chun (Host) - I was thinking about something yesterday.

Freddie Dang (Co-host/Producer) - Oh no.

Jooney - Why is that the reaction? Why are you making that face?

Freddie - 'Cause you say this whenever you're about to get super philosophical about something and I haven't had any coffee yet.

Maisie Chun (Co-host; Jooney's Mom) - No coffee yet, Frederica? How come?

Freddie - (*heavy sigh*) Okay, so I went to Starbucks on 5th and Lantana this morning, right, but when I got there the line was all the way to Saturn. So I left. Went to CVS. You know the lipstick that unnie was talking about yesterday? Yeah, I got that instead of a coffee.

Maisie - That lipstick is very nice, yes, but you have no coffee 'cause you give up? You're a quitter? Boo-hoo. You know who else is a quitter, it's Jooney. In 2nd Grade everybody in class had a hula hoop, glitter hula hoop, light up hula hoop, whatever. So Jooney's papa, he gets him a hula hoop. Nice hula hoop! Expensive, so many colors! Like rainbow but if it threw up, pah, all over the place.

Freddie - Oh, wow. This imagery.

Jooney - Tie dye. It's called tie dye.

Maisie - (*ignoring Jooney*) Yes, the image! Make image of Jooney in your head. He tried to hula in the hoop like two, three times. Then he said, I give up! This is stupid! Hula hoop went in the garage, never come out again. Quitter!

Freddie - I've learned my lesson. I'll stand in line next time.

Jooney - Anyway! Anyway I was thinking about something, folks! And I wanted to bring it up on the show because of last week's news that 12:12's Jinyeol is leaving the group.

Freddie - That just reminded me of how you spell the word "folks" like f-o-l-x on Twitter and I'm honestly just... so mad all over again.

Jooney - Um, the news —

Freddie - Like, I can't believe I've been your friend since sixth grade even though you type f-o-l-x instead of f-o-l-k-s on a regular basis.

Maisie - Oh! That's right, you been friends a long time now! At least Jooney's got good taste in friends. Clothes, not so much. See what he's wearing? Ratty shirt. Ugly palm tree on front. Cost $90!

Freddie - You had ninety bucks to spend on that t-shirt but you're still a lousy tipper?

Jooney - Uhhhhhh anyway, I think everyone knows that 12:12 is a pretty successful boy group; they debuted in late 2018 and were quickly hyped as 'monster rookies' due to their instant popularity.

Maisie - Why's this boy leaving, then? Everybody leaving these days.

Freddie - Oh, the scandal! That's why.

Jooney - No mention of the, err, incriminating

text messages reported last month. The press release from BlueSky came with the usual vague statements about deciding to part ways with mutual respect and all that. So, nothing juicy there, sorry.

(Disappointed noises from Freddie and Maisie)

Jooney - You know, some groups have lost multiple members since debut and I honestly always wonder how everyone copes with that. When these groups become so close to each other, practically like family, and they lose someone? That's gotta hurt.

Freddie - But what about the ones who leave? We hardly ever hear about them once they bow out of the industry or try to set out on their own, establish a solo career. Granted, there are exceptions. Some have done really well for themselves even after leaving.

Maisie - Sure, sure. That boy with the big muscles, seems happy now, lost a lot of money though. Oh, plus the boys who had that big lawsuit. And those girls from Jewell, old-time group. Made their own agency and now they're big bosses.

Jooney - Ah, you mean Haewon and Soyeon, the ones who founded Emerald Entertainment? Only Soyeon left Jewell back then, though. Right?

Freddie - You're both wrong. Soyeon was thinking of leaving Jewell, but she changed her mind and stayed. Jewell made it to their tenth anniversary before disbanding.

Jooney - Man, how'd I forget that? I must've mixed them up with that other 90s group, Hera. In any case, I do agree with Ma, feels like everyone's leaving their groups left and right over the past few months.

Maisie - Mm-hmm. Before, too hard to quit. Costs too much. Pay more than Jooney's ratty t-shirt.

Jooney - (*clearing throat*) Err, that's a very good point. Not the part about my shirt! The part about how hard it was to break an idol contract, back in the day.

Freddie - It was so hard. Agencies had all the power. And if you ask me, they still have too much power. Quitting is not a decision anybody is making lightly, you know?

Jooney - Oh boy, this is one of Freddie's pet subjects. Buckle up.

Freddie - Look, this is just the kind of nerdy shit — ooh, sorry Auntie Maisie, don't kill me — nerdy *stuff* that you get into when your parents had *Law & Order* on loop throughout your whole childhood. (*squeals*) Help, she's going to forcibly wash my mouth out with soap...

Maisie - Not me. Calling your dad, he can do it.

Jooney - Wait, wait. Let her explain first, she has valuable knowledge.

Freddie - But you'll feed me to the wolves right after? Get stuffed in a locker, Chun.

Maisie - Your daddy not answering, keep talking 'til he picks up.

Freddie - (*nervous laughter*)

Jooney - You mentioned agencies having a lot of power.

Freddie - It's a lot to go through, probably deserves its own episode, but mainly agencies could make it a financial nightmare for idols to break contract.

Jooney - Right. It was stay or go broke, pretty much.

Freddie - Plus, before the legal reforms, agencies were free to include all kinds of restrictions in their contracts, many of which are thankfully very rare now. Like banning dating outright, controlling what artists ate, or penalties like forced disbandments. Agencies could require that idols work insane schedules. A contract could even last for over ten years. That phrase about signing your life away is very appropriate here.

Jooney - But from what I understand, it's not as bad now, right? Oh, but dating bans are still a thing.

Freddie - Yeah, there's at least one agency that doesn't allow artists to date in the first three years after debut. The amount of time varies but there always seems to be a policy against dating. Speaking of Emerald, they're not allowed to date if they still live in the dorms. Pretty strict. I personally feel like the agencies ban dating but it's the fans who enforce it. Some fans get soooooooooo mad when their idols try to be normal freaking people.

Jooney - I think it's crazy that most idols make the choice to potentially live this kind of life when they're just kids. Most start training around the age of thirteen. I knew nothing about life when I was thirteen. (*pauses*) I know nothing about life right now.

Freddie - Better to live at home and make podcasts, eh? I mean, look at Jooney. $90 t-shirts.

Maisie - Pah!

22

If Denny Han ever needed a new job, he'd do well to consider hiring himself out to do wake up calls. The man was an alarm clock you couldn't snooze. Eunjae had woken at 4:32am to find him standing over the bed, a walking mountain somehow gifted with powers of stealth. It shocked all the sleepiness out of him. They were at Wanna Waffle by 5am sharp, firing up the irons and pulling down all the dining room chairs.

Now it was midmorning and Eunjae occupied a seat behind the counter, a quarter of the way through his mandatory reading assignment: an old hardback copy of *Molly Merriweather and the Clockwork Knight*. Inside the front cover was a fading Bookmobile sticker and the name 'Emma Jiyeon Han' scrawled in shaky cursive. Denny had inscribed his own name underneath hers at a later date. His cursive was clearer, more precise. Neither could agree on rightful ownership of the book and Eunjae had stepped in to mediate.

He made swift progress through the first *Molly Merriweather* book as the morning ticked slowly away and Jeannie shuffled around the empty dining room with a broom. She possessed a bottomless supply of soda candy and even plunked a handful beside the register for Eunjae. By force of habit, he chose a flavor that none of his younger brothers would squabble over.

"Oppa-yah," Jeannie drawled shortly thereafter, removing one earbud and pointing the broom handle at Eunjae. "Has anyone ever told you that you look like Ari from Apollo?"

Denny exploded out of the kitchen. "Who are you out here calling oppa?"

"Ryan," said Jeannie. She popped another candy in her mouth. "He looks just like —"

"He looks just like *not* anyone's oppa!"

"Denny-boss, you're getting old. Like, you used to babysit me. So it makes sense that your eyes are getting bad and you can't see that this new guy is totally an oppa. His oppa energy is intense."

"Insubordination," scolded Denny. "And you! Ryan! How can you just sit there while some girl calls you oppa? You didn't even react. You're either as empty-eyed as I said you were, or you're a coldblooded serial killer, which I also said you were."

Of course Eunjae hadn't reacted. Sunshines were forever addressing him in this manner. Although the honorific was meant to be used by girls when talking to an older brother, 'oppa' had evolved into something more flirtatious and affectionate in certain contexts. After nine years, it just bounced right off him. Being accused of resembling Ari from Apollo had been much more concerning at the time.

He lowered the book. "Um, I didn't notice. I was reading. Like you told me to."

Denny's wrath subsided as quickly as it had flared. "You're damn right you were reading. Do it fast 'cause there's still four books left in the series and we're watching the movies, too."

He stormed back into the kitchen just as Jiyeon came out, balancing a tray. Eunjae jumped up to hold the door open for her and she thanked him through the pair of plastic-wrapped boba straws she was carrying in her teeth.

"You don't have to read the whole series in one day," she said, shaking her head. "No need to watch all the movies, either. He's just really excited."

"I don't mind," said Eunjae, truthfully.

Jiyeon set the tray down on a table near the big window. It held a waffle with a pristine scoop of ice cream on top. She dusted the whole thing with powdered sugar and then adorned the plate with strawberries sliced into little hearts.

"How about it, Miss Vho? You feel like being a waffle model today, right?"

In answer to this question, Jeannie whirled around and tugged Eunjae forward. "Use him! He looks just like Ar—"

"Ryan's too shy for modeling work," Jiyeon said easily, arranging and then rearranging a pale pink smoothie and a boba tea around the waffle with a practiced eye. She thumped the waffle straws on the tabletop so that their sharp ends pierced through the plastic wrap in one go. "Do you think the tea should be on the left or the right? I say left."

"Left. You know I'll drop this tray, Sis."

"You won't. Come on, help me. Denny only ever posts pictures of the same waffle on the shop's Instagram over and over again. He thinks taking it from a new angle makes it different. We're overdue for some video."

"I'm too young to be trusted with this. Ask Denny-boss, he'll tell you."

"I'll braid your hair tomorrow."

These were the magic words. Jeannie jumped into the task with sky-high motivation. Eunjae looked on from the sidelines, wary of getting in the way. Jiyeon had appropriated her brother's phone for the project and went about it with her usual certainty, filming the components of several videos in a batch. It struck Eunjae that he had yet to see her fumble or hesitate, no matter the task or circumstance. Whatever it was, she just did it.

"I think that's enough," Jiyeon concluded, ten minutes later. "Ryan, smoothie or boba?"

Noting his teenage co-worker's covetous glances at the boba, Eunjae went for the smoothie. Jiyeon handed it to him, then insisted that he take the waffle too.

"By the way," said Jeannie, slurping away at her tea, "did you cut Ryan's hair? Cause it looks good. Like, *really* good."

"That's concerning. I was supposed to make him look more wholesome. Denny's orders."

"Wholesome," hooted Jeannie, taking another loud slurp through her straw. "We'd get a hundred million views if you put him in a post. This haircut is too powerful. Sorry, but you failed for sure."

"Darn. I knew my greatest failure had to happen sometime." Jiyeon looked up from the Instagram story she was posting, smiling at Eunjae. Her earrings were pink enamel roses. Eunjae smiled back at her, but the rose motif reminded him of Jungwoo, and thinking of Jungwoo naturally led to thinking about the rest of his brothers. This dissonance between the two worlds he occupied left a temporary ringing in his ears.

Misdirecting Emerald Entertainment into searching for him in the wrong places could only ever earn him a temporary reprieve. What Eunjae needed was a solution to the bigger problem. That solution was unattainable without a better understanding of the contract that bound him — and the whole group — to their agency.

When had he first requested the copy of his contract? Sometime after that second global tour, maybe. The tour itself had been difficult enough, all the months of near-nonstop travel and the film crew following them around for the entire North American leg. Or did he request the contract after last year's gauntlet of holiday show performances?

Eunjae had been so tired for so long. He could think of any number of catalysts. But it was discomfiting to remember that he'd never asked for a copy until things felt unbearable. He'd signed the thing twice without really reading it. This was embarrassing to admit, even just to himself.

Regardless, Eunjae had his contract and the time to go over its terms, if not much expertise in that regard. The pages sat untouched in his inbox for months while Apollo got through the grueling promo period for *Never Too Late* and then Jaehwan's enlistment. It had continued to sit there as Eunjae went straight into recording for the unit project with Jungwoo and Max. But he'd opened the file yesterday, at last, and was still working through it. The font was tiny, the formal language broken up into long, convoluted sentences. It didn't help that the whole thing had been written in very formal Korean. Eunjae could read and write well enough, but legalese was a struggle in any language.

Eunjae delivered the tray to the kitchen, where he munched on the waffle and thought about his options. Then he looked for Denny, finding him by the door with Jiyeon as she prepared to leave for work.

"Do any of your resources offer legal advice?"

Denny looked at Eunjae as though he'd sprouted a third eye in the middle of his forehead. "Now you're lawyering up? For what? You can't possibly have committed any crimes. You're you!"

"He's... him?"

"You know what I mean, noona!"

Jiyeon removed her sunglasses for the express purpose of glaring at her brother. "Woosung-ah. Not so long ago you were shouting about Ryan being an international crime lord. Now you're shouting the opposite."

"Our HR department wouldn't hire a convicted felon," scoffed Denny, "because our HR department is me."

"There aren't any crimes involved," Eunjae quickly cut in. "I just have some questions about, uh, this thing I was reading online. I thought you might be able to recommend a lawyer who could answer them."

"For fun? Or a murder trial?"

"No murders involved. I swear."

"That's what the murderers always say."

But Jiyeon brought out her phone. "Hmm. Arthur is a lawyer." She paged through her contacts list while Denny spiraled into a fresh round of derision.

"You're suggesting *Arthur Hong* for this?"

Eunjae's thoughts snagged on the name. Arthur Hong. Where had he heard this name before?

"He finally passed the bar exam, didn't he? So yeah, he's a lawyer."

"An *estate* lawyer, Yeonnie."

"Still a lawyer. And if he doesn't know the answer, he'll ask Arthur Senior. I'll text him, okay?"

Eunjae nodded. "Okay. I can pay. Will you tell him that? I don't want him to think he has to help me for free."

"I doubt he'll accept money, but it's nice to know the Han Corporation pays you enough to afford legal fees. The management loves some free labor."

"What's that supposed to mean?" bristled Denny. But Jiyeon was already out the door, laughing.

23

After the sixth episode of *I Loved You*, Eunjae concluded that it wasn't a drama he'd seen before. It seemed improbable that he'd forget an entire carousel on a beach, for starters. Why was it even there? Where were the other rides? Had they built this carousel for the drama, or was this a real location? Eunjae hoped quite fervently that it wasn't. Jungwoo would want to visit.

"And see," said Mr. Han, who sat on Eunjae's left, "this was where he met the girl when they were kids. But he didn't remember that, of course."

Mrs. Han patted Eunjae's right arm. "They come back later. It's where she dies."

"Oh," Eunjae said. "I... should've seen that coming."

A brisk knock sounded at the front door. Jiyeon, who always alerted them before using her key. Eunjae figured this was to ensure that no one mistook her arrival for a home invasion. It had been explained to him that such an event would trigger what Denny cryptically referred to as 'Red Protocol.'

Eunjae leapt up from the couch even before Jiyeon came in, knowing she'd be loaded down with bags. During the time he'd spent at the Hans' apartment, he'd rarely known her to show up empty handed. Peaches that were on sale when she stopped at the grocery store, thick slices of chocolate cake in a plastic clamshell, a magazine full of celebrity gossip for Mrs. Han. The random treats were a daily occurrence.

Jiyeon surrendered the evening's haul to Eunjae. She shook her car keys at the TV. "What's this? Are you making Ryan watch *I Loved You* again?"

"It's research," her father replied.

Mrs. Han agreed. "For the amnesia."

"But you already spoiled the ending for him yesterday. Three different times."

"Important to make sure he's prepared. Nobody wants a surprise like that. Boom! Pretty girl is dead on the beach. Boom! The pony ride keeps turning. Boom! The hero is crying. So stressful!"

"That is stressful," admitted Eunjae.

Denny strolled out of his room with a teetering pile of blankets. "Noona, you got the popcorn?"

"Yeah, and some candy. You need both for a movie night."

"Aigoo! Movie night, how nice!"

"Not for you!" barked Denny. "Everyone over the age of sixty is going to bed. We need the big TV for this. It's part of Ryan's education."

While Denny chased the Han parents out of the living room — they accepted their early bedtime with good grace — Eunjae trailed after Jiyeon with the shopping bags. She was wearing the blazer covered in poppies again, red petals a burst of riotous color against the kitchen's neutral grays and whites.

"So, Ryan Kim. What did you do today? Other than *Sad K-Drama Hour with Joey and Lizzie.*"

"Jeannie showed me how to clean the waffle irons. She was out of soda candy so we ate a whole bag of Hi-Chews." Jeannie had also confessed to Eunjae that, in elementary school, she'd wholeheartedly believed Denny Han was the President of the United States. ("He had to be the President, right? Secretly. There was no other explanation.")

Jiyeon began unloading her purchases. "I should grab her some candy tomorrow. The Asian market's just around the corner from work. Did you finally get to meet Evan today?"

"Ah, yeah. I learned everything there is to learn about the California two-spot octopus." Evan was the other part-time Wanna Waffle employee. An aspiring marine biologist, he worked slightly fewer hours than Jeannie due to his packed extracurricular schedule.

"No way. Evan talked to you? Like you guys had an actual conversation?"

Eunjae nodded. "It's great that he has an internship at the aquarium. Didn't seem like he enjoyed their cafeteria much, though."

"He told you what he thinks of the food?" Jiyeon's eyes were wide with awe. "Explain what you did to make Evan like you so much. Tell me right now."

"I... sat there?"

"I've known that kid since he was this tall," Jiyeon said, gesturing at about hip-height, "and I've gotten maybe two sentences out of him per day, max. I think you have some kind of superpower."

"Maybe it was too much chatting, though. I didn't make it to the last Molly Merriweather book. I think Denny might send me to bed early, too."

"Please," Jiyeon replied, handing Eunjae a candy bar and laughing. "He's never read the last book either."

"Really?"

"Uh-huh. He decided that if he just didn't read book five, the series wouldn't be over. I think he was in fourth grade. Once he makes up his mind, that's it. He's never budged on that."

Eunjae pondered this for a bit. "Do you think he's made up his mind about me already…?"

Jiyeon took her own moment to ponder. "I'm gonna say yes."

"Is that good or bad?"

"You're still here, aren't you?"

"Ah. Fair point."

Jiyeon unloaded the last of her shopping and started on the popcorn. Eunjae decided to go ahead and eat the candy bar while trying to remember the last time he'd even had one. In the event that he might acquire such an indulgence, one or multiple brothers could be counted on to insist that Eunjae split it with them.

Yesterday it was the biggest cupcake he'd ever seen, replete with rainbow sprinkles. That would've been divided into slices so small that he'd barely get a real taste. Eunjae had so many luxuries here.

"Hey, I've been meaning to tell you… thanks for hanging out with my parents," Jiyeon said, nudging him with her elbow. "The only thing Mom and Dad love more than watching dramas together is forcing one of us to watch with them. Neither of us has much time to do it anymore, though, between Denny running the shop and me being at the salon most days. I thought I'd have more time with them once I moved back. So much for that."

Once I moved back. From where? But Eunjae decided not to pry. "I should be thanking them. They took me in, no questions asked."

"True," she conceded. "It's not every day you meet kind strangers who diagnose you with amnesia on the spot."

"I think about that every day."

"I bet you do."

"I've missed watching dramas more than I thought I would," Eunjae found himself admitting. "They're all crazy in some way but Miss Vivi loved them. She had this tiny TV in the kitchen at our house in Brisbane and we'd watch while she made lunch or dinner. My brother, Jungwoo, he…"

Eunjae trailed off, realizing what he was doing just a beat too late. Jiyeon paused in the middle of shaking popcorn into a bowl. Slowly, she prompted, "You have a brother?"

"I have, uh, a lot of brothers." He finished the candy bar without choking. "But what did you do today?"

The look on Jiyeon's face hinted at a number of questions she was refraining from asking. "The longest cut and color of my life," she replied. "That's why I'm so late tonight." Her phone buzzed on the countertop. "Oh, it's Arthur."

"Man," said Denny, barging into the kitchen. "You seriously roped Arthur Junior into this? How can he even stand to talk to you?"

"Arthur couldn't hold a grudge if you super glued it to his hands. Here, Ryan. He said to give you his email address and he'll help with whatever."

Eunjae hurried to take a picture of the text from Arthur, which contained the email address and also a bunch of squares that were supposed to be emoji. Jiyeon's phone had a very limited range in that regard.

He knew exactly what he wanted to ask. The sooner he sent the questions, the sooner he might have answers. "I'll email him right now," Eunjae told them.

"Why is everyone obsessed with Arthur Hong?" muttered Denny. "Except Yeonnie, I guess. Since she's broken up with him — what? Two times?"

Jiyeon corrected this statement. "He broke up with me the second time around. You guys all love to forget that part."

Eunjae accidentally minimized the email he was composing and sent it to drafts. It was *that* Arthur Hong. Victim of the Arthur Hong Betrayal, capital letters. He knew he'd heard the name before.

There was a rustle as Jiyeon dumped more popcorn into a purple plastic bowl. It had Halloween bats printed all over it. "I like Arthur. He's an amazing person and I'm probably supposed to love him, because people tell me that I should. Kinda like how I should love my job just because I'm good at it. I don't think that's any reason to stay with someone. Do you?" She was talking to Denny, but she glanced at Eunjae for just the barest flicker of a moment. It happened so quickly that he thought he must have imagined it.

"Hey, I didn't say that. I just felt bad for the guy. He probably still needs space. Maybe getting a text from you made him want to light himself on fire, you know? The anguish, etcetera."

"If it makes you feel better, he's never in anguish for long. He's Arthur."

"Makes sense. He's got a lot going for him. Stable financial situation, respectable job, peak physical fitness. In a contest to become my next brother-in-law, he'd definitely be a finalist. Kind of a big weirdo sometimes, but still. Really strong contender."

Jiyeon searched an upper cabinet for more popcorn bowls. "Wow. A contest, huh."

"It's an exclusive contest. Most don't even meet the requirements."

Eunjae sent his email. He reached for the bowl Jiyeon wanted, the red one that had somehow been returned to the highest possible shelf when the clean dishes were put away the other night. "What are the requirements?" he asked.

Denny's nostrils flared. "Why? Who wants to know?"

"Ah, nobody."

"That's what I thought."

"Okay, point made," said Jiyeon, ushering them into the living room. "You're both ridiculous. Can we watch the movie now?"

24

Arthur was fast. He sent a reply to Eunjae's questions before the second movie even hit the halfway mark. This was both good and bad. Good, because the answers made things clearer for Eunjae, narrowing the number of potential paths to take. Bad, because the answers and their implications inevitably consumed his thoughts. The rest of the second movie whipped past him in a blur.

Did he want to leave Apollo? If he did, he would drag the whole group through hell. There appeared to be no way around that, based on the contract. And after this, what would he do? Imagining an ordinary life was easy. The building of an ordinary life was decidedly not.

But what if he didn't leave? He would resume a life that was, by most standards, extraordinary. Eunjae would continue to long for an escape, but as the years wore on, he'd lose both strength and conviction. He and his brothers would follow the natural cycle of a career in their industry. They'd stay together, likely seeing higher and higher success until it was time to gracefully fade from the spotlight, and all the while Eunjae would dedicate even more of himself to a dream he'd never chosen.

He didn't realize that he'd fallen asleep. Awake, he'd been

thinking about the contract. Dreaming, he'd paged through it and never questioned why it seemed to have no end. When Eunjae opened his eyes, it was 1:41am and he was under a striped blanket, sprawled on the floor in front of the TV. Denny's deep breathing evoked the rumble of a dragon stirring in its lair.

No one had played the next movie in the series. The darkness was tinged a silvery blue as the TV rotated through a screensaver of ocean scenes, slowly moving from one underwater landscape to another. Shafts of sunlight pierced a curving wave. A kelp forest swayed with the current, fish threading through the fronds.

Eunjae searched for Jiyeon amid the pillows she'd claimed for herself, within arm's length of where he'd settled earlier, but she wasn't there. He happened to catch a glow coming through the living room window on the way back from refilling his glass of water. It was too bright to be moonlight peeking through the gap in the curtains. On a hunch, he padded over to the front door and peeked outside.

Jiyeon sat in a rattan chair parked outside the Hans' front door, feet propped up on a plastic crate sourced from the trunk of her car. She had Denny's laptop balanced on her knees and looked up when she heard Eunjae shuffle out.

"Everything okay?" he asked.

"Yeah. I just couldn't sleep. Did I wake you up? I did drop my car keys on the floor at one point."

Eunjae shook his head. "I'll sleep through almost anything." He hesitated, keeping one hand on the doorknob. "Can I sit with you? Just for a little while."

"Oh, sure. Go borrow that chair over there. The neighbors won't mind."

But Eunjae opted to sit on the ground, in a patch of moonlight that came and went as clouds scudded across the sky. He was wary of getting too comfortable. He'd said he wouldn't stay too long, and maybe Jiyeon was busy with something important.

She assured him that she wasn't. "Looking at listings. Retail spaces, something that might work for a salon." Jiyeon closed the laptop and leaned back, the chair creaking softly. "A place of my own. Then I could quit, you know? Go live the real dream."

"I guess you haven't found anything yet?"

"I've found plenty. Nothing that really seems right, though. I think I just like to look, and remind myself where I want to be one day, especially when it feels like I'll never get there."

Eunjae glanced back at her from where he was sitting. "You'll get there."

"So will you," she replied. "Wherever it is you want to be."

Where he wanted to be. Eunjae felt like he was starting to get a sense of that destination, catching glimpses through a thick scrim of fog. But if he'd known where he wanted to be, and if he'd been able to see with Jiyeon's level of clarity, maybe he wouldn't be here now. He might never have auditioned for Emerald back then.

He'd been so young when he went to Sydney to sing for Haewon and Soyeon, and the only clear thought in his head at the time was that he needed to do well. That was the only way to fix everything. His mother had said as much, and at the age of fourteen, reeling from both shock and grief in the wake of Vivian's expulsion from his life, Eunjae had still believed in some of Leila's promises. But he'd also realized, by then, that nailing the audition might open the door he'd been searching for.

If they liked him and his voice, he could leave. No more living in that house without Miss Vivi's slippered tread on the stairs, trapped in rooms which no longer held the warmth of her presence. All he had to do was stop rejecting the dream his parents had assigned to him.

"The real dream. When did you figure it out? How did you decide what it was?"

Jiyeon hugged the laptop to her chest, thinking on it for a while. "For my eighth birthday, all I wanted was to get my hair cut in a real salon. My sister had already been going, but I was still having mine done at home, by Dad. I wanted it so badly that Mom decided I could go. That wasn't just because Dad gave me and Denny the exact same bowl cut, either."

Eunjae laughed at that. The memory teased a laugh out of her, too. "We have pictures. Unless my brother destroyed the evidence."

"So those are gone, then."

"Long gone. Never to be seen again." Still smiling, Jiyeon said, "I had this doll, you know, where you could cut her hair and it would grow back. It was just extensions that stuck on with Velcro, but I think that's partly where my fixation came from.

"Besides, I always wanted whatever Janie had. If she was doing it, I had to do it, too. She's four years older than I am. It seemed so grown up, to go to a salon. I wanted to know what it was like to have an appointment, I thought that was really special. Not for the dentist or the doctor, but a fun appointment."

"That's a pretty reasonable goal."

"Right? And when I got there, it was even better than I imagined. Everyone was talking and laughing. It seemed to me like people came in as their normal selves, but when they left they were brand new again. They had hope for something better around the bend. All because of a haircut."

Jiyeon sighed. The smile faltered, and her gaze slipped a little further away. "I wanted to do that: help people feel brand new. I wanted to make my own magical place in the world that felt something like that salon we went to as kids. It didn't have to be fancy, and it didn't even have to be very big. If it had one chair and one mirror and a spot where people could sit and wait, that'd be fine. It's the feeling that matters, right? That's the magic."

"It is," Eunjae answered softly. "That's the magic."

The producers have assembled a variety of artifacts relating to the members' lives before and after they began their journey to stardom: photos, videos, objects of significance. These were sourced from family, friends, and the agency's archives. Through the cameras, we are offered a chance to observe as Ari comments on what the producers have brought him.

First comes a set of photographs. Here is Ari as a baby, wailing furiously in a bassinet trimmed with blue ribbon. Then he appears with his father, Simon Song, on a tarmac that shimmers with heat haze. A vintage plane is parked in the background. Ari, four years old, wears an oversized pilot's cap and smiles shyly at the camera. "So your dad flies for Qantas," we hear the producer say, off-screen. Ari glances up at them and nods.

This segment was filmed late into the night, after Apollo's tour stop in Miami. Signs of his exhaustion are everywhere if you care to look: the slump in his posture, the occasional stifled yawn that couldn't be left on the cutting room floor. But perhaps because it is so late, and perhaps because Ari is so tired, he is actually more forthcoming than usual in this interview.

"Dad was away for most of the week," he recounts in Korean, staring down at the photograph in his hands. Viewers are given a closer view of the image as it fills the screen. "Mum would usually be gone, too. She had performances back then, and rehearsals, so she only commuted home from Sydney every other weekend."

Here, the picture transitions to footage of Ari's mother, American-born model and actress Leila Goldsmith-Song. Willowy and blonde, she walks runways as cameras flash. Some years later, she appears in a stage production of Shakespeare's *Othello*, adopting a somber expression as she stands before a painted backdrop of medieval Venice. While Leila is partially obscured by the actress playing Desdemona, this shot provides a clear look at her features. Mother and son are nearly mirror images of each other, except when Ari smiles. There is a warmth to Ari's smile that is absent from Leila's.

"I had a guardian," says Ari. He hesitates over the word choice here, briefly murmuring to his manager in consultation. He communicates the rest in English. "Sorry, wasn't sure how to say that in Korean. I had a nanny who took care of me because my parents were so busy. She loved music. We used to sing together all the time."

A video clip plays, grainy and dimly lit: Ari's birthday. Eight candles have been arranged on a chocolate sheet cake, dispersed among plastic Disney figurines. Young Ari watches with bated breath as the woman beside him prepares to light the candles with a match. Before she can strike it, Ari can be seen whispering something in her ear. She nods in reply, one hand resting briefly on his thin shoulder.

This woman is not his mother, and indeed we can see Leila's graceful figure off to the right, her back turned to the camera, laughing with a party guest. It's safe to assume that the woman who helps Ari blow out the candles is the aforementioned nanny. Since she is looking at Ari for the entirety of the clip, we only see her face in profile. She has dark hair threaded with strands of silver, pulled into a bun and secured with a large tortoiseshell hair clip. The name 'Vivian Romero' appears on the screen.

"I can't even tell you how much she did for me, everything she gave me," Ari tells the producer. A faint tremor can be detected in his tone. "She had three kids and had to leave them behind while she worked overseas. The whole time she lived with my family, she never got to fly back and visit them. I always felt like all the love she couldn't give her kids in person, she gave to me instead."

In the next clip, we've jumped forward to the aftermath of the birthday party. The video camera sits on the dining table, recording while Ari takes a wrapped package from Vivian's weathered, sun-browned hands. It looks to be about the same size and shape as a paperback book. His elation fairly leaps across the years, reaching us through our screens somehow.

Disembodied, Vivian's warm, sonorous voice sings the last lines of the birthday song. The camera refocuses on the adult Ari as he encounters this remnant of the past. At the sound of that voice, a spark of joy transforms his entire demeanor, as if he's caught up to a familiar figure in a crowd of strangers, but then the spark fades just as quickly.

Happy birthday, dear Eunjae, happy birthday to you.

Ari bows his head. He covers his face with one trembling hand. We hear him utter a muffled, "Sorry." The manager, identified on the screen as 'Nami Seo,' comes forward to check on him. "I'm okay," Ari tells her. "I'm fine."

"What happened with Vivian, Ari?" the producer prompts him.

"She left. It was a few months before I flew to Sydney for my audition."

"Where did she go?"

"I don't know. After my parents fired her, I never saw Miss Vivi again."

In the background, Ari's manager opens her mouth as if to say something, but she never actually speaks. The producer continues this line of questioning. "Why was she fired? Do you know?"

Ari takes the tablet used to show him the clips from his past and flips it face down on the table in front of him. Dully, he replies, "Because I ran away."

25

The next day, Eunjae found himself promoted from dishwasher to general kitchen drudge. His duties expanded to include wiping tables, rolling utensils into napkins, and refilling glass bottles of maple syrup from a gargantuan jug.

Wanna Waffle was packed that morning. It helped to have so much to do and not enough time to brood on the contract, its myriad clauses and the scope of its penalties. Eunjae embraced his rota of menial tasks, finding satisfaction in completing them. Since they were shorthanded until Evan arrived from the aquarium, Denny even risked deploying him to bus tables. That was how Eunjae ended up with his apron pocket stuffed full of crumpled $20.00 bills — an overly generous tip from the family at Table 7.

"Dennis honey, did you know that this nice boy over here speaks English, Korean, *and* Japanese?" the family's elderly matriarch exclaimed, having stopped at the register on her way out. "We're hosting another exchange student for the summer, see? She's from Kyoto and needed help ordering. Thank goodness he offered to help."

The exchange student waved enthusiastically at Eunjae. Eunjae waved back.

"I did *not* know that, Mrs. Garza," admitted Denny, "but it's very valuable information."

"You should give him a raise. He didn't even blink when she started crying on him." Mrs. Garza motioned for Denny to lend her an ear. "Rina's feeling homesick. And her boyfriend sounds like an ass."

Denny's laser beam vision hit Eunjae right between the eyes as soon as the Garza family filed out of the restaurant. "So, Mystery Ryan. You're fluent in three languages."

"Um, and conversational in two more."

"Which ones?"

Eunjae gulped. "Mandarin. And Thai." He could also articulate the phrase *We belong to our fans* in about ten more languages, but sharing this would require him to provide an explanation.

"Interesting."

"Ryan," hissed Jeannie, popping out of the kitchen. "Why was that girl crying into your apron? Auntie Lizzie thinks it's 'cause she asked you to marry her and you said no —"

"Insubordination! Back to work, Vho!"

The rest of the day flew by. Eunjae wiped down tables and washed dishes, knowing all the while that this was exactly the kind of job his parents never wanted him to have. They would deride it as a waste of the gifts he'd been given, according to their estimation: his height, his looks, his voice.

Make something of yourself. As if they'd ever trusted Eunjae to handle this monumental task. Leila had been set on dragging him into stardom since he was six years old, even if he went kicking and screaming. His father was less invested but also disinterested in opposing her. Simon echoed everything his wife said.

It wasn't until late in the afternoon that he had a moment to wonder: if this became his daily existence, would he grow weary of being Eunjae just as he'd grown so deeply weary of being Ari? From where he stood right now, it didn't seem likely. But before he could even begin to dig deeper into that question, it was crucial to sort out what *being Eunjae* entailed. Who was this person he had only just begun to embody? In which direction was he headed? Every time he thought the answer was within his reach, doubt came sailing in.

These worries threw their long shadows across Eunjae's path as he followed Jiyeon and Mr. Han up and down the aisles of a grocery store after work. They'd been sent to stock up on milk and coffee filters, vanilla ice cream by the gallon tub and many, many cartons of eggs. While Mr. Han went off on a quest for steel-cut oats, Jiyeon pushed the cart into the produce section.

"What did you do today?" Eunjae asked her. All the pondering had worn him out. He needed a break.

Jiyeon rearranged egg cartons to make room for a veritable bushel of bananas. "Hmm. I thought of you, actually."

He froze, one milk carton in each hand. "Is that good or bad?"

"Oh, pretty bad," she teased him, laughing. "Someone came in for a color correction this afternoon. They'd tried to go from brunette to platinum and it was a disaster. Took me hours to fix. It made me think about your silver hair, you know? Since I won't be able to cope if you do that a second time."

Eunjae had to laugh, too. "I won't."

"You'd better not."

"I'm never changing my hair again. This is it."

Jiyeon relieved him of the milk cartons, continuing her game of shopping cart Tetris. "Same haircut 'til you're eighty, then? That's the plan?"

He pulled his mask down for three seconds, just so she could see that he was serious. "That's the plan."

"I'd tell you to make an appointment, but Olivia would just pressure me to sell you twenty bottles of volumizing spray that won't even work very well." She rolled her eyes. "And when I refuse, like I always do, she'll make a big deal out of *not* giving me any silly trophies, bouquets, or medals."

"Hold on. That's why you don't have any at your station?"

"Uh-huh. She really wants us selling, selling, selling. I won't do it. I've had enough of that for one lifetime." Jiyeon sighed. "I feel bad for Olivia sometimes, to be honest. I'm... really not what she expected."

He wondered what she meant by that, but it would have to wait. This conversation topic had reminded Eunjae of something he wanted to show her. He pulled it up on his phone while they lingered near the check lanes, waiting for Mr. Han to come back. "Look at this," he said, angling the screen in her direction.

It was the website for a new shopping center, still under construction, some twenty minutes from the Hans' apartment on Ivy Lane. He'd remembered passing by on the way to the optometrist with Denny. Although he couldn't remember the exact address, Eunjae was able to find it on his lunch break with a bit of aggressive Googling.

Only a few of the spaces in the development had been leased so far, with most of the buildings still under construction. Some of those spaces offered more square footage and came at a higher price than what she'd been looking for. But there was one on the corner that seemed just right, even though it was small. Eunjae liked that the architect's rendering showed a wide front window facing west. Never mind the uninspiring parking lot views; the evening sunsets would more than make up for it, he thought.

"There aren't any salons listed as tenants yet," said Eunjae, scrolling further down the page with his thumb. "And it won't be ready for a few more months, so that gives you time."

He let her take the phone. Jiyeon studied the pictures, absently tucking a stray tendril of hair behind one ear. "I think I know where this is," she murmured. "I might even be able to afford it. I've seen some spaces with similar square footage, reasonable rent but awful location." And Eunjae watched as hope began to blossom there, lighting up this face that he'd come to know so well in such a short amount of time.

It felt like nailing the high note in a song that challenged him, expanding to an octave outside his range. It felt nothing short of intoxicating.

He shook his head in an effort to clear it. "There's this, too." Eunjae switched to Google Maps, navigated to the address he'd saved, and zoomed in. "Just down the block, there's a florist. You could stop for flowers every day if you wanted."

Jiyeon lifted her head to stare at him. "Flowers?"

"Yeah. You're always wearing flowers." Case in point, today's outfit involved a black shirtdress with buttons shaped like daisies. Three more daisies featured on the silver clip she'd used to pin her hair into a knot at the nape of her neck.

"I think you like them a little," said Eunjae.

"Just a little." She smiled. "You're something else, Ryan Kim."

He shrugged, suddenly a touch too warm in his Wanna Waffle t-shirt. "I'm just some guy from Brisbane."

"With a lot of brothers."

"Uh, eight of them."

"*Eight?*" But Jiyeon clapped a hand over her mouth, backpedaling instantly. "Nope, forget I said that. And I never heard you mention having eight brothers, either."

"Probably for the best. I think I'd tell you anything if you asked."

"That's not very mysterious of you." Great, he'd said that out loud.

She found a pen in her tote bag and scrawled the leasing office's phone number on the inside of her arm. "I'll leave them a voicemail on the drive back. Maybe we can go see it tomorrow. Ask Denny for the day off, okay? I'm off too."

They really needed to crank up the air conditioning in this grocery store. "Me? I'm going with you?"

"Well, yeah. You found it, after all. You've gotten yourself involved. You have to stick around, at least until after tomorrow."

Mr. Han came ambling back, then, having successfully acquired the steel-cut oats. "Not instant!" he proclaimed. "Denny said *no* instant oats. This is the right kind, steel oats. Steel, you know, like swords. Won't get a lecture this time. Rolled oats, quick oats, blah blah oats. So confusing. And the boy has to be so strict all the time."

"Sorry, I just need to check and make sure: they're sword-cut oats?"

"You know my meaning, Han Jiyeon!"

They went to check out. The line moved at a glacial pace. Eunjae parsed through the latest reply from Arthur. Then he read a text from Kazu that contained an email address for the founders' former executive assistant, the closest thing to contact information that they'd been able to scrounge up so far. It was a stretch, but better than nothing. He'd work on that later, after he figured out how best to petition Denny for a day off.

Unfortunately, these plans were dashed. Even before Eunjae got out of the car, he saw the two figures standing by the front window at Wanna Waffle. Figures in baseball caps pulled low over their faces, their identities instantly obvious to Eunjae despite the masks they wore. Jungwoo and Max were there, waiting for him inside.

26

Long after he'd set the grocery bags in the kitchen, and long after the initial wave of emotion — shock, relief, confusion — Eunjae still couldn't settle on how he felt about his brothers' arrival. He struggled to contend with the nagging notion that this should be simple. Jungwoo and Max were here. He loved them. He'd missed them. So he should be glad to see them, right?

But he wasn't. The joy of seeing them was tempered by a creeping apprehension that filled him with shame. And then there was annoyance, even a glimmer of rage. Eunjae battled the urge to push Jungwoo and Max back outside so that they stood on one side of the door and he stood on the other. *This place is mine. You don't belong here.*

And yet, Eunjae didn't belong in the life he'd been borrowing, either. His brothers were a physical reminder, an encroachment of reality. That was what he resented, Eunjae corrected himself. Not Jungwoo, not Max, but the impossibility of his situation. This truth that he would never be able to outrun.

"Why do they keep calling you Ryan Kim?" asked Jungwoo. The three of them sat in the empty dining room, at the same corner table where Eunjae had eaten on Waffle Wednesday. The shades were drawn and the door had been locked. Muffled voices could be heard in the adjacent kitchen as the Hans restocked their fridge and pantry for the Sunday rush.

"I mean, it's not like hyung could give them his actual name," said Max, sounding scornful and superior in the way only a fresh-faced twentysomething can manage. Not wanting to tell the whole rambling story, Eunjae nodded his head in agreement. This proved somewhat challenging with Max's arms draped around his neck.

"Sure. That makes sense. Smart of you, really." Jungwoo reached out to swat at Max, who swatted right back at him and continued clinging to Eunjae like a barnacle. "Let go, you big baby. Weren't you just yelling at him the other day?"

"I never did that."

"You kind of did," said Eunjae, but he made no move to displace him. "How did you find me?" he asked Jungwoo.

"You mentioned a door like the one in that book. There aren't many interesting doors within walking distance of where we went on our last day. It was trial and error from there."

Max said, "We tried to come by in the morning but it was way too busy. Couldn't risk it, even with the masks on."

Eunjae kept his eyes on Jungwoo. "Hyung, I told you that I need more time."

"Yeah, and I wanted to find out why. What could possibly make you act so crazy all of a sudden? This isn't like you, Ari."

The kitchen door swung open just a crack. Jiyeon peeked out at them. "Time to go home," she called to Eunjae. "Oh, or I can come back for you later. Whichever."

Jungwoo flinched at the word *home*. Then, Denny's voice ricocheted through the sliver of open doorway. "I don't care if they claim to be his brothers. They could be anybody. I'm that idiot's employer, I'm responsible for him —"

Eunjae made a valiant effort to get up from his chair. Jungwoo intercepted him, though. He walked over before Eunjae could pry himself free of Max.

"Hello," Jungwoo said, taking Jiyeon by the hand and drawing her fully into the room. "I wanted to thank you for taking care of my brother." To Eunjae's bewilderment and Max's disgust, he gave her the most dazzling of his smiles. "I've explained it all to your mom and brother, but Ari's coming back with us tonight. I'll make sure you guys are fully compensated for being so kind to him."

Jiyeon looked over at Eunjae. Then she carefully freed her hand from Jungwoo's grip. "It cost us nothing to be kind to him," she said firmly. "You can keep your money. We'll keep Eunjae."

"Eunjae." There was a discordant note to Jungwoo's voice as the name rolled off his tongue. Turning his back on Jiyeon, he let the dazzling smile go out like a light. "You told her that name? Why? Who is she to you?"

Max released him, confounded by how drastically their reunion had iced over. Free to move, Eunjae pushed past Jungwoo in order to reach Jiyeon.

"It's okay," he told her, even though he felt the exact opposite. "I'll meet you outside. Just give me a few minutes."

She cut another glance at Jungwoo. With no small amount of trepidation, she said, "Alright. I'll be at the car when you're ready." And then Jiyeon slipped away, the silence acquiring a bladed edge in her wake.

"I'm not going with you," Eunjae said.

"That's enough," Jungwoo snarled back at him. "This is done, okay? Game over. You've had your fun, you've had your little adventure, but you've gone too far. You're taking it where I can't follow."

"What the hell are you even saying?" Max blurted out. "Is this about the girl? You can't be upset that he might be dating someone in secret. That would make you the king of all hypocrites, hyung. It's not like we don't know what you've been doing with Hazel behind the company's back."

"Ha. Sneaking around with her is nothing compared to what he's doing. If I get caught, I get caught. Emerald will deny everything, I'll get slapped on the wrist, we wait for the media to shut up about it and then we move on. But Ari's mess," said Jungwoo, glaring fiercely at Eunjae, "won't be so easy to clean up. There's no moving on from that. And there's no turning back, either."

Eunjae refused to concede. "You're acting like it would be the end of everything, but it doesn't have to be."

"So you're admitting it, then? You're telling me that I'm right, and you — you're —"

Here, Jungwoo faltered. So did Eunjae, because he had failed to anticipate the full measure of how much this would hurt. It was a pain that cleaved flesh and shattered bone. It was a sorrow that filled his lungs and threatened to drown him.

"He's what?" demanded Max. "Quit fucking talking around me like I'm not even here!"

"Leaving." Eunjae forced himself to look Max in the eye as he said it. "I want to leave, Max."

"But you already left. You're here, aren't you?" And then understanding dawned, bringing unwelcome clarity. Max removed his baseball cap and slumped into a booth, stunned.

Jungwoo shook his head in disbelief. "How can you even be considering this? After all these years of working so hard to get here, you just want to give up? Ari, for god's sake. This is our dream. It's been our dream since we were kids. Are you telling me that it means nothing to you anymore?"

It was never my dream.

This thought struck instantaneously, a spark devouring dry tinder, and then it went up in a blaze. Eunjae felt half blinded by the truth of it. "It was never my dream," he whispered. Jungwoo heard him loud and clear. Eunjae could tell by the way he staggered backward, as if the sentence was a violence enacted physically.

They stood in the same room. They stood a thousand, thousand miles apart.

"This can't be real," said Max, looking younger than ever. "I never thought this would happen to us. I never thought one of us would want to leave. Is it something we did to you, hyung? Are we the problem?"

Eunjae gave him an emphatic denial on that count, but Jungwoo said, coldly, "This isn't about us. This is all on Ari. We could support him in every way, be strong when he's weak and pick up the slack when he needs a break, but the willpower has to come from him. And right now, he's decided that he can't take it anymore. Right now, he's making a mistake."

As he made this declaration, Jungwoo took out his phone. He chose a name from his contacts and began composing a message. Eunjae's heart sank as he realized what was happening.

"I can't let you do this. As your brother, as your best friend, I have to stop you before it's too late."

"No. Please, Jungwoo."

But he sent the message anyway. Now the company knew exactly where to find them. Made cruel by grief, Jungwoo echoed Jiyeon's words from earlier.

"Time to go home."

27

Eunjae ran through the kitchen and burst through the back door, out into the parking lot behind Wanna Waffle. Jiyeon's car was there, the hood silvered in moonlight, but the Hans' Camaro remained as well. They had all waited for him.

The family stood in the empty space between their vehicles, parents on one side and the Han siblings on the other. Jiyeon and her brother had adopted similar postures: backs straight, arms crossed.

"What can we do?" fretted Mrs. Han, her voice carrying on the breeze.

"I'll tell you what we can do," Denny began, but Jiyeon cut him off before he could really get any wind in his sails.

She said, "Nothing. We can't do anything, okay? If it's time for him to go, then that's it."

"How can you be so negative like this? Right away, your answer is no."

"Dad, he's got another life. We all knew that from the beginning." And she sounded so resolute, but still so sad, that Eunjae felt as if he'd reached out and hurt her with his own hands. Perhaps, in a way, he had. By using their world as an escape route from his own, maybe he had brought them more trouble than he ever meant to cause. Meanwhile, they'd given him nothing but care. A sense of belonging he'd only ever found with Miss Vivi and his brothers.

He walked up to where they'd gathered. His shoes scuffed the pavement and Denny was on him in a flash, glowering even harder than usual. Mr. and Mrs. Han hurried to bring Eunjae into the fold, both peppering him with questions in Korean, competing with Denny for his attention. Only Jiyeon maintained her distance. It was as if she already knew the ending. He would leave. Their time was up.

And this hurt, but in a different way. It was foolish to fight the current, perhaps, and Eunjae had certainly subscribed to that belief before. But this didn't have to be the end. He could still find a solution. He could still work on this, figure out an alternative.

"I'll come back," he told them, all of them, but especially her. Jiyeon seemed to pick up on that — on his need to change her mind, in particular — because suddenly she couldn't look straight at him anymore, and Eunjae realized she was blinking back tears.

"Of course," said Mr. Han, gruff and unsmiling, clapping a heavy hand on Eunjae's shoulder. "Of course you'll come back. You're a good boy, a smart one."

Mrs. Han sniffled. She reached up, up, to pat Eunjae on the cheek. "We're not part of the amnesia, okay? You remember us. You remember us always."

"I will."

"Don't cry! Oh, no. No, no. Now I'm crying."

"You," thundered Denny, pointing at Eunjae, "still work here. So you'd better come back. And that's all I'm saying!" Then he retreated so quickly that one might think he was running away.

Eunjae dropped into a bow. A tear splashed onto the asphalt. "I'll come back," he said again. It was as if all other words had evaporated from his vocabulary. When he looked up, Jiyeon was there in front of him, the others packing into the Camaro with a slamming of doors and a brief blare of noise from the ignition.

She wrapped her arms around him. It was so easy to do the same, so strangely habitual to hold her close despite the fact that this was an action Eunjae had never taken before in his life. This startled him. He'd been awake, wide awake, since the moment he spotted that orange door — or so he'd thought, until now.

I wish we had more time.

"Promise me you'll still go, tomorrow. I can't come with you, but you should still go."

"Okay." She took a deep, shuddering breath. "I'll go. I promise."

Maybe they hadn't repeated Jungwoo's explanation to her yet. Maybe his secrets were still his to keep.

"Do you know who I am yet?" *Please say no. Please pretend.*

A new set of headlights cut through the dark. Jiyeon held on for just a moment longer.

"Yes."

28

They marched him straight to the agency, of course.

Eunjae didn't drag his feet. He didn't ask to stop at the dorms for a shower and a change of clothes. His eyeballs felt like they'd been rolled in sand and then pushed back into their sockets, but he made no appeals for sleep. *Let's get this over with*, he thought to himself, following Nami-noona through the gleaming halls of Emerald Entertainment. *Let them hit me with whatever they've got.*

He watched the numbers change on the panel above the elevator doors: six, seven, eight. The executive offices were on this floor. All along the main corridor, enormous illuminated panels featured the faces of Emerald's biggest stars, past and present: soloists and groups, actors and actresses, all dressed for their headshots in vivid, arresting green.

Eunjae remembered when Apollo had earned the right to have their images hung in the executive hall. He and his brothers were here too, photographed in threes because nine was too many for one panel to hold.

Despite his earlier conviction, Eunjae paused at the images of Haewon and Soyeon flanking the entrance to CEO Yoon's office, lagging behind even as Jungwoo pushed straight through. They hadn't spoken to each other since the confrontation at Wanna Waffle. Max looked back for a second, concerned, until Nami-noona urged him onward.

"Come on, Ari," she said softly. Her voice was kind but worn down, unraveled by the stress and anxiety of the past week. It occurred to Eunjae that his time with the Hans had been the longest he'd gone without at least one of his brothers nearby and also the farthest he'd ever strayed beyond Nami's oversight.

When he still wouldn't budge, Nami sighed and sent the security staff back to the elevator. Together, she and Eunjae stared up at the founders' faces on either side of Yoon's door. The photographer had gotten his shot while Soyeon was in the middle of laughing at something; her happiness was effervescent, impossible to contain within the bezeled frame. On the opposite panel, Haewon's smile showed no teeth, but she had eyes that spoke volumes. Her earrings were heavy emerald drops that trapped the light and held it within.

They were here, larger than life. They were nowhere, and too far for him to reach. But if he could only talk to them, reason with them, surely the founders would listen. Once upon a time, they'd lived this life, too. Once upon a time, they'd cared and understood. Eunjae wanted to believe that they still did. He wanted to believe that Kazu was wrong, that hoping for a compromise wasn't just an exercise in futility.

"Where are they?" he asked Nami. But this time she only pulled him away. Maybe she didn't know. Maybe she couldn't or wouldn't tell him. It was impossible to guess.

Inside the office, the walls were all windows, sheets of sparkling glass allowing an unobstructed view of the rooftop garden on the adjacent building, which housed a dining hall and also belonged to the Emerald Entertainment complex. No one sat at the chair behind Yoon's desk. Instead, Eunjae's brothers were ranged throughout the room.

Everyone was there except Jaehwan. The oldest present, Kazu and Nicky had taken the chairs closest to the desk. Namgyu sat with Kei beneath a framed aerial photo of Seoul. Max and Jesse huddled next to the CEO's vintage record player.

Only Jungwoo stood apart. How many times had Eunjae taken the spot beside him? And now he stayed away, remaining in the center of the room. But it wasn't the first time Eunjae had been surrounded by others while feeling completely alone at the same time. He attempted to settle into that state of being, a familiar discomfort. It didn't come very easily. Perhaps too much had changed already.

Jesse spoke up first. He sat with his shoulders hunched, his usual energy dimmed to an ember. Sniffling, he asked the question hanging heavy and unspoken in the air between them.

"Are you leaving, hyung? Is it true?"

"You can't just leave," Kei blurted out. "That isn't fair to the rest of us. You know it's not."

Kazu turned to cut him a warning glare. "If he wants to go, then we have no business holding him back."

"That's easy for you to say. They're about to put you out to pasture anyway. You, Nicky, even Jaehwan-hyung. You're all halfway out the door."

"Keiichi," admonished Namgyu, but Kei pressed on, pinning Eunjae with a flinty stare.

"You've had your time. I guess that's good enough for you. But what about the rest of us? Me, Max, and Jess? We're the youngest members in the group. If we disband —"

"Nobody said anything about that," Nicky was quick to interject. "You're jumping to conclusions. Groups can lose a member without disbanding. It happens."

Kazu nodded. "And Ari hasn't even gotten to say anything in his own defense yet. We need to hear him out."

Tell them, urged the part of Eunjae that had somehow become braver than the rest of him. *You can't put it off forever. You can't keep hoping you just read the contract wrong. Just tell them everything.* But in the end, he didn't.

"Losing a member could have serious consequences for all of us," Kazu went on, "especially when you consider what Ari contributes to our overall sound. We have to be fair, so that's something to think about."

With a grimace, Nicky said, "There's no way we'd ever match what we've got now. We need everybody for that. The fans would be upset, too."

"Maybe Apollo would bounce back. Seems like lots of groups do, even when they lose someone. But what happens to Ari if he leaves?" Namgyu leaned forward, frowning out of genuine concern. "That could be the end of your career, man."

"I know," said Eunjae.

"Just to be really clear, it could be the end of all our careers. Because we're successful as a group, first and foremost. A lot of us haven't had as many chances to do stuff on our own. So without the group, what the hell are we? Why should people care about us if we aren't Apollo anymore?"

Max took a step toward Kei. "What are you getting at? We can't force him to stay. That's not right either." Automatically, Eunjae grabbed Max and Kazu took hold of Kei before things could escalate.

"I don't get how it's come down to this. I thought Ari-hyung just needed a break. Now he might never come back?" Jesse swiped at tears. "Can everybody just stop fighting and yelling, at least?"

"You should be yelling too," Kei argued at him. "If this idiot walks out now, it's never going to be the same again. *We're* never going to be the same again. We might as well look at it as the beginning of the end."

"Between the enlistments and Ari leaving, it would be hard to keep up the momentum."

"That's true. Nicky and Gyu are supposed to go next year. It'll be forever before all nine of us are on stage again."

"Let's say we keep going as a group," said Nick, beginning to pace. "That's fine, but we'll always be one man down. We'll know it. Sunshines will know it. We've been nine members for almost ten years. That's not easy to forget or erase."

"You guys have a unit project dropping next month. That won't happen if hyung quits now."

"I don't give a shit about that, Keiichi," Max was quick to say. "Seriously, can you guys figure out what's more important? Why are you being like this?"

"Because this is all he knows how to do," Kei raged back at him. "He just runs away!" And Eunjae couldn't defend himself because it was true.

Someone else interjected, and then that interjection gave way to more. Soon the room rang with raised voices, a growing cacophony of opposing viewpoints and high emotions. Eunjae had no idea how to make himself heard above the noise. Jungwoo, who had always spoken for him, had still not uttered a single word. To Eunjae, his silence was an ongoing rebuke. Of all the reactions, it was the most painful to endure.

"We said we'd stay together," said Namgyu, partly drowned out by Kei and Max as they lobbed accusations at one another. He looked up at Eunjae, face drawn with misery. "We're supposed to be brothers."

There has to be another way, Eunjae wanted to scream. As if on cue, the office door swung open and CEO Yoon stepped in at last. An abrupt hush fell upon them all as they realized that he had a pair of guests in tow.

Following close behind him were Choi Haewon and Sun Soyeon, the founders of Emerald Entertainment.

Excerpt from Jewell's entry on Wikipedia

Jewell was a South Korean girl group formed by <u>Polaris Media</u> in 1998 and consisted of members <u>Sun Soyeon</u>, <u>Nam Jinseol</u>, <u>Choi Haewon</u>, and <u>Lee Eunmi</u>. The group was one of the most popular and successful acts of the late 1990s and early 2000s, credited for their significant role in the cultural movement which came to be known as the <u>Hallyu Wave</u>. Some of the group's most enduring hits are <u>"Too Many Boys"</u> (1998), "Spring Love" (1999), <u>"Secret Garden"</u> (2002), and "Last Goodbye" (2005) from the Korean drama <u>A Rose in Winter</u>.

Jewell officially disbanded on August 12, 2008. Eunmi branched into acting with a breakout role in the 2010 historical film *Fallen Flower*. Jinseol stayed on at Polaris Media as an in-house choreographer. In 2009, former members Haewon and Soyeon jointly founded <u>Emerald Entertainment</u>. While Soyeon pursued a brief solo career, Haewon primarily dedicated herself to songwriting and production.

HISTORY

1998: Formation and Debut

The eldest member and leader of the group, Sun Soyeon, was scouted while waiting to be seated at a restaurant in Myeongdong. According to an interview with a former Polaris Media executive, Soyeon was heard singing to a song on the radio and immediately drew his attention with the clarity and range of her voice. The next member to be scouted was Lee Eunmi, who auditioned with some friends from school. Nam Jinseol joined as a trainee after initially pursuing a career as a ballerina. Last to join the lineup was Choi Haewon, discovered two months later when she won a songwriting contest sponsored jointly by Polaris, <u>Wonder Music Korea</u>, and <u>M7 Entertainment</u>.

The four girls debuted as Jewell in 1998 with their first album, <u>*Ruby Red*</u>. Defying late 90s K-pop trends, Jewell focused less on cute, catchy pop, becoming known for poignant lyrics and a distinct R&B sound, as with their debut single "Too Many Boys" and its equally popular B-side "Sunshine Smile." In the back half of their career, they shifted to include melodic power ballads that showcased the members' impressive vocals, particularly Soyeon's.

It is rumored that member Haewon is an uncredited lyricist and composer on a significant number of Jewell's hit songs. Polaris Entertainment has neither confirmed nor denied these rumors. Haewon has never addressed them either, despite continued speculation among fans and industry experts. Notably,

Haewon went on to co-found Emerald Entertainment, which houses multiple self-produced groups (<u>Athena</u>, <u>Apollo</u>) and singer-songwriters (<u>Ye-ri</u>, <u>Flora Jung</u>, <u>Ryeowook/SKYLINE</u>).

1999-2001: *Sapphire Blue* and *Jeweltones Live*

Jewell's sophomore album, <u>*Sapphire Blue*</u>, arrived in May 1999 to wide critical acclaim. Its lead single "Spring Love" reached the number one spot on multiple South Korean airplay charts upon release. At the 1999 <u>Seoul Music Awards</u>, Jewell won a daesang (grand prize) as well as Song of the Year.

Between 1999 and 2001, Jewell saw a massive increase in popularity. Seeking to capitalize on the tremendous success of *Sapphire Blue*, Polaris Media announced a special album in the first half of 2000 entitled <u>*Jeweltones*</u>. For this album, each member of Jewell had a solo track in addition to two songs by the full group.

In September 1999, Jewell's leader Soyeon also released a song for the Korean drama <u>*Until You*</u>. The song ("<u>When You're Here</u>") became the only track on the drama soundtrack to break into the Gaon charts. Shortly after *Until You* finished airing, several news networks reported on an alleged copyright dispute between Jewell member Haewon and Polaris Entertainment CEO <u>Jang Minseok</u>; Polaris disputed the claims and threatened legal action against all three networks.

In January 2000, the group starred in a commercial for <u>Korean Airlines</u>. Brands such as <u>Pepsi</u> and <u>Lotte Department Store</u> reported a surge in earnings due to their endorsement deals with Jewell.

During the summer of 2001, Jewell embarked on a concert series called _Jeweltones Live_. They performed in cities all over Asia and ended their tour with back to back concerts in Seoul. The group finished touring and went straight to the studio to begin recording for their third album.

2002: _Crystal Clear,_ Production Delays, and Soyeon's Hiatus

In early spring of 2002, Polaris Media issued a statement which explained that a series of health problems among the members of Jewell necessitated the delayed release of their third album, _Crystal Clear_. Originally slated for April 2002, it was postponed until May as member Eunmi recovered from a compound fracture and Soyeon was hospitalized due to complications from an untreated illness during 2001's _Jeweltones Live_ concert tour.

Crystal Clear smashed all of Jewell's previous sales records. The title track "Secret Garden" earned the group their second perfect run on South Korean music charts. It also earned them Song of the Year and Album of the Year at the Mnet Asian Music Awards (MAMA). Polaris Media announced an impending Japanese debut for the group in July 2002 with a repackaged album forthcoming in the next year. However, promotions for "Secret Garden" were interrupted when Soyeon experienced a panic attack while filming their performance on the music show _Inkigayo_.

Jewell completed the final week of promotions as a four member group. Abruptly, Soyeon posted a message on Jewell's fan cafe which stated her intention to leave the group and end her exclusive contract. Just as abruptly, Polaris held a press conference the following day. At the press conference, the agency's CEO confirmed that Soyeon would remain a member of Jewell, resuming group activities after a hiatus of approximately two months. This hiatus eventually lasted eight months total.

29

As the women drifted past him — Haewon in a brutally crisp white button-down shirt, Soyeon with her face hidden behind massive Ferragamo sunglasses — Eunjae was almost afraid to look away. Was this a hallucination? Here were the two people who controlled his fate. Now that they were right in front of him, now that his silent pleas to the universe had been answered, should Eunjae be grateful or wary?

Soyeon acknowledged him with the barest inclination of her head, nothing more. But Haewon paused to flick a lock of hair out of Eunjae's eyes, murmuring, "You've had a haircut. It suits you."

Eunjae bowed his head, a gesture of respect for his superior but also a tactic for self-preservation. The intensity of Haewon's gaze felt like something to be avoided, much like staring into the sun.

"Why don't you sit down, Ari? There's a lot to talk about."

"Thank you," he replied quietly, head still bowed, staring at his shoes. "I think I'll stand, if that's alright."

"Whatever you like," said Haewon. She left him and went to perch on the glossy wooden expanse of Mr. Yoon's desk while Soyeon took the leather chair behind it. The upholstery seemed to swallow her slight figure, as if she'd curled up in the palm of some monstrous hand.

"Would you like me to try and get Jaehwan on the line?" inquired Mr. Yoon, addressing the women who had taken over his desk. Soyeon dismissed the suggestion instantly.

"We shouldn't disrupt his duties. Jaehwan can be notified once a decision has been made."

"I agree. No need to cause a commotion just yet. And there may be no reason to call him at all. That depends on Ari, but I'm confident he'll make the right choice."

Haewon smiled at him from across the room. Eunjae couldn't help noticing the way this smile failed to reach her eyes. It reminded him of his mother and summoned, from the depths of memory, a rising tide of dread.

But Haewon hadn't always been like this. Eunjae remembered her fingers flying over piano keys, drawing melodies out of guitar strings. There was a period when, every time she ran into him, Haewon would make an exaggerated show of bribing Eunjae into a solo debut. She and Jungwoo were ready to write all the songs, produce the whole record themselves. She'd buy him a dozen new cameras. He could ask for anything he wanted in return: a pony, a library, her firstborn child.

They used to laugh together. And Soyeon, she used to pop up at Eunjae's voice lessons every week if she had time. When Apollo stopped in Sydney on their first tour, it was Soyeon who came to his hotel room and listened, patiently, as he explained why he didn't want complimentary tickets sent to his parents, or seats reserved for them in the front row. She never judged or tried to change his mind. It was also Soyeon who arranged for Ezra to come watch, with two friends, when Apollo performed in Singapore.

What happened? When did it all change, and why?

A hand gripped Eunjae's shoulder. Kazu stood beside him now, mouth set in a firm line. "I'm the eldest here," he said, with a formal bow. "I take responsibility."

"Kazuhiko, how admirable. Please, lift your heads, stop looking so sad. This isn't an execution." Haewon punctuated this statement with a laugh. Light and airy, it somehow managed to set Eunjae's teeth on edge nonetheless.

"Let's just get started," Soyeon sighed. Juxtaposed with the sound of Haewon's brittle laughter, the weariness in her tone stood out in sharp relief.

Mr. Yoon took over. "Ari, we're relieved to have you back. You gave us quite the scare. And I have to admit that I never expected this kind of behavior from you. It's grounds for termination, really. Missing your flight, getting yourself adopted by strangers like an abandoned dog. Forcing us to send staff to Australia when you were right there, just a few miles from the original hotel. And your parents have been distraught, of course. We had to plead with them not to pull Ezra out of school and go searching for you themselves."

Eunjae bit his tongue. The thought of those two scouring the globe for him was only marginally more ludicrous than Ezra being jolted out of his regular life on Eunjae's behalf. Leila and Simon would never do something like that.

His younger brother was fourteen now, leading a busy life at his illustrious and expensive international boarding school. The tuition came out of Eunjae's share of Apollo's album sales and concert tours. He received quarterly dispatches from Blackridge Academy, by request; over the years, he'd seen pictures of Ezra on intramural sports days, winning medals, having some of his artwork shown in the school's front hall for an event. On Eunjae's birthday and at Christmas, there would be a card from Ezra or a letter on Blackridge stationery. Sometimes he'd get an email out of the blue. Just a few lines in polite English, businesslike and concise.

If Ezra needed it, Eunjae covered the cost. It was never the money that bothered him about this setup. Rather, it was the experience of watching his parents protect Ezra's childhood so zealously. They showed up for his awards ceremonies and attended family days. There was no pressure on Ezra to work with a voice coach or take piano lessons. In his latest Christmas card, he'd mentioned maybe becoming an accountant. How freely he could choose — it was beautiful, and it hurt.

Fourteen years old. The same age Eunjae had been when he signed with Emerald and gave up his own normal existence for the foreseeable future. For the entirety of his youth, or possibly even more.

And the founders didn't intervene, even though they should know how preposterous Yoon was being. Bitterness welled up inside him. "You can tell my parents that the money will keep on coming. There won't be any issues with Ezra staying at that school." Eunjae knew how much he'd saved. There was more than enough to cover tuition until his brother graduated, even if this mess resulted in legal fees. He'd been so careful to make sure Ezra wouldn't be affected because he didn't think that would be fair.

"I'll accept whatever punishment you think I deserve. No one else should be blamed, though. Just me."

"We're aware that you asked your brothers to help you, Ari. They deliberately concealed your location from us, and even if they weren't lying outright, they were lying by omission. These breaches in behavior have cost Emerald a fair amount of money. We had to cancel a fanmeeting and refund tickets at short notice. Venue deposits were forfeited. All of that, just so you could have a little holiday."

"But it wasn't just a little holiday," Haewon said, interrupting Mr.

Yoon midsentence. "According to what Jungwoo told us, you want to break your contract. And you want to do that with our blessing."

Behind the desk, Soyeon shifted in her chair, a frown marring the flawless impassivity of her expression. "Is that true?" she asked Eunjae.

He'd lived almost a straight decade in the public eye, every move and every breath monitored by millions of people he didn't know and would never meet. Even so, it took every ounce of strength to endure the pressure of his brothers' stares in that moment. The bonds that held them together were powerful enough to exert their own gravitational pull. These were the bonds that Eunjae might sever just by making the choice that felt right to him — the choice that would save him.

He took a deep breath. "Yes," he told them. "It's true."

30

All around him, voices lifted in alarm. Although it was no surprise to the rest of Apollo, hearing the words come out of Eunjae's mouth must have felt like having the decision carved in stone. The founders traded glances, speaking in that wordless vernacular so particular to sisterhood, and to brotherhood as well.

Haewon's frosty smile had vanished. She said, "Then you'd better tell your brothers what happens next. Because you've figured it out, haven't you?"

This finally compelled Jungwoo to address Eunjae from beyond the invisible wall that had gone up between them. "What's this about, Ari? What else have you been hiding?" *What other secrets have you been keeping from me?*

Eunjae didn't know where to begin. Or rather, he knew where to begin but had no idea how to soften the blow.

"There's nothing hidden about it, really," said Haewon. "It's only that so few of you bothered to look. Did the intern make those copies I asked for, Mr. Yoon?"

"Yes, they're right here." Yoon slid a stack of documents out of a folio in the top desk drawer. Soyeon eyed the stapled pages with cool detachment, then turned away when she was offered a set. Yoon proceeded to distribute the rest until all the members had their own.

Only Eunjae refused. He'd guessed what the documents were, by then: generic copies of the contract they'd all signed, first when they debuted and again upon their renewal with Emerald Entertainment in their seventh year as Apollo.

"Just the highlighted part, boys. You can read the rest on your own time."

It was Jesse who finished reading first. His head snapped up, and he looked right at Eunjae. "This says... this says if one member breaks contract, the whole group has to disband. At least, I think that's what it means."

Max lowered his copy, eyes wide. "That can't be legal," he protested.

"It's not illegal, either," murmured Eunjae. He couldn't admit it without sounding defeated. The agency could force disbandment if even one member bowed out of his exclusive contract before the next renewal. These terms were uncommon nowadays, but also violated no existing laws.

He'd done as much research as he could, sifting through the convoluted legalese, staying up too late even though Denny would be hustling him out of bed as early as 4am. Every article retrieved from Google search and every resource from the South Korean Fair Trade Commission led to the same conclusion. And when he asked Arthur to help him understand it, the contract's restrictions only seemed even more impenetrable.

"Wait," said Namgyu, the pages crumpled against his chest. "Just hold on a second. Ari, you knew about this? You knew and you didn't say anything to the rest of us?"

"I didn't know it for sure until a few days ago." *And I didn't want to believe it.*

"Maybe you never told us because you didn't care about the price we'd be paying for you."

Kazu whipped around, hackles raised. "That's enough, Keiichi."

"You can't prove that he really meant to talk to us about this. Last I checked, he ran off to California like a coward. Who's to say he won't bail on us like a coward? Isn't that the logical next step?"

"He's not the one you should be mad at," Max exclaimed. "Can't you see that? How can we be mad at him for not wanting to live like this anymore?"

"He knew what he was signing up for," Jungwoo volleyed back, siding with Kei. "We all did."

"Shut the hell up, Jungwoo. Did we, really? What did any of us know? We were just stupid kids."

"No, I won't shut up! I'll never shut up about this!" Jungwoo balled up the contract and hurled it to the floor. "I wrote those songs. The terms say that if Emerald disbands us, they keep the rights to all of them. Even the songs I've written since debut that haven't been released yet, or never will be. Are you listening to me? Aren't these your songs too? We all chip in, don't we?"

"That's another thing I just couldn't figure out," said Eunjae, addressing Haewon. It was one of the industry's most badly kept secrets, that she'd written songs for Jewell without even being credited. So much of her work from that era was iconic now. None of Haewon's lyrics and compositions had been attributed to her. "After what you went through with Polaris, why would you deny the rights to our own work? Why put us through that?"

"I'm not denying you anything. If Apollo had decided not to

renew with Emerald two years ago, ownership would've reverted to you. We keep your songs if you break our trust. You break our trust by violating contract terms. Fair enough, to me. It's all written into that same penalty clause."

"Even our name, though?" murmured Nick, shaking his head in disbelief. "You'd go so far as to keep the name 'Apollo' if we're disbanded?"

Max exploded. "That's petty as all hell!"

"And it's nothing we'd have to worry about if Ari just stays."

Max informed Kei exactly how he felt about him in that moment. The sheer number of expletives had Mr. Yoon threatening to kick him out of the room. Then Jesse remarked that Apollo would be signing contracts again in just two more years anyway, since renewals lasted for shorter durations. Could Ari just hold on until then? But Namgyu thought it was cruel to force him to wait if he was unhappy now, and Kazu was just plain incensed at the degree to which they could all be controlled by a stack of paper.

No consensus could be reached. Chaos erupted again. Mr. Yoon roared at them to settle down, but Haewon scarcely batted an eye at any of it. She didn't react until Nicky approached her.

"You'd really disband us? We're one of Emerald's flagship groups. Our sales have never been higher, we've won awards for our work, and we break records with every comeback. Apollo's never let you down. How can you justify doing something like this?"

"No, you haven't let us down. We're very proud of what you've accomplished and we won't deny that Apollo has majorly contributed to the agency's success. But will Ari let you down? Isn't that the real question, here?"

Eunjae decided not to take the bait. He looked to Soyeon instead, voicing a theory that had been percolating in his head for a while. "You had the same clause in your contracts, didn't you? Back then, when you were still part of Jewell. When you wanted to quit too, just like me."

The arguments died down. Soyeon did not respond, but her knuckles were white as she gripped the armrest, nails digging into the leather. Haewon predictably spoke for her.

"Yes. *All for one, one for all.* The musketeer clause, as it was known at the time. This may be difficult to understand, but the clause is meant to keep groups together. It's designed to remind us that we're part of something greater and there's no room to be selfish — that the group comes first. We're all human, aren't we? And humans are self-centered. Inevitably, we lose sight of what's important. Rules like this one prevent us from making terrible mistakes."

Haewon went to join Soyeon behind the desk. She wrapped an arm around her co-founder, her sister, her oldest and dearest friend. Eunjae couldn't help noticing that, for her part, Soyeon remained as cold and distant as the moon.

"Soyeon stayed with Jewell because of that clause. It helped her find the strength to continue, for the dream we shared and for the sake of keeping the four of us together. We were a family, just like you, and that's why I was determined to have the same clause written into your contracts: it saved us. And it can save you, too. All you need to do is endure the pain, like she did. But again, ultimately it's up to Ari. Will he set off on his own, leaving the rest of you high and dry? I'd like to think he wouldn't. Surely he has too much love for you and what you've built together."

From the beginning, Apollo had felt like its own independent universe, nine planets sharing a single, bright dream that blazed like the sun. Up until that moment, Eunjae's love for his brothers had acted as a force that kept him tethered to his place in the world, a place where he belonged. With the founders watching him, and while the others waited for his choice — a choice that hardly felt like a choice — those invisible bonds of brotherhood reforged themselves into chains.

Eunjae had hoped that speaking to Haewon and Soyeon would change their minds. Now, he saw that it was simple, really. There was only one answer and he gave it.

"Don't disband us," said Eunjae. "I won't break my contract. I'll stay."

Sourced from unused footage recorded for Ari's episode of *Sunshine 24/7: Apollo on Tour*, cut from the docuseries at the request of Emerald Entertainment

"Because I ran away." These words are scarcely out of Ari's mouth before the interview is interrupted by a scuffle out in the hall. The cameras are left rolling, forgotten, as a muffled argument takes place off-screen. The producer steps out of the session to deal with this outburst. Ari stays seated at the foot of his hotel room bed, staring at the photos gathered for the segment. He doesn't acknowledge the noise emanating from the doorway.

Nami walks past the camera. Wringing her hands, she slows down to talk to him. Her words are unintelligible. We see Ari nodding mechanically in response, then falling backward onto the mattress as soon as his manager steps away. He lies there in silence, staring at the ceiling. It's as if he's withdrawn into his own head, leaving nothing but a shell behind.

When Jaehwan strides into view, his mood is evident from the start. One scathing glance sends the remainder of the film crew packing. None of them return for their equipment. "You should've told them to drop it," he tells Nami. "You're supposed to be looking out for him. Isn't that your damn job?"

"Just go," says Kazu. Anger smolders in every syllable, kept in check only through careful control. He's speaking to their manager, but his eyes are on Ari. "We've got him. Take the rest of the night off. We won't be needing you."

Nami scurries away with one last backward glance. Jaehwan sits on the bed. "Who did they get that stuff from?" he asks. "Leila?"

"Yeah."

"That's what I figured, but I was hoping to be wrong for a change." He scowls down at Ari. "They're gone. You won't have to record this interview again. They can ask, but only if they get past me."

Ari sits up. He blinks at Jaehwan, whose frightening expression is completely at odds with the rest of his appearance. The man is dressed from head to toe in a cashmere loungewear set that seems to have been spun from actual fluffy clouds. The sweater and joggers are the same color as the top layer of a cold foam latte. These soft details combine with the icy beauty of Jaehwan's face, a study in contrast.

Apollo's leader is an avenging angel come to deliver judgment while looking as cozy and luxurious as possible. No one ever made matching sweats look so formal. Meanwhile, Kazu looks like he tumbled out of bed two minutes ago because this was the actual chain of events. His hair is mussed, both feet are bare, and he didn't bother tying the hotel bathrobe when he raced out of his room. If Apollo fans were to see this footage, they'd be peeking through their fingers at the amount of skin Kazu's showing on camera. And are those the same silk pajama pants he wore down the Vuitton runway two months ago?

The easiest thing to see is how much comfort Ari derives from having his brothers here — the calm certainty of it, like the beacon of a lighthouse sweeping across an expanse of dark water.

"I should've declined to answer," he murmurs. "I wasn't thinking straight."

"And they knew you weren't. Why else would they schedule your interview right after we walked off the stage tonight? They wanted you to come in exhausted because then they could catch you off guard, dig into your business." Jaehwan shakes his head. "If I'd known that the producer was playing this game... but I guess it's too late to do much about it now."

"I'm sorry, hyung."

"Don't be sorry," Kazu protests. "You haven't done anything wrong."

Ari tries to compose himself. He fails. "I can't do this anymore," he says, burying his face in his hands. "I just can't."

Instantly, Jaehwan's arms are around him, and then Kazu's arms are around them both. They sit this way for a while, and most of what the older brothers say to Ari is pitched too low for the camera to pick up. We do hear Jaehwan say this: "There's a fire pit downstairs. We can burn that picture of your mom."

"Hey, let's make some of those things Max was talking about. What were they? Snores?"

"S'Mores, hyung."

"Yeah! Some-mores. I knew I was close."

"Whatever you feel like setting on fire, Ari." Jaehwan's expression softens. "We could find her, you know. Miss Vivi. If you want to."

Ari's tentative laughter dies down, a spark extinguished. He shrinks back, retreating again to a place far removed from here. He glances at the photos scattered on the hotel's snowy white sheets.

"My parents always told me that I couldn't be anything else. This was all I'd be good for, and anyway, every other option was a waste of the one talent I'd been born with. Miss Vivi didn't agree. When she found out that I didn't want to audition, that even thinking about the audition was making me sick to my stomach every single day, she loved me enough to try and help me skip it. She helped me run away."

This is news to both Jaehwan and Kazu, who swap concerned glances over Ari's head. "She helped you? How?"

"I was supposed to fly to Sydney with her because both of my parents were busy, as usual. We'd just stay at the hotel, not show up to the audition at all. We could say that I didn't make it in. But Miss Vivi didn't realize that Dad knew someone who worked at the audition venue. That's how he heard that we never went. When Mum found out, she was furious. Beyond furious."

"You didn't miss your audition, though," Kazu points out. "There's a recording of it."

"That was six months later," says Ari. "I came back to Sydney when Emerald did their next round."

"You didn't even want to be there." Jaehwan's eyes are downcast. "This isn't even what you wanted to do with your life. At least the rest of us had a choice."

"No, I thought I wanted it by then. It was the only way to escape. And I was stupid, so I believed it when Mum said Miss Vivi could come back if I got in, as long as Emerald took me as a trainee." Now his laughter is barbed, rueful. "I don't want to find Miss Vivi. How could I ever face her? She'd take one look at me and be so sad."

"I doubt that, Ari."

"She's been waiting all this time just to see you again. I'd bet money on it. And you know I don't just say things like that."

"Hyung, they made sure she couldn't find another job after. Refused to write a reference, reported her to the police. Child endangerment. Kidnapping. Mum even tried to accuse her of stealing jewelry. That's how angry she was. My shot at becoming a star, ruined. It was unforgivable."

"Fucking Leila," mutters Jaehwan.

Ari is about to say something more, but then a small army's worth of footsteps comes thundering up the hall. Jaehwan and Kazu swing their heads toward the door, listening to the slap of flip-flops and slides on carpet. Rambunctious chatter gradually seeps into Ari's room. That's the rest of Apollo and there's no mistaking it.

"My god. Those idiots came up straight from the pool."

"How'd they even find out? You didn't call anybody but me, right?" Kazu pauses. "Oh damn, Hwannie. That producer probably ran through the lobby crying his face off. What did you say to him before I got here?" He crosses his arms. "Is there a body under this bed?"

"That would be sloppy. Not my style. Nicky extorted it out of Nami, most likely. He's got a sixth sense and it's only for gossip."

Jaehwan gets to his feet. "If Jess tries to bring that giant unicorn float in here, I'm stabbing it."

"Hyung, you have a knife...?"

"We'll send them away if you want," Kazu offers. But Ari turns him down.

"It's okay. They can come in."

"All of them? You want everyone to come in here right now?"

Too late. The others tumble in, swarming over to Ari in a clamoring mass. Is he okay? Does he need anything? Where are the people who bullied him? How do they contact Netflix about it? If they combine their bank accounts, can they sue? Actually, could Kazu just pay for it since he's the nephew of a known millionaire?

Jesse dashes off in a blur of pumping legs, sandals hitting the floor with a wet thwack. He says something about ice cream. Nicky bawls at him to stop at Kazu's room for the credit card, earning himself a smack in the shoulder. Max rants at Ari for being a doormat while clinging to his arm like a sailor in the middle of a shipwreck, and Kei hints darkly at revenge. But this is only after he's finished shouting, "Why's Zuzu always naked?" at the top of his lungs.

Jungwoo is in shock upon learning how the producers found out about Vivian; how could Ari's mother possibly sink lower than before? ("I'm his mom," snaps Jaehwan.) Namgyu announces that the solution is to build a pillow fort. He saw it on some American TV show and is certain that this will make Ari feel better. It's only a matter of minutes before he's managed to drip chlorinated water all over the place.

In this crucible of total chaos, Nicky jostles the camera by accident and catches it just in time. He alerts the others to the fact that it's still recording and shuts it off.

31

The day had worn down to a sliver of fading blue-gray sky by the time Eunjae made it back to the dorms. He'd been ferried there on his own after a separate meeting with Mr. Yoon in which the expectations for his future conduct were duly delivered. Eunjae had endured it, numb to just about everything at that point.

Inside the double that he shared with Jungwoo, all the common areas were immaculate. Mopped floors, scrubbed counters, not a single dish languishing in the sink. Jungwoo tended to clean when stressed or unhappy. His door was shut and his lanyard and keys missing from their usual hook on the wall. Eunjae stumbled into his own room, relieved.

His bedroom was still in the same state of disaster in which he'd left it last week. Clothes strewn all over the furniture, a scattering of shoes and random electronics littering the floor. Eunjae unceremoniously swept everything off his bed and crawled in. He plummeted into merciful, dreamless sleep not even five minutes later.

For a moment right after waking, as his eyes adjusted to the dark, Eunjae felt okay. But then he remembered again and misery surged back in, a riptide dragging him under.

He thought back to that first night: the orange door and the flight he'd missed, the question Jiyeon had asked him afterward. *What do you want to do?* A question that was so simple and yet imparted so much power. A question Eunjae had not been asked by his parents at any point along the way. Only Vivian had ever asked him how he felt about it.

But whenever Eunjae had the opportunity to make choices for himself, it seemed as though he could never get it right. Or, the choice would feel right for him and wrong for everyone else. Selfish, weak, thoughtless, off in his own little world — criticisms from his parents, a familiar refrain throughout Eunjae's childhood. Many of the same words cropped up during the fight with Jungwoo and again in the lecture he'd just gotten from Mr. Yoon. That had to mean something, didn't it?

He wasn't supposed to make choices that prioritized his own happiness or well-being. That was selfish. He wasn't supposed to turn away from what made him miserable, seeking any escape he could find, whether he did this through a book about a magical door or by zoning out in the middle of a photo shoot. That was weak.

If he broke his contract, Eunjae would be free. He'd known there would be a price to pay, financially and professionally, but the cost was far steeper than he imagined. He couldn't do that to his brothers.

His phone buzzed, buried somewhere under the covers. It was still the phone from California because he'd never bothered to charge the one that had been forgotten in his luggage since last Wednesday. The buzzing continued, relentless, and at last he fished the phone out of the blankets. The name shining out at him from the screen was 'Jiyeon.'

He'd let it ring too long and the call dropped. Eunjae thought about just rolling over and pretending to be asleep. Did he want to talk to Jiyeon? Yes. When did he ever not want to talk to her, in retrospect? Actually, he'd grown so accustomed to the routine of waiting all day to talk to Jiyeon after work, saving up the things he might tell her, that it pained him to deviate from that pattern now.

But did he want to tell Jiyeon that he wasn't coming back? No. Saying it out loud was bound to make it real, and he didn't want it to be real.

Still, Eunjae stared down at the phone in his hand. He missed the Hans and their comfortable chatter, their bickering, their kindness. He missed Denny's glowering face. He missed Jiyeon's laugh, and the sound of her key turning in the lock as evening fell.

Throwing the blanket back over his head, Eunjae swiped to his missed calls and dialed her number.

Jiyeon picked up immediately. "So, it's possible that we Googled you," she said.

Eunjae took a beat to process not only this, but the sound of her voice on the line, directly in his ear while the rest of her was physically out of reach. "Is that good or bad?"

"Hmm. Well, I guess I should clarify that it was my parents who Googled you. Denny claims he already knew everything because of his investigation, whatever that means, and I..."

He waited, watching as the luminous digits of his bedside alarm clock changed from 10:39 to 10:40. Eventually, Jiyeon said, "I heard you singing."

In his rumpled bed on the other side of the world, Eunjae went stock still. But then he remembered that there was nothing left to conceal; Jiyeon knew exactly what he was. "I've been told I'm not bad at it," he managed.

With a smile in her voice, Jiyeon replied, "Oh, sure. You can sing a little." And Eunjae had to laugh, despite everything that had gone so wrong.

"There's been some talk of converting the Austen shrine into an

Apollo shrine, although really it would be a Ryan Kim shrine. Seems like we play favorites in this household." She paused. Softly, Jiyeon amended, "Sorry. It's Ari, isn't it? That's your name. The real one."

"No." This response came out of him with such vehemence that it practically blistered his mouth. "Ari's just the name my mum picked out for me. When I came here, that's what Emerald wanted me to use. But back when I was a kid, when Miss Vivi was still around, she always called me by my Korean name: Eunjae. She thought I should have some connection to the part of me that was Korean."

On the day that Eunjae discovered he had a second name, it was like being handed a second chance. This brand new person named Eunjae didn't have to meet anyone's expectations. Ari, however, had always belonged to other people. First, he belonged to his parents and their visions for a future where he was a brighter, better, more promising version of himself. Then, Ari belonged to the agency. They owned the rights to his name and the use of his image. They owned his voice. Ari belonged to his brothers and his career. He belonged to his fans. But Eunjae belonged only to Eunjae.

"Whatever the Internet says, I'm just Eunjae. And when I was there, when I was with you, I could finally just be me."

"For what it's worth," said Jiyeon, "whether you're Eunjae or Ryan or Ari, or all of those at once, we miss having you around. Even if you can't come back, I'm grateful you were here. We all are."

"That's worth a lot," Eunjae replied, tears blurring his vision. "More than you know."

"There's something I wanted to tell you. When I heard you sing... I knew I wasn't gonna forget it, ever. Not just because you're talented, but because you sounded so happy. I felt happy too, just to hear you. While you were singing, while you were with your brothers, I felt like that was the truth of you. That's who you are, regardless of the name you use."

She was right. Singing used to be something Eunjae did solely for the sheer joy of it, and that joy was still there, buried but not lost.

On the call, the background noise shifted from indoor quiet to a rush of wind that whistled through the receiver. Eunjae calculated the time and realized she must be walking to her car, heading over to help Denny with the morning rush. She'd woken up so early to call him.

"But you know what else? Your singing isn't even the best thing about you. I get to say that because I never heard you sing until my parents went on a YouTube binge after you left."

"Oh, no. You guys really do know everything about me now."

"I think Denny's been watching the one with the top five wardrobe malfunctions on a loop. That one and the clip of you being really mad about someone stealing your snacks."

"Great," groaned Eunjae.

"The silver hair looked weirdly good. I mean, I'd rather not encourage you to go back in that direction, but I'm trying to be fair. It looked so good that I was mad about it for at least two hours. But the color you've got now is still the one I love best. And the haircut isn't bad, for being my greatest failure."

He kicked the covers off. When did the thermostat go up ten degrees? "No worries. Never changing my hair again." And then it hit him. "You went to the leasing office, though?" He'd taken much too long to ask. Eunjae felt like an ass.

"Yeah," she answered, with uncharacteristic hesitance. "I did. I took pictures but I didn't want to bother you with them."

"I want to see. Send them, okay?"

"Okay. I'll do it when I get to the shop."

She was quiet for a while, driving to Wanna Waffle in the morning fog. Eunjae sat up in bed, reaching over to open the blinds and let the night fill his window. "Why did you help me?" he asked Jiyeon. It was something he'd been wondering for a while. "I was just a stranger standing outside your door."

"What a thing to ask." Jiyeon sighed. "You seemed so sad. And you looked like you were running away from something. I know how that is. I've done my share of running, too."

"All I do is run," he said, all the pain surging back in full force. "I'm not much good at anything else."

"That's not true," she protested. "And you know what? Sometimes running is the only thing you can do. Sometimes you're just not strong enough for anything else. They say you shouldn't be a quitter, quitting is for cowards, losers, whatever. But it can be so much harder to quit something that's hurting you. It's easier to just... stay there, broken and sad, pretending you're fine. Because that's what you know best. And running could take you somewhere you've never been.

"Eunjae, forget what's been said to you before. Running away isn't the only thing you're good at. Singing isn't the only thing you're good at. Whatever you're going through right now, even if it's hard, you'll find a way. You're thoughtful, you know? You pay attention, and you give your time so generously. You listen, really listen. Those are strengths, too."

32

The call with Jiyeon ended. Eunjae swung both legs out of bed, feet landing on wrinkled shirts and a pair of jeans half spilled out of his duffel bag. The hurt from the past few days continued to crash through him, a dull roar ever present in the back of his mind. Jungwoo's betrayal, his brothers fighting, those lines in their contracts like prison bars — it all congealed into a weight that only grew heavier. He didn't know how he could possibly bear it alone for much longer.

Maybe that was his mistake: trying to bear this alone.

The agency was counting on pain to keep him down. Eunjae couldn't let it happen. And they knew he would be feeling guilty, blaming himself for everything. He was willing to bet that none of them — the founders, CEO Yoon — expected him to get up right now. They were waiting for Eunjae to bury the truth he'd found about himself. After all, he'd diligently buried that truth for years with his own two hands. They were probably also betting he'd stay away from his brothers out of shame. Apollo would remain divided.

Divided, they would lose. Not just him, but all of them, together. Eunjae couldn't let that happen. How many times had he been the one to broker peace between them? He could do it again.

He began clearing the detritus out of his room. As he cleaned, he thought back to various instances when they'd fought amongst themselves, as brothers are wont to do. It was impossible to live so closely with a group of eight other peers, to see each other night and day, without getting into fights on a pretty regular basis. They really were like siblings. And yet they were also friends, the best of friends.

Friendships outside the walls of their agency were a lot harder to forge and maintain once they started training. It only became more difficult as Apollo saw higher and higher levels of success. In a way, they'd had no choice but to turn to one another, to lean on one another through the years. But Eunjae remembered the day Haewon and Soyeon called him into that meeting room. He hadn't been allowed to choose whether or not he would pursue this career, but when it came time to decide between a solo track or joining Apollo, hadn't Eunjae chosen his brothers? And no matter what, he would continue to choose them.

They didn't deserve to be trapped like this. Eunjae shouldn't be locked into a position where his departure could unravel everything they'd achieved together, and the others shouldn't be forced to go down with him. That clause in their contracts wasn't fair or right.

As for Haewon's assertion that the musketeer clause had saved Jewell from disbandment, enabling them to continue together as a group for a full decade... Eunjae wasn't sold. The clause had been instrumental in convincing Soyeon to stay, sure. But how did Soyeon really feel about reversing her decision to leave? He wished he could ask her.

All for one, one for all. Brow furrowed, Eunjae excavated his laptop from a desk drawer. There was plenty of material about Jewell online. It wouldn't be hard to learn more about them, and the years after Soyeon's long hiatus. But first, he navigated to the digital copy of his contract.

He'd thought he was doing better, before. Finally standing his ground. Eunjae saw now that his initial decision to leave the group really was just another form of running away. The same could be said of his decision to stay. Neither of these was a real solution. For as long as that penalty clause remained in their contracts, no one in the group was safe. Eunjae had to fight this. But he would do it his own way, trusting himself to see it through.

Singing isn't the only thing you're good at.

Paragraph by paragraph, line by line, Eunjae surveyed the bounds of his cage. He went back to Arthur's emails and notes saved to the app on his phone. He added more notes, nearly exceeding the word limit. From memory, he typed out things that were said during the confrontation in Yoon's office, his brothers' fears, hypothetical steps to take.

As he worked, it occurred to Eunjae that the prison bars could fulfill two purposes: to keep you in, but also to keep danger out. To offer protection at the cost of freedom. While many of the terms were written with the intent of safeguarding Emerald Entertainment's interests, the contract included safeguards for artists too.

Not everything within those pages was a weapon to be wielded against them. Maybe he couldn't persuade the agency to do away with the musketeer clause, and maybe he'd never succeed in appealing to the founders for empathy, but there could be another way to protect everyone. To make sure all of his brothers had the choice to stay or go, in the future.

"The key is in here somewhere," he murmured to himself. "I just have to find it."

So absorbed was Eunjae in scouring the contract that he fell asleep there, slumped over with one cheek pressed against the laptop keyboard. He woke in a haze to someone knocking urgently on his bedroom door.

33

"Ari? Hello?"

It was Nami knocking on the door, and she wasn't alone. "Let us in," ordered their other manager, Doyoung. "We don't have time to waste."

Eunjae checked the alarm clock. Then he made note of the light cutting through the blinds, or rather, the absence of it. It was just shy of 5:00am, sunrise only the merest suggestion on the horizon. What did the managers want with him at this hour? He had nothing scheduled. Nothing that he knew about, anyway. He was supposed to be under disciplinary restrictions, all privileges revoked. No leaving the dorms without supervision, no social media, no interaction with the outside world unless Emerald Entertainment approved it first. They'd confiscated his other phone without knowing about the one on loan from Jiyeon.

"Sorry, I was still asleep," Eunjae answered, letting them in. "Am I late for something, noona?"

Nami chewed on her bottom lip, trying to work out what to say. But Doyoung went straight to the freshly emptied duffel bag at the foot of Eunjae's bed. He held it up, muttered that it was too small, and set it down again. Alarm bells began to ring inside Eunjae's skull.

"What are you doing?" he demanded, breaking away from Nami. Doyoung dragged a rolling suitcase from the closet, the largest suitcase Eunjae owned. It hadn't been used since March, when he'd stayed in Busan with Jungwoo. Eunjae's following trips had required nothing more than an overnight bag.

Nami said, "I know it's short notice, Ari, but we've been told to take you to the airport this morning. The email said to make sure you're at Incheon by 6:30am at the latest. We'll help you pack, okay?"

Eunjae recoiled. "What? No, it's not okay. The airport, noona? Why?"

"To catch a flight," Doyoung snapped at him. "What else? Use your brain. And start packing or we'll be late."

"It's nothing bad, I promise. Just a trip back home." In response to Eunjae's panicked, questioning look, Nami expounded with, "Home to Brisbane, Ari. Your parents requested it after what happened. They think you need to go home and rest. Looks like Mr. Yoon agreed with them. I do wish we'd been given more time to prepare, but it's nice that you can be with your family for a while. I know you've had your issues, but maybe they're trying to be part of your life, now. Give them a chance."

Brisbane. His parents. *Leila*. Eunjae felt like he'd been shoved in front of a train. That was because Yoon knew exactly what he was doing.

While the other members felt homesick for actual people and locations, Eunjae felt homesick for a time that was gone, impossible to relive again. He was homesick for Vivian, driven from his life with such finality. And now he was homesick for that apartment on Ivy Lane, for a waffle restaurant on a boulevard lined with palm trees. By sending him to a place that was never going to feel like home again, Yoon had chosen to hit him where it would really hurt.

Here was his true punishment, then. Yesterday's events were only the opening act. Haewon and Soyeon both knew the state of Eunjae's relationship with his family; they were under no illusions that sending him to Brisbane would result in a happy reunion, a peaceful retreat. They knew exactly what they were doing, too.

"Let me talk to Mr. Yoon, to the founders. There's something I have to tell them. It's important."

Doyoung sneered at him. "Who do you think you are? The higher ups aren't at your beck and call. They don't have anything to say to you, kid. Take the free vacation and be satisfied that you got away with murder."

"Didn't you need some time to rest?" Nami asked, wringing her hands. "That's what all of this was about, right? You can't be upset about going home. You're getting what you wanted."

"That's not my home," Eunjae said fiercely, wresting the suitcase out of Doyoung's grip. "I won't go." And he was about to bolt when Jungwoo stepped into the room.

Eunjae watched, warily, as his brother finished typing a half-composed message, then punched the Send key on his phone. Jungwoo's gaze took in the managers and the open suitcase, the expression on Eunjae's face, before saying, "They can't ship Ari off to Australia right now. Our unit debut was postponed, not canceled. How are we supposed to get through promotions without him?"

"Jungwoo, this isn't your business. Leave so Ari can pack, please."

"Well, aren't you being polite today, Doyoung-hyung? What a nice surprise. A lot nicer than finding out my next project's getting sabotaged by Yoon himself. But I had to deal with enough shit when Ari ran away, and I'm not dealing with more, so I can't let you take him to the airport." Jungwoo crooked a finger at Eunjae. "Come on, we're taking this to the

CEO. Apologize, beg, bribe. I don't care as long as you convince him to let you stay. It's the least you can do for me."

"Boys, you can't bother Mr. Yoon at this hour. I understand what you're saying, and the timing does seem kind of strange, but we can schedule a video call once Ari's safely with his family. The scheduling will get ironed out later."

That was Nami's most placating tone. It usually had a decent success rate, paired with her gift for compromise, but not this time. Jungwoo behaved as if she hadn't spoken at all. Phone buzzing nonstop, he replied to another message. "Let's go, Ari. I'll call Yoon on the way over." Pointedly, Jungwoo added, "Unless you'd rather be in Brisbane. Which I doubt, but I won't pretend to know you as well as I thought I did."

A chasm still yawned between them. This was only the first step in potentially bridging that gap, repairing the damage done. But there was no time to hesitate. There wasn't even time to do more than assemble the rudimentary beginnings of a plan, like wending his way down a twisting path with only limited visibility. It would just have to be one foot in front of the other, from here on out.

At least he wasn't alone.

Eunjae snatched up his laptop and the jacket he'd worn on the flight from California. His passport and wallet were tucked into the pockets, right where he'd left them. He threw these essentials into the duffel bag, in too much of a hurry to add anything else, then checked that he had Jiyeon's phone as well. "Noona, you tried to stop us. You did everything you could, okay? This isn't your fault."

Nami gaped at him. "Huh?"

"Tell the story any way you want," urged Eunjae, backing away, "as long as you blame it on me. I was uncooperative. I pressured Jungwoo into helping."

"Say that we tripped Doyoung when he tried to chase us," his brother added for good measure. "He fell on his face. It was embarrassing but he made a good effort."

Doyoung started toward them. "What are you two —"

"Okay," Eunjae said to Jungwoo. "Let's go."

Jungwoo turned on one heel and sprinted for the apartment door. Eunjae was right behind him. On their way out, they overturned every piece of furniture in their path: two bar stools, an end table, a life size cardboard cutout of a masked, tuxedo-wearing anime character that had been gifted to Jungwoo by a fan. And in the hall, they broke into an all-out run.

Jungwoo - I'll be on my deathbed saying this, and you'll have to admit that I'm right —

Ari - (*laughing*) Will I?

Jungwoo - Yes! Because the best Jewell song is obviously *Secret Garden.* It's not even a question!

Ari - (*bowing*) To our founders, Haewon-noona

and Soyeon-noona, I love *Secret Garden* but I respectfully disagree with hyung —

Jungwoo - How dare you! (*pretends to shove Ari off his chair*) Which song do you think is the best, then? It's some random B-side, isn't it? You always pick some random B-side, you do the same thing with Apollo songs. What's wrong with my title tracks, Ari? Why do you have to be like this?

Ari - (*bowing again*) Boss Jungwoo, please accept my sincere apologies, but the best Jewell song is a random B-side called *Say There's Tomorrow*.

Jungwoo - I knew it! You picked a B-side! Wait, which album is that from?

Ari - *Crystal Clear*. Oh, but I also think *When You're Here* is really good. That was from a drama soundtrack. It was Soyeon's first solo track anywhere, if I remember it right.

Jungwoo - Alright, fine. *When You're Here* is amazing.

The lyrics are so good. And obviously the vocals, too, but the lyrics. (*low whistle*) I hope I can write that well, someday. I bet I could write that well if I found… true love.

Cartoon wedding bells pop up over Jungwoo's head

Ari - (*laughing*) Good luck, hyung.

Jungwoo - She's out there, Ari. (*winks at the camera*) Sunshines! Maybe it's one of you!

The occupants of the neighboring room begin pounding on the wall; we hear a chorus of muffled voices yelling 'Ari, make him stop!' and 'Did he wink when he said that? I hate it here!'

Jungwoo - (*gets up to pound on the wall as well*) Shut up! I'm not asking for much! One, find my soulmate. Two, write a song for Red Velvet. Three, sing at Ari's wedding.

Ari - You can't all sing at my wedding.

Jungwoo - What? Who else said they're singing?

Ari - Everybody. And there's eight of you. If you all sing, the wedding will take eight extra hours.

Jungwoo - Which is exactly why I'm the only one who should be singing! Of course it's me, I'm your best friend. That time you broke your ankle in Dubai, who carried you on his back? Me! (*epic instrumental music starts playing in the background*) Who did all your laundry for two years? Me! And that time you broke your glasses on tour, who read all the signs for you? Me!

Ari - Okay, plenty of time to figure it out, right? No one's getting married in the near future.

Jungwoo - (*nods*) Fair point. Your love life is completely dead.

Ari - We belong to our fans.

Jungwoo - (*exaggerated conspiratorial tone*) Fans, I can confirm that this guy has never — to my knowledge — dated anybody. Not even secretly. If he did, I'd know. Well, I guess everybody would. All the members know the passcode to Ari's phone.

Ari - (*shrugs*) I wouldn't want to keep her a secret. If I found someone, anyway.

Clapping and whistling from the other side of the wall, along with cheers of 'Lion-niiiimmm!'

Jungwoo - Our dorms have zero privacy and Ari has zero relationship experience.

Ari - (*blinks*) I don't need any secrets. I'm too busy keeping all of yours.

Jungwoo - No comment! But I think the real answer here, Sunshines, is that anytime Ari is talking to a girl, she ends up crying all over him. True story. (*pauses*) Well, I guess it's anybody, not just girls.

Ari - It does happen a lot.

Jungwoo - I need you guys to cry on me. Don't you want some songs written about your broken heart?

Thumping on the wall. 'Jungwoo, shut UP!' 'I'd rather cry on Ari.' 'Yeah, he smells nice.'

Ari - Hey, remember when we were trainees and you used to write song lyrics on any piece of paper you could find? Those brown bags from the bakery, when they let us go there on Saturdays. Oh, and the backs of receipts.

Jungwoo - We weren't allowed to have phones back then so I couldn't type them in the notes app. Man, how did I survive those days?

Ari - And so many of those songs are out there in the world now.

*Montage of Apollo singles, starting with **U Shine** in 2014 and*

ending with the most recent at the time of this video, Trickster

Ari - I hope you keep writing songs, hyung. I'm really proud of you.

Jungwoo - (*pretends to wipe away a tear*) Ari! Please sing at my wedding! Even though you fall asleep halfway through every drama episode I ask you to watch with me!

Ari - (*calls out to the ceiling*) Nicky-hyung! Please let me skip dance practice tonight! I'm so tired!

Jungwoo - (*also yells at the ceiling*) Please, hyung! Why is the choreo so hard this time!

Both continue laughing uncontrollably until Max busts through the door with a croissant stuffed in his mouth

Max - You guys are so annoying. Are we doing this or what?

Jungwoo - Wait, wait. Max, what about you? Is your love life also dead?

Max - Gross! Obviously it is! We belong to our fans!

Ari and Jungwoo, in unison - We belong to our fans!

Max - (*mouth full of croissant*) And anyway, you know, it's so hard to date because of you people (*pointing at the camera*) always getting mad about it. Like, what is that? I don't get mad when you date.

Jungwoo - I get mad. It hurts my soul.

Max - (*swatting Jungwoo with printed song lyrics*) Everything hurts your dumb soul!

Ari - That's true. But maybe that's why Jungwoo's songs are so good.

Jungwoo - Sunshines! Keep hurting my soul so I can keep writing the songs!

Max - (*laughing in spite of himself*) Hurry up! I told Jess I'd go to lunch with him! I'm starving!

Jungwoo - Okay, okay. We're doing it. Let's go.

Ari picks out the first few notes of Jewell's **Secret Garden** *on the keyboard; Jungwoo checks audio equipment; Max starts on his second croissant, which was apparently in the pocket of his hoodie the entire time and will become a meme five minutes after this video posts on YouTube*

Jungwoo - (*as the scene fades*) Ready? This is Apollo's Jungwoo, Ari, and Max with *Secret Garden* by Jewell. This one is for our founders. It's been a while since the last time we saw you, and we know you're very busy, but we hope you see this video and think of the good days we've had. There are more good days in the future, right?

Ari - (*smiling*) More good days — that's right.

<u>Note</u>: *Fans have made multiple video compilations of Apollo members jockeying to sing at one another's weddings. This running joke began in a 2018 episode of the group's popular reality series (Shine with Apollo) in which the members had to vote for who among them was most likely to get married first. Four of the nine members voted for Ari (Jaehwan famously explained his choice by saying, "It's always the quiet ones"), Jungwoo voted for himself (one of the fandom's most enduring memes), and the rest voted for Max just to make him mad (this video goes viral again every few years).*

34

T he elevator doors had never shut more slowly in Eunjae's life. They could hear Nami crying out for them to stop, to wait, and that was definitely Doyoung shouting orders to the building's security team.

"They'll be waiting for us at the bottom, now that he's called for help," said Jungwoo, punching the button for the fourth floor. That was just one floor below theirs. "I say we get out and take the stairs."

"Yeah. The emergency exit would take us to the courtyard. We could take that back gate to the street, easy."

Jungwoo's phone buzzed with another message. He tapped out a reply as the elevator began its descent. "Kazu was already in the lobby. It's so early that they don't have a lot of guards on duty, just the night watchman and one other. He says he saw them go running past the gym a second ago."

Eunjae reeled after him as soon as the doors opened again. They exited the elevator just as Max, Kei, and Jesse spilled out of their own rooms around the corner, summoned by Jungwoo's flurry of text messages. He must have been sending them to the group chat the entire time. Eunjae hadn't received any notifications; his borrowed phone number had never been added.

"This is so fucking funny," wheezed Max, loping toward the stairwell on his long legs. He was so overcome by mirth that he'd acquired a stitch in his side already. "These people really think they can catch us."

"We could take them," Kei said grimly. "They've never had to perform four songs in a row at an awards show before. We're in way better shape." This only had Max wheezing even harder, and then Jesse started laughing his head off as well.

"Where's Namgyu?"

"He's recording for Idol Pop Radio today. Left ages ago already."

"Oh yeah. Well, he can catch up with us when he's done."

"You babies shouldn't be here. I was just telling you the situation, you didn't need to join in."

"Shut up, Jungwoo. We can help Ari escape, too. We're more qualified since we didn't betray him like you did."

"I didn't *betray* —"

"Et tu, Jungwoo?"

"Yeah, spoken like a true traitor."

"But for real," said Jesse, "no fighting! Hyung, it's better if we all go. More of us for them to worry about."

It's better if we all go. A crazy thought slotted itself into the half-formed plan coming together in Eunjae's head.

In the stairwell, Nicky shouted down at them from the fifth floor landing. He'd taken the stairs from the start, as was his habit most mornings. He was on his way to meet Kazu at the gym on the ground floor when Jungwoo's texts popped up. "Brisbane? Has Yoon lost his shit completely?"

"Ari really pissed him off. Never thought I'd see the day."

"Like we'd ever let them take hyung back to his horrible parents,"

Jesse huffed, taking the concrete steps by twos like a lunatic.

Kei had made a very good point when he brought up the intense endurance contest that was their four-song marathon at the Golden Disc awards last December. What ordinary cardio workout could compare with singing and dancing for fifteen minutes straight, all kitted out in leather pants and full makeup? Running from a bunch of company goons was nothing.

Yes, this was the easy part. It would only get worse from here. And yet, Eunjae wasn't half as worried as he probably should be. Perhaps the fear would hit him later, all at once like a slap to the face. But for now, his brothers were here. How could anything seem insurmountable for long? They had a knack for making him feel that way.

Apollo was magic, too.

Kazu met them in the empty courtyard. Together, they dashed for the back gate and split up, reconvening at a hole-in-the-wall noodle place down the block. At a signal from Nick, who had called ahead, the owner shunted them inside. Drapes were yanked shut and face masks passed around. This wasn't her first time colluding with them.

"The goddamn wind sprints are finally paying off," rasped Max. He sagged against Eunjae, downing a glass of water provided by their kindly collaborator. She even brought some towels to mop up the sweat they'd worked up on the way there.

"Ajumma," Nicky hollered into the back room, "I think you need a new Hermès scarf to go with that apron. I've got you."

"You're too much, Nicky!"

"What's the plan?" Kazu demanded. He pointed to a tower faced in mirrored glass. It loomed on the skyline, the top just barely visible through a gap in the flowered curtains. "I can get a helicopter to the roof of that hotel over there, but I need to call for it right now if you want it to be waiting for you when you get there."

Jesse gawked at him. "That's one of *your* hotels? I thought it was a Hilton!"

"You can get me a helicopter?"

"My aunt decided to invest in a company that does helicopter tours of Seoul."

"Gross! How do I always forget that Kazu's from some millionaire family in Tokyo?" groaned Max.

"It's because Grandpa Zuzu acts like spending money is the same as bleeding actual blood. Like one pint of blood for every hundred won."

"Yeah, hyung doesn't act like a normal filthy rich chaebol man at all. Well, except for the clothes, I guess."

Kei threw his hands up in the air. "What clothes? Do you ever see him wearing the expensive clothes? We're all just lucky we caught him before he ripped off his shirt at the gym this morning."

"YA! I'd have clothes to wear if some of you could quit robbing my closet! And there's nothing wrong with being frugal!"

Kazu's roaring scattered his critics to the four winds. He turned to Eunjae again, steam still pouring out of both ears. "So? How are you getting out of here? The helicopter can get you wherever you want to go in the city, and Emerald will have a hard time chasing you that way. Seoul's huge. It's easy enough to disappear for a day or two once they've lost your trail, so long as you don't go out much. Personally, I'd leave the country again. They'd hate that."

"Don't let them win, my son," said Nick, making a mess of Eunjae's hair. "Leader-nim said to tell you the same thing."

"Actually," Jungwoo corrected him, "the text says *We're winners in this family so get up and start winning before you embarrass me*, with five exclamation points."

Eunjae's eyes burned with unshed tears. He looked at each of his brothers, his mind supplying the images of those who weren't there, filling in the gaps where they would otherwise be standing. "I'm sorry," he told them, voice breaking. "I'm sorry for everything."

"Why the hell are *you* sorry?" Max exclaimed. "*We're* sorry!"

Kazu wrapped Eunjae in a bear hug. It was somewhat sweaty, but none of his brothers could beat Kazu at giving hugs, and no one ever complained when they got one. "Let them disband us, Ari. They couldn't break us up if they tried. Maybe we wouldn't be Apollo anymore, but only we can say when Apollo is over, right? Apollo is us. And if quitting is how you end up happy, then I say you should quit. *We* say you should quit."

Eunjae hugged his brother back. He couldn't string the right words together, what with the sob caught in his throat, so this silent demonstration of gratitude would have to suffice.

"Wow, did you know we have a real dad sometimes?" Kei whispered to Jesse.

"Right? He sounded like a real dad just now."

"That was some leadership shit," Max concurred.

"YA!"

"Don't forget the other part of Mom's text!" Jesse treated everyone to some dramatic drum roll noises before reading Jaehwan's message out loud. "Here it is: *We don't need a piece of paper to tell us that we're brothers, you goddamn idiots.* Gosh, I want that on a shirt. Can we get that on a shirt?"

Well, now Eunjae really was going to cry. He did his best to master the emotions, knowing that they didn't have much time. "I'm not the only one who deserves to be happy," he said fiercely. "Everybody in the group deserves that. For as long as that clause is in our contracts, we're trapped. One person can make a choice about staying or leaving, but the others won't be able to choose whether or not to disband. In the end, none of us gets to have a say. It isn't fair or right."

Eunjae stood up straighter, aware of the implications and the consequences of what he was about to ask of them next. "That clause needs to be removed. I know I can't make it happen on my own. The company can ignore me, bully me, ship me back to Brisbane until I've had enough, but they can't silence all of us at once. We'll leave the country like Kazu said. The world is always watching us — let's use that. Let's tell everyone the truth."

"Like, have a press conference?"

"Let's hire one of those planes that fly the big banners through the sky."

"And the banner will say what?"

"WE QUIT!"

"We can't quit," said Eunjae. "Breaking contract triggers the penalty clause that allows them to disband us and keep our music. But if we tell our story, it could be enough pressure to make Emerald remove it. So come with me. Help me win this. I know we can't lose if we fight them together."

Jungwoo frowned, still apprehensive. "What if this just makes them even madder?"

"Oh, they'll lose it," Kazu answered. "But if they retaliate when so many eyes are watching, it'll only make them look bad. The last thing they want is for the company's reputation to take a hit. You know how they are." He turned to Eunjae, a glimmer of pride in his dark eyes. "Just tell us what to do next, Ari. It's all for one, right? And one for all."

"What a stupid fucking catchphrase," muttered Max.

Jesse feigned offense. "That's from *literature*."

"I'll tell the others," said Nick. "We can just meet up at the airport."

"How will we even make it inside without being mobbed? The fans are always watching."

"None of our schedules put us at the airport today. Hopefully they won't know until it's too late."

Kei picked up the backpack he'd brought with him from the dorms. "You guys don't even have anything to wear. I'm the only one who remembered what Jaehwan said about always having a go bag."

"He said that? When?"

Kazu kept on typing in the group text. "We'll just buy whatever we're missing."

"International Bank of Kazuhiko!" Jesse and Nicky shouted together, fists in the air.

"His money is blood and blood is money!"

"Our dad is rich!"

Eunjae laughed helplessly. Even Jungwoo cracked in the end, shaking his head and pulling up an app for flight bookings on his phone. He was laughing so much that he kept entering the destinations wrong. But he closed the app a second later, an epiphany written plainly on his face.

"Hang on. Zu, does your uncle still have that jet?"

35

"Aww, how could you give a heroic speech when I wasn't there?" lamented Namgyu. "You couldn't wait an hour?"

He was in the middle of handing out the t-shirts he'd bought for everyone at the airport gift shop, a purchase funded by Kazu. All the shirts were the same size and color, printed with the word JEJU in massive block print across the chest. Silhouetted behind the letters was a design featuring one of the island's famous haenyeo divers in full gear, swimming for the surface.

Namgyu tossed a shirt at Eunjae. "You need to give the speech again so I can hear it in person. It's not my fault I missed the jailbreak!"

"It really wasn't much of a speech, Gyu," Eunjae maintained, catching the shirt with both hands.

Jesse layered the souvenir shirt over his long-sleeved pajama top, which looked suspiciously like something filched from a certain brother's Vuitton collection. "I loved the speech. I felt a lot of feelings."

"Aww! I wanna feel the feelings too!"

"Why do we all have to wear the same thing?" groused Max, even as he pulled his own wrinkled shirt over his head and changed outfits right there in the terminal. A scandalized granny glared at him from her seat a few rows away. Max noticed and glared right back at her.

"I shouldn't have to wear this. I didn't run to the door looking like a clown this morning."

"This is a family jailbreak, Keiichi," said Nick. "You're part of the family. Put the damn shirt on."

"Yeah, you cried all over the one you were wearing, anyway. And on Ari's hoodie, too."

Upon fully absorbing what they were about to do, Kei had insisted that he be allowed to punch Eunjae in the face for 'emotional damage and potential career destruction.' When this permission was granted, he'd dissolved into a sobbing wreck and ended up punching approximately no one. Now he donned his new Jeju Island tourist apparel and began lecturing on the itinerary, sniffling every once in a while.

"Jeju to Singapore, six hours. After that we're all on different flights to LAX, good luck to Emerald if they're trying to catch us. It's me and Grandpa to Tokyo — Haneda instead of Narita because that'll throw the agency off a bit. Five hour layover for us. Nicky and Namgyu are stopping in Taipei. There's only an hour before the connecting flight so don't get distracted and wander off."

"Kazu and Jaehwan are the same age. Shouldn't they both be grandpa?"

"I only have one grandpa and his name is Ueda Kazuhiko."

"Can't decide if I should be flattered or not," said Kazu.

"Okay, and why were you looking directly at me when you said not to wander off?" asked an affronted Nick. "Namgyu's the one who wanders off."

"And then you go and follow him," said Kei, exasperated. "Anyway! Ari, Max, and Jess have a flight from Singapore to San Francisco. The earliest flight from there to LA was the next morning at stupid o'clock, sorry. So long as there aren't any delays, cancellations, or weird weather patterns, we should all be in California by Wednesday. Well, Wednesday-ish. Or is it Thursday? I dunno. I haven't gotten enough sleep to calculate time zones."

There was a brief but enthusiastic scatter of applause for Kei's mental gymnastics. He accepted this with grace. Then he stopped short, turning slowly to Jungwoo. "Hyung, you never told me which group you were going with. Ari's, I guess? Were you able to get another seat on that flight for yourself?"

But Jungwoo shook his head. Eunjae realized that his Jeju shirt was folded neatly on the empty chair between them.

"This is as far as I go," said Jungwoo, addressing the whole group but making eye contact only with Eunjae. "I'm flying back to Seoul."

This announcement brought stunned silence in its wake. Jungwoo pressed on. "I can't... I can't risk anything more, Ari. I know you've said this isn't your dream, and even though I didn't realize that about you until a few days ago, you probably knew from the start that it's *my* dream. To work in this industry, to make it big. To write music and produce for other people."

Jungwoo looked away. "I want to have a career when this mess is over. If I come with you, I have a feeling that won't be possible. Emerald has too much power. They can make sure none of us ever makes it any further than this. Maybe I can still talk to them. Get this done a different way."

Nicky recovered first. "You're siding with the agency? Are you serious?"

"I'm not siding with them," Jungwoo insisted. "I won't help them find you guys. I won't say anything at all."

"Hyung, you could write more songs. You're so good, you'll never run out of them. I just know it."

"That's easier said than done, Jess."

"This isn't just for Ari," said Kazu. "It's for all of us. You get that, don't you? Everyone is risking everything, and it's for the whole group. If we lose, you lose. If we win, you win too. There's no way to separate yourself from it, not from the agency's standpoint. Running back to Seoul might not even save you."

"Yeah. I know."

"There's probably no way to get off easy on good behavior, Jungwoo. Too late for that."

"I know that, too."

"So you might as well come with us," ventured Namgyu. Nicky and Kei murmured their agreement with this suggestion. They received no response.

Max threw his balled up basketball jersey at Jungwoo, who didn't even try to dodge it. "Unbelievable. You're the fucking worst, hyung. You always are. Every time I think you're not so bad, I just end up disappointed." He stomped away with Jesse and Nicky peeling off after him, concerned.

As for Eunjae, he stared across the fissure that divided them, breaking their long friendship into Before and After. Not a clean break, but then again, how often does that happen? And even broken things might someday be whole again.

It took him a little while, but eventually he nodded at Jungwoo and said, "Okay. I understand. Thank you for being there for me when I needed you."

Because Jungwoo had been there that morning, when the company tried to send him to Brisbane. He'd been there for Eunjae dozens and dozens of other mornings before that, and afternoons and evenings, and sleepless nights in studios or on planes. Jungwoo had been there — that was the important thing, the part he couldn't lose sight of. Eunjae wanted to believe that Jungwoo would still be there in the future, that they could support each other even if their paths diverged. But bridges must be built. Wounds take time to mend.

Eunjae had to take this chance to follow a dream that belonged to him, genuinely. He didn't even know the full extent of that dream; so much of it was still hazy, nowhere near as crystalline and focused as Jungwoo's. It would be his choice, though. He cherished the ability to make that choice. Jungwoo should be able to choose, too.

Half an hour later, Eunjae walked his brother to the gate and said goodbye.

36

It turned out that when Kei described their departure time as stupid o'clock, he meant that they'd need to be at San Francisco International Airport by three in the morning.

Eunjae spent a lot of time in liminal spaces: baggage claims, backstage corridors, hotel lobbies, airports. Airports, for him, held a uniquely strange atmosphere. At this hour, that strangeness seemed more pronounced. Their terminal was a ghost town. Most of the shops were shuttered and dim, resulting in a sort of artificial twilight. Fellow travelers were either bleary-eyed and partway catatonic like Max, or infused with fathomless, manic energy like Jesse.

Eunjae fell somewhere in between, as usual. Exhaustion had become his whole personality at this point, but he didn't feel as though he could rest, either. His brain wouldn't stop long enough for that. While his two younger brothers slept like the absolute dead in their adjoining rooms, Eunjae volunteered to gather the supplies they'd failed to bring during their escape from Seoul. Three duffel bags, new phones for Max and Jesse so that Emerald couldn't track their old ones, a few sets of clothes.

Taking care of the other two left him with little time to dwell on everything that could go wrong. Alas, there wasn't much to do now except wait.

Their flight to Los Angeles would board soon. Jesse had gone to stock up on three days' worth of snacks that would be demolished in less than an hour. Eunjae worked on his backlog of messages, sending and replying while the Wi-Fi was decent. He wrote another email to Arthur, who replied with his usual speed.

Max was sprawled full length along four seats in the empty row they'd chosen, swaddled in a Golden State Warriors hoodie and swearing under his breath at yesterday's crossword puzzle. When he suddenly hauled himself upright, Eunjae was prepared to be accosted for another four-letter word that might possibly be the name of a country smaller than Sicily but larger than Mallorca. He'd been stuck on that one for hours.

Max surprised him by choosing to jettison the puzzle entirely. "I'm sorry about the door," he said, out of the blue. "It was me. I'm the one who found it."

"What do you mean?"

"You know, the door. That orange door at the waffle place, like the one in your book. When Jungwoo called you that first time, like the day after you went missing, you said something about it. I remembered. We'd walked past the waffle place a few times, looking for you, and I thought about how that was the only interesting door around there. I just kept feeling like it had to mean something, so we came back on another day."

"It's okay. You're not the one who told them where to find me, that was all Jungwoo. How did you connect it to the door in my book, though? Have you read it before?" Everyone in the group knew about Eunjae's attachment to his worn copy of *The Brass Key,* but he couldn't recall ever discussing the plot with any of them in much depth.

His brother heaved a sigh. "Yeah, I read it once. I just... I saw that you always had it in your bag, back then, if we were traveling or whatever. I wondered why it was so important to you. I figured that Jungwoo probably knew why. That made me so damn mad. Why couldn't I know, too? Why was Jungwoo always the one you picked, and why did he always pick you? Why wasn't there any room for me?"

Max kicked at his luggage, refusing to look Eunjae in the eye. "I thought reading the book might give me something to talk to you about," he went on. "'Cause I really wanted to talk to you about a lot of things. Like how you were always nice to everyone and we didn't always deserve it. And how you always let Jungwoo do all the talking, even when it was obvious you didn't agree. And I just wanted to be your friend on the same level that he was."

Here, Max made an incoherent noise that was part disgusted groan and part wail of despair. "I can't believe I said all that! Augh!"

Eunjae let the incoherent noises pass. When Max had quieted down, he said, "I hope you still want to be my friend."

"Idiot, why wouldn't I? Anyway, we're brothers. Can't change that ever."

"You're right," said Eunjae. "So good luck getting rid of me."

"Ha." Then, very quietly, he added, "About Jungwoo, though."

"What about him?"

"He hurt you, hyung. How could you just forgive him like that?"

"I hurt him too." Being honest about this was like voluntarily twisting the knife, but Eunjae felt lighter as soon as the words left him. "And you just said it, didn't you? We're brothers. Can't change that ever."

"Gross! I never said that!"

"You did say it, and you were right."

Max's brown eyes were ablaze. "I won't forgive him. I don't care if I was right."

"I'm glad you're around to be mad enough for both of us. Because you do care — you care so much. I hope you never stop."

"Oh, what the hell, hyung? I'm not crying at this airport. I've never cried at an airport even one time and I won't start now."

"I'll cry, then. I'm fine with it." Eunjae hooked an arm around his brother's neck. "My life is so much better because you care about me, Max. Sorry I haven't told you enough."

"Gross!" But Max returned the half hug with bone-crushing force. Then he squirmed away, flopped back down, and returned to the crossword. Muted sniffling came from the depths of the hood pulled over his head. "Greek goddess of victory. Four letters."

"Too easy," said Jesse, hurrying over to them with a casual tonnage of snacks. "It's 'Nike'. Like the brand. And, um, I think we're in trouble."

"Duh, Jess. We've been in trouble for days now. And Ari's been in trouble for like two weeks straight. Big deal."

"This is new trouble. Here, hyung." Jesse already had his phone out. He showed it to Eunjae, rapidly swiping between screenshots.

At first he thought the fatigue had finally done him in. Each of Jesse's screenshots looked almost the same. He tried blinking again, even removing his glasses and glaring until the pixels came into proper focus, but it wasn't the hallucination he was praying for.

Max sat up again. "Shit. Aren't those...?"

"Yeah. They got us."

These were Apollo's personal Instagram accounts. Eight of the nine members had their own. The only exception was Nick, who mainly used his phone as a vehicle for gossip. It had taken years for them to be allowed their own accounts. Now, each of these had been reduced to just one post, all their photos and videos archived or perhaps even outright deleted.

Everyone's grid showed a simple emerald green square. The agency had taken over their social media.

"We had to use company email addresses to sign up for these. Should've thought to go in and change everything before we escaped."

"What about the main account? The one for the whole group?"

"It's got a green square on it, too. Sunshines are posting conspiracy theories already."

Max scowled. "I assumed they'd take that one away from us. Not the personal ones, though. Damn."

"What will we do now, hyung? This makes it a lot harder to get our message across."

Eunjae didn't have an answer ready for that, but he wasn't about to give up yet, either. "It's fine," he told his younger brothers. "We'll figure it out. Let's just try to get where we're going."

"Yeah," said Jesse, plopping down beside him. "And we won't let them win!"

"You're right. We won't."

Denny - Ryan. What's the fastest you've ever run a mile?

Eunjae - 5 or 6 mins?

Denny - Passable. Under duress, do you think you could successfully pilot a plane through an emergency landing?

Eunjae - Wait what

Denny - If all hell breaks loose

Denny - Do you think

Denny - You could pilot a plane

Denny - And save everyone on board???

Eunjae - I hope so? I mean I'd try?

Denny - Noted. On a scale from 1-5, rate your accuracy with an automatic longbow at sniper range.

Eunjae - Am I moving or standing still

Denny - CORRECT.

Eunjae - No which one

Eunjae - I had to shoot a bow from a motorcycle once

Eunjae - Music video

Eunjae - Wait my brother says it was a crossbow

Eunjae - It's on YouTube

Eunjae - *Break Point*, 2021

Denny - Ryan, for god's sake!

Denny - You're WASTED on the South Korean entertainment industry!

Denny - PLEASE consider a career pivot!

Eunjae - To what

Denny - I can only transmit that information through secure channels. Stand by until further notice.

Eunjae - Got it

Eunjae - I have a question though

Eunjae - You know how you gave me a job

Denny - Sure, I made you a functioning member of society.

Denny - What about it?

Eunjae - Can that be made official

Denny - Official? Like with paperwork?

Eunjae - Yeah

Eunjae - Idk what you need from me but if you can email it I'll fill everything out and send back

Denny - Sent.

Eunjae - That was fast

Eunjae - How did you know my email address

Eunjae - Oh right

Eunjae - Resources

Denny - Actually, you left the laptop open while you were VERY BUSY helping my sister get more popcorn the other night.

Denny - Rookie mistake.

Eunjae - I have a lot to learn

Denny - Nothing that can't be fixed with six weeks of rigorous mental and physical conditioning in high-stress environments.

Eunjae - Will this help me qualify for the contest to be your next brother-in-law

Denny - Are you testing me, Ryan Kim? Cause I'll play ball.

Eunjae - Batter up

Denny - LOL.

Denny - HAHAHAHA.

Denny - Man, you're hilarious.

Denny - See you when you get back.

Denny - DON'T FORGET TO CHECK IF YOU'RE BEING
FOLLOWED.

37

As he led his brothers across the tiny parking lot at the Ivy Lane Apartments, Eunjae realized that he'd arrived without a camera again. His favorite Nikon had been left behind in Seoul for a second time. Using one of his phones was fine, but insufficient. He didn't trust either device to adequately capture what was here: the evening shadows that softened every angle, the lights in the windows and the wisps of cloud reflected in puddles. It had rained again while he was away.

He'd been away forever. He'd never left, not really. Magic worked in strange ways. And it was still here, despite everything, unsullied and unchanged.

It didn't matter so much about the camera, Eunjae concluded. It wasn't possible to fully preserve everything he felt so deeply about this return, and no photograph could convey the scent of dinner cooking in multiple kitchens at once, or the sound of the wind chimes as they seemed to be welcoming him home. A picture couldn't record the comfort of having his brothers at his back, bickering and laughing amongst themselves. And a video couldn't replace the sensation of just being here, either.

A picture would've been nice to have, though, if only so Eunjae could memorialize the look on Denny Han's face when he opened the door.

"Am I drunk?" he muttered, studying Eunjae's face and then the figures behind him. Louder, he repeated the question. "Yeonnie! Am I drunk?"

Jiyeon's voice floated over to them from further inside the apartment, bemused. "How? You don't even drink."

"Then why am I looking at like, fifty copies of Ryan Kim? This can't be real."

There was a thump of crockery against the kitchen counter, set down with a bit more force than intended. The Han parents both doled out admonishments for being heavy-handed with the dishes. Eunjae listened with bated breath as Jiyeon's footsteps approached the front door, closer and closer.

"It's too early for it to be Ryan already," he heard her say. "I checked. Traffic was terrible, as usual."

"Yeah, well, this is definitely Ryan Kim. Plus six other Ryan Kims, which makes it a grand total of too many Ryans."

"Who's Ryan Kim?" Jesse whispered to no one in particular. Eunjae didn't respond because by then he was face to face with Jiyeon, the brief history of their relationship replaying before his eyes. There she was again, standing behind her brother, staring at him from the threshold. Here he was again, in need of a place to stay.

Jiyeon slipped past Denny to stand on the doormat in her bare feet. "Eunjae," she said, smiling, and it was only another thing he couldn't take a picture of: that sense of being exactly where he should be, and the sound of his name imbued with such wonder, with tenuous joy. The way the rest of the world seemed to fall away so that nothing existed beyond the pool of light where they stood.

This didn't last very long. Denny soon came to his senses and launched into a full scale interrogation. He did this after commanding everyone to get inside the apartment *right now*. Eunjae hadn't witnessed his brothers obey orders with this much alacrity in months. Not since Jaehwan left for basic training.

Initial discussions revealed that no one had informed Denny of the size of Eunjae's entourage. "I thought it was just you coming back! Not eleven billion clones of you."

Eunjae bowed an apology. "I thought I mentioned it. Didn't I?"

"Probably! To my sister!" There was some mumbling about 'Ryan's freaking priorities' which certainly piqued the interest of every Apollo member within earshot. Eunjae squirmed inwardly. Why was he still in this jacket? It was much too warm for long sleeves.

"Sorry, Den," said Jiyeon, not sounding sorry at all. "We decided Dad would get too excited if he found out, but I thought Mom was gonna tell you."

"Surprise!" trilled Mrs. Han.

"Is that scary man trying to say we all look like Ari?" Namgyu whispered to Nick. "Because I don't think we all look like Ari."

Nicky pinched his cheek, hard. "Calm down, Gyu. You don't look like Ari. One: you're shorter. Two: you're way uglier. And three —"

That argument never built up steam, what with Mr. Han avidly making his rounds. He pumped each member's hand with enough enthusiasm to power three squads of cheerleaders. He'd also memorized everybody's names, including nicknames. And when he reached Eunjae, he snatched him up in a bear hug that made his back pop in at least two different spots.

"RYAN!" Mr. Han roared. "Lion-nim! You're here! You came back!"

"I did," said Eunjae, gasping for air. He was here. He'd made it back.

In that moment, he felt like he could get through anything.

"Ah, hold on. I just remembered." Eunjae pulled Kazu and Kei out of the group and positioned them in front of the Han parents. "In the seventh or eighth episode of *I Loved You*, there's a song that plays in the ending credits."

When he heard it, he'd recognized his brothers' voices in an instant. What with Apollo's burgeoning discography, it was hard to keep up with all the projects the members had undertaken since 2014. Kazu and Kei had contributed a song to that soundtrack, though. They'd collaborated with success on multiple occasions, despite the chronic bickering.

"Just the chorus, Kei," coaxed Eunjae.

"But I barely remember the lyrics!"

"Kazu's got them on his phone."

"You're ganging up on me now? I hate it here so much."

"What a big baby," scoffed Max, in English. "Keiichi is a big, sad boo-boo bear." Which did the trick, of course. Kei scanned the lyrics, opened his mouth, and began to sing. Kazu took over the second half of the chorus, and even before they were done, the rest of Apollo had broken out into deafening whistles, cheers, and applause. Jesse went so far as to doodle a sign on his phone that read 'JAPAN LINE 4 EVER'. He waved this in the air like fans did at their concerts.

Mrs. Han fanned her face with both hands, bubbling over with tears. Jiyeon dashed for the box of Kleenex and brought it back to her. Mr. Han gave a loud sniffle, then started another round of hugs. Even Denny appeared fairly awestruck. Eunjae was not surprised. Anytime those two could be convinced to sing together, the result was a revelation. The slight rasp to Kazu's voice provided a perfect balance to the unexpected sweetness of Kei's.

Eunjae was glad to have thought of this as a gift, but there was still so much he needed to repay somehow. Not only to the Hans, but to his brothers. When all of this was over, he would keep chipping away at that debt. He'd work on it forever if he had to.

There was no way of peering into the future. He could secure no real guarantee that the battle would be won, but he would hold these people close, regardless. And there was one thing Eunjae knew for sure: any place was magic as long as they were with him.

It was worth it. It was everything.

38

Obliged to make room for seven additional bodies, the Hans' apartment seemed, mystically, to expand. Kazu made a beeline for the dining table, but Nicky went into the kitchen, asking if he could help with dinner. Namgyu parked himself on the rug in front of the TV. Kei took the couch, yawning, and Jesse collapsed into Mr. Han's recliner with a satisfied sigh. A very harassed Max stalked into the hallway to return a call from his eldest sister, Madison. His other two sisters called right after, back to back.

While his brothers settled in, Eunjae drifted toward the back patio with Jiyeon. If she noticed the extra pairs of eyes tracking her every move, she gave no sign of it.

Denny noticed, though. He prowled onto the patio too, but not before averting all the curious gazes with the sheer power of his aura.

"They're still building it," Jiyeon was saying. "You probably saw in the pictures. The outside is done but the inside won't be ready until September, they said."

Eunjae came through the glass doors right behind her. "Do you think there's enough room for everything you need?"

"Uh-huh. I don't need much, really. A chair, a big mirror, a sink.

Oh, and some counters. That would be helpful."

"You should get a couch if there's enough space. We'd have to measure."

"I think the light will be really nice."

"I thought it might be."

They were interrupted by an abrupt barrage of throat clearing. The sound was reminiscent of two thunderstorms locked in a fight to the death, or possibly five Siberian tigers growling in concert.

Denny inserted himself in the space between Eunjae and Jiyeon. They stepped apart like repelled magnets. "That's enough canoodling," he barked at them.

"Canoodling?"

"You heard me, Han Jiyeon! Now, pay attention. It's time for the mission brief."

This mission brief was apparently Eunjae's responsibility. Denny communicated as much with his piercing glare. And so the events of the past few days were retold in full: his disastrous return to Emerald Entertainment, the penalty clause that could disband them, the future of Apollo still hanging in the balance.

"They were going to ship me back to Australia," said Eunjae, stomach turning again at the mere thought, "but I ran away again. With help."

"How could they do that to you? Don't they know how things are between you and your parents?" Jiyeon fumed. She leaned against the porch rail, face bare, hair tumbling down in slightly frizzy waves. Her shirt might have once been blue but had faded with repeat washing. She'd padded out in a pair of slides that obviously belonged to her father or brother. They looked like kayaks on her feet.

It was the most casual outfit Eunjae had ever seen Jiyeon wearing so far, but when he looked, he found it: the black band of a hair tie on her wrist, dotted with tiny red flowers. Her floral motif, alive and well.

She crossed her arms. "I'm glad you ran away."

"Me too," he replied, having realized he was staring.

"But you decided to run back here? To us?" Denny grinned at him. "Well, hey. That's pretty smart for a guy whose eyes were 75% empty when I first met him."

"75%."

"Give or take."

"Where is that number coming from? Because his eyes were definitely not empty then, and they're not empty now —"

"There will be zero staring into his eyes in my presence, Yeonnie!"

"Uh, anyway," Eunjae cut in, "the plan was to do a livestream once we were all in the same place. I thought that with enough pressure from the public, Emerald might at least agree to remove the clause from our contracts. But they've cut off our social media access. Even our personal accounts are off limits."

"Take it to the actual press," suggested Denny. "I know a guy."

"We will, eventually. It would take time, though. More time than we wanted to lose. Ideally, we'd be doing this tonight. And on social media, we could reach fans everywhere, right away."

"You want them on your side."

He shrugged. "We belong to our fans."

Eunjae didn't say it out loud, but he was afraid that Emerald would try to control the narrative. The longer he and his brothers took to tell their story, the more they risked the company telling it for them.

"Hmm." Jiyeon turned away from them, pacing to the porch rail and tilting her face up to the evening sky. "How many followers do you guys have?" she asked Eunjae over her shoulder. "It doesn't need to be exact."

Eunjae wasn't sure. He rarely even used his Instagram account, posting mainly when they were traveling, and then of course once a month or so when Nami or Doyoung started prodding him to do it. "It's in the millions. I'll have to check to be sure. My older brothers have even more, though. Here, I can go ask."

As it turned out, Eunjae had guessed correctly. Jaehwan and Kazu both had a mind-boggling number of followers. Combined, they had higher counts than all the younger brothers put together. Max had a surprising amount, himself; every surly remark on someone's podcast, magazine editorial, or variety show only seemed to gain him another hundred devoted souls.

"Jungwoo's gotten a lot more over the past month," reported Nick. "Now he's tied with Ari."

"Gross. Why the hell does anyone want to follow him? His posts are so lame. *'Hey Sunshines, look at these raindrops on my window.' 'Here's my favorite line from Romeo and Juliet with clouds in the background.'*"

"Seems like they got him too. The latest post on his Insta is exactly the same as ours."

"That's what justice looks like, Jess," Max was quick to retort.

Jiyeon tugged at the hair tie on her wrist, brow furrowed, her expression deeply pensive. "Do you have an official account that the whole group shares?"

"We do," Kei confirmed. He read the number out loud. "That's higher than what I remember. Must be all the theories people are posting about those stupid green squares that Emerald posted."

"Hmm."

It was at this point that Eunjae finally noticed the signs of dismay etched onto Denny's face, growing rapidly more pronounced as he watched Jiyeon like a hawk. "Yeonnie," he said, in a warning tone. When this didn't register, Denny took his sister by the shoulders and marched her into the kitchen. An urgent conversation ensued, too low for Eunjae to parse except for the occasional snippet with no context: *mistake, heroics, bad idea*.

"Hyung. Ari-hyung." Jesse was waving both hands less than an inch from Eunjae's nose. "Hyung!"

"Do a backflip," Nicky suggested wryly. "Maybe that'll do it."

"Sorry, I'm listening. What's wrong?"

He realized that the others were clustered around Kei and his tablet. Apollo's Instagram account filled the screen. Now, the cryptic post with its green square had been bumped down by a newer one.

"It's an event announcement. The same one is posted on everything — Star-Connect, social media, the fan café."

Eunjae stared at the photo that came with the event details, horrified and yet transfixed. Emerald's marketing team had layered the event details on top of a picture that showed a familiar street, palm trees evenly spaced down its length.

Max turned to Eunjae, slack-jawed. "Hyung, isn't that...?"

"It is," Eunjae replied faintly. He'd seen it too, right away: there in the background was an unmistakable orange door.

39

Just like the attempt to send him back to his parents, the choice of venue felt like a personal attack. Of course, that was the precise intent. Eunjae recognized this move as an incursion. A way of shoving him off balance, desecrating a place that was important to him. He gripped the back of the nearest chair, dizzy with the sense that this was a loss for him and a win for Emerald. It felt so wrong, a few nights ago, to see his brothers standing in the dining room at Wanna Waffle. This was different. It was a thousand times worse.

There were no concrete details in the post except for an address — not Wanna Waffle's but the karaoke bar two doors down — and tomorrow's date, minus a specific time. It was a tactic the agency had used before, since vague announcements garnered huge interest. The secrecy never failed to goad fans into a frenzy.

"Another surprise fanmeeting," grumbled Kazu. "I hate the surprise fanmeetings."

They all did. Surprise fanmeetings were a mess. Already, Kei had discovered multiple news mentions of Apollo fans converging on the area. Two different Apollo-related hashtags were trending across multiple social media platforms. When Namgyu clicked on these, he found a video that showed a line forming in the shopping center's parking lot. The most dedicated Sunshines had brought tents to sleep in, determined to hold prime spots in the queue.

Hearing this, Denny took a break from his intense conversation with Jiyeon. He whipped out his phone and berated the owner of the karaoke bar for renting their space to Emerald. "Sandra, please explain to me where my customers are supposed to put their cars in the morning if the circus has moved into town." A pause. "I don't care that your granddaughters love Apollo. I care about providing adequate parking to the patrons of my small business. Jesus."

"Emerald sucks," mumbled Max. "Bringing the fans into it isn't even kind of fair."

"I guess Yoon's betting that we won't pick a fight with the agency at a fanmeeting."

"They're using our own fans against us. No, wait. They're using our fans as meat shields."

Nicky shook his head at Kei. "We let you play too many of those violent video games and it shows."

"I have to get my aggression out somehow."

Jesse winced as YouTube auto-played someone's vlog about their undying love for him, how handsome he was, and how ardently they wished to be his bride one day. He locked his phone in a panic and buried it under Max's discarded hoodie. "I don't get it. Why did Emerald announce that we'll be here? I mean, doesn't this make them look bad? First Ari ran away, and now the rest of us did too."

"It's smart," Eunjae replied. "If the company can claim that we're here on official business, the media can't claim that we ran away. It isn't a potential scandal if all we did was leave Seoul with their permission."

The agency had gone into aggressive damage control. It confirmed

Eunjae's theory that waiting too long to speak would give Emerald the devastating power of speaking for them.

"Let's make new accounts," he announced to the table. "We have to post tonight. If we end up in a position where we're just reacting to whatever they've got planned tomorrow, we lose the advantage."

"Won't people just think these are fake accounts?"

"We'll make them anyway. Emerald is trying to keep us quiet. We need to be as loud as we can. New accounts won't have the traction or the reach that we would've gotten with our actual accounts, but it's better than —"

"Better than nothing," Jiyeon argued at Denny in the kitchen. They were back at it again. This coincidental echo of his words caused a temporary glitch in Eunjae's brain.

"It's better than nothing," he continued, recovering some momentum. "I wish we could have more time to rest, but Emerald isn't pulling any punches. We shouldn't either."

His brothers reacted with trepidation at first. Eunjae understood the mood very well. No one really felt that they were prepared for this battle now that it was here. He was no exception.

"While we're all waiting backstage," he said quietly, "I know we're thinking the same thing. Can we really do this? Sometimes we've barely had three days to learn the choreo. In New York last year, we'd gotten no sleep and only had one chance to rehearse before we performed. But we went on stage anyway, because there were people out there waiting to see us. We weren't about to let them down. And we knew we wouldn't let each other down, either. That's why Apollo works. It's why we're good at what we do. We trust each other to do the job."

Even without Invisible Jaehwan issuing reminders, Eunjae remembered to stand tall, to speak with conviction. "We'll never feel like we're ready. We just have to go ahead and do it the way we always do."

Kazu smiled at him from the head of the table. "We're on it, Ari. Just say go."

"I don't think I've ever heard him talk this much in my whole life," Nicky whispered to Namgyu.

"Aww, I'm so glad I got to hear an inspirational speech after I missed the last one!"

"Now he won't talk for another year just to make up for it."

"Can you guys shut up and get on Instagram? Hyung just said to sign up for new handles. See if 'Tweedle Dum' and 'Tweedle Dee' are already taken."

"How can Keiichi be so mean but still sound like an angel when he sings?" Jesse wondered aloud.

"I've been asking that question for way too long, kid."

"Haha, isn't it too bad he always gets more rap lines than singing lines?"

"Gyu, get off me, I can't see the screen —"

Nicky threw back some coffee that he probably shouldn't be drinking at such an advanced hour of the evening. "Never thought we might get into this much trouble 'cause of something Ari came up with. Would've been on brand for Max, though." He raised his mug in a toast. "No offense."

"None taken, jackass."

One by one, the members of Apollo went to work. The Hans' dining table became a mess of gadgets and charging cables. Galvanized into action, operating on varying levels of sleep deprivation, they compared the notes and screenshots assembled piecemeal during the exodus from Seoul.

Eunjae waded into the thick of it, pulling the disparate parts together, building the case he'd envisioned in his head. He knew the contract left to right and backwards. He knew exactly what they should say in order to be persuasive while also credible. It was only a matter of trusting his own ability to see it through. There was room for neither error nor doubt. This was their side of the story, their chance to show the truth beneath the shining surface. And if that truth came into question, if the company assailed it with lies, it needed the strength to withstand every blow.

Preparing their statement and all its components required careful attention to detail. What was essential to include? What could be left out? Eunjae lost track of time for a while, wholly absorbed in the task at hand. But then he felt a tug on his sleeve.

"Got a minute?" Jiyeon asked, motioning for him to follow. Her tone came across as strained, but determined. "I think I've found a way to help you."

40

As he followed Jiyeon down the hall, Eunjae wondered if he would ever develop the ability to be alone with her without simultaneously fearing for his life. He kept bracing for impact, searching for Denny in every shadow. At least she didn't shut the door and lock it this time. Eunjae had only narrowly survived that experience and was not confident he'd do any better now.

Jiyeon's room remained as he'd left it on the night before returning to Seoul. The only difference was a set of clean sheets. "Dad found your camera, by the way," she said, "and the hat you were wearing when we met you. Look on top of the dresser." Then she hauled out the cardboard box under her bed. "Can you help me with this one? I have more in the closet."

Eunjae bent down to grab the box. Crammed with tripods and ring lights, it was the same box he'd stubbed his toe on at least once a day during his stay with the Hans.

"I've been telling myself that I need to donate all these things," Jiyeon mused as she dragged her desk chair to the closet. "I guess it's good that I haven't. You guys can use some of it later, while you're recording."

He watched as she balanced on top of the chair in order to retrieve another box from a high shelf. This one turned out to be a plastic storage bin stuffed to the gills with more equipment: some headsets, a collapsible green screen panel, even a sound boom that folded down to half its actual size. Entombed somewhere behind a row of winter coats was a jumble of umbrella reflectors for adjusting the lighting.

"Do you know how to set up in there? I can rig something together, otherwise. The overhead light in the living room is decent. You'll all fit in the frame if we move some furniture around, don't you think?"

Eunjae knew a little bit from helping Jungwoo record his YouTube series during the long months of lockdown. He wouldn't claim to be much of an expert, but as he took stock of the evidence, he realized Jiyeon might be.

"Before you threw your phone into the Pacific Ocean," began Eunjae, only for Jiyeon to shake her head, stopping him from fully formulating the question.

"I'll tell you later," she answered, breaking eye contact. "I promise I will. Speaking of phones, though, can I borrow yours?"

"You're asking me to let you borrow the phone... that you're letting me borrow?"

This earned him a smile at last. "You heard me, Song Eunjae."

"Sorry. Had to do it."

Still, though. Still, something about this was troubling, like a splinter working itself under his skin. He recalled the grim look on Denny's face, glimpsed through the kitchen doorway as he argued with Jiyeon, and the splinter evolved into a sense of pervading unease.

What had gotten Denny so upset, back there? It started when Jiyeon asked about their follower counts. Eunjae made up his mind to pursue the topic further, and Jiyeon must have sensed the direction his thoughts had taken because she requested the phone again.

"You'll use it to film the livestream, right? I can do it for you."

"Ah, yeah. I have to make another Instagram account first. I didn't get to that yet."

"About that. We'll lend you the Wanna Waffle accounts, that's got around two thousand followers between Instagram and Facebook. There's tons of people we can ask to share it out, and Denny's probably on the phone with that guy he knows at Channel 4. But you can use my Instagram, too." And she sounded so calm on the surface, but something was off and Eunjae knew it. Especially when she added, "I can't compete with Apollo's numbers, but 1.3 million followers is —"

Eunjae set the box down at the foot of the bed. "Better than nothing," he said, filling in the rest. "You have 1.3 million followers on Instagram?"

The microphones, the tripods, the way she moved through filming a video like it was a dance with steps long since memorized. The phone she'd hurled into the sea. The phone she preferred to use now — a plastic brick for calling and texting, nothing more.

"Well, Emma does," Jiyeon replied, still refusing to look at him. "Emma Han. That's who I am, online. Those counts were higher around six months ago, and I don't have updated numbers for the other platforms, but I'm not surprised the count went down. That's a natural consequence when you post that you're quitting and not coming back."

He felt that this had to be about more than just making a personal choice to leave social media. Having over a million followers was no small feat. Building that kind of platform took time and investment, and at a number like that, it evolved into more than a platform. This had been her livelihood. An endeavor like that was not so easily abandoned.

There was a time when I was Emma, just Emma, and Jiyeon was harder to reach. I sort of forgot how to be her. But she was always there. I just needed to learn who she was, again.

"Why did you quit?"

She didn't respond right away, and her smile had vanished by the time she did. "When you're Ari, do you ever feel like nothing is real anymore? Like *you're* not real anymore?"

Wide-eyed, Eunjae said, "I do."

"I thought you might say that." Jiyeon heaved a sigh. "It's a long story. We don't have time right now, but I swear I'll tell you later. All you need to know is that I couldn't take it anymore. That's why I quit."

"And has that changed?"

"Ha. No, I don't want to go back to being that person or living that life. It got to be so miserable. Just thinking about typing my Instagram password is making me nauseous, honestly. Please hurry and give me the phone so I can get this over with." A rueful laugh. "I might lose my courage and run away again."

"This is too much. You made a choice to put this down and I can't ask you to pick it up again just for me."

"You're not asking," countered Jiyeon. "I'm offering. Using my account gives you much better visibility than any of your new accounts combined. I'm verified, I have a longer reach, and I'm willing to bet that a big part of my audience overlaps with yours."

She was right, and Eunjae had no doubt it would do them a great deal of good to take her up on the offer, but there would be a price to pay. Once she got tangled up in this situation, there might be no going back. How could he allow that to happen? He didn't know Jiyeon's reasons for running away, but that was beside the point.

She'd built a quieter world for herself. Doing this would almost certainly herald the end of that world as they knew it right now. Eunjae couldn't bear the thought of it.

"No," he told her. "Thank you, with everything I am, but no."

Their eyes met. All he could get out of her was, "Hmm."

"No. I can't accept, okay? I mean it."

"Eunjae-yah," she said, approaching him with an upturned palm. "You're so sweet, but please just let me borrow my own phone."

He caught her hand. "You've helped me enough. You've helped me so much that I'll never be able to pay it back. I have to say no, this time."

"Didn't you say you could pay me back with a song?" she asked, lacing her fingers with his. "Let's do that."

"Just the one? Doesn't seem fair." He should've stripped this jacket off when he had the chance. Why were they keeping the thermostat at subtropical temperatures?

"Three, then. Can I have the phone now?"

Eunjae used the last of his wits to remember where the phone was, dig it out of his pocket, and surrender without a fight. She thanked him for it. And from just outside the bedroom door came an awestruck, loudly whispered, "Oh, hell."

"He really tried, though."

"Stupid of him, but yeah." A crunch. Was that popcorn? "Good effort, Ari."

"When I grow up, I wanna be a total goner like hyung."

Eunjae dropped Jiyeon's hand like it was made of molten mercury. Just in time, too, because Denny's voice boomed down the hall in a tidal wave of sound. "Who left the fridge open? Do all ninety of you share one brain cell that you pass around every five minutes?"

This swiftly flushed all of Eunjae's brothers from their hiding places, triggering some primal instinct that counseled survival. They scrambled back to the living room and Jiyeon watched them go, biting her lip to keep from laughing.

"Ready? I'll pick out what we need from this box over here if you'll get the other one."

Silently, Eunjae went over the reasons why he'd invited his brothers to come here with him. All of these reasons seemed very, very foolish now.

"Yeah," he said, shrugging his jacket off and tossing it on the bed. "I'll be right there."

41

"Was that everything? Did we say it all?"

In his head, Eunjae paced through the recording they'd just made. He replied, "We talked about the contract — penalty clause, disbandment, copyright. Jesse got us some comparison contracts from other idols, anonymously. Nicky covered how much of our work Emerald will keep if they force us to disband. Kei did the part about current South Korean laws governing contracts and Max, uh, complained really well about our schedule over the past few years under Yoon."

"It's fucked up, okay?"

"Don't forget that I looked up all that stuff about Jewell!"

"Good job, Gyu," said Kei. "You listened to a podcast like a champ."

"It's a great podcast! *Omma Gosh*, that's what it's called. They know a lot about us! They even knew about that time I got lost in Vegas. Haha!"

"You mean the time you wandered off at Caesar's Palace and a bunch of Sunshines mobbed you at the fake Roman fountain? Cause I still have nightmares about that."

"Aww, Keiichi looked for me *everywhere*."

"I'm just really glad Zuzu remembered to bring Mom," Jesse chimed in. He smiled fondly at the prop he held in his hands. This was a life-sized photo of Jaehwan's head, backed with cardboard and mounted on a popsicle stick like a mask to be worn at a grade school play.

"Of course I brought Hwannie. This is war." Kazu unfolded his legs and got up from the couch, swatting Kei for commenting about how loudly his knees cracked in the process. "The Internet seems to think this thing's happening in the morning. There's no specific time listed on anything the agency's posted to official channels, but the fans could be right."

"I hope the fans are right. I can't brain anymore. I'm too tired."

Eunjae chose this moment to share the next phase of the plan, something he'd discussed with Denny and Jiyeon while they were setting up for the livestream. "I don't think we should wait until morning," he said. "The fans are already lined up and waiting. If we go there now, maybe we can beat Emerald to the punch, talk to the audience directly. We can make sure they know everything we said in the video was real."

"Now?" sputtered Nick. "But I look like garbage!"

"Calm down, Nicky. We all look like garbage. I mean, especially you."

"You know what's annoying? Zuzu doesn't look like garbage. Funny how it turns out that way when he remembers to wear a full set of clothes..."

"Ya! I could show up naked and still look better than you," Kazu shot back, sparking an argument with Kei that was conducted entirely in Japanese.

"Waaaah! Stop fighting!"

"You all look like heroes!" declared Mrs. Han. She swept into the room, clapped her hands, and went to fetch car keys. "Now, men! To battle!"

A flabbergasted Denny grabbed his own keys and headed for the door, towing Mr. Han along with him. "Jesus, where'd she get that from? That's not a line from *Pride and Prejudice*."

"But it could be," Jiyeon pointed out.

The members of Apollo went pelting out of the apartment. Eunjae rushed to steer both Max and Kazu away from Mrs. Han and the Camaro.

"We're riding with Denny," he informed them, recalling that Lizzie Han's driving would fit right in on the streets of Monaco during an F1 grand prix. Not a good match for the two Apollo members who habitually carried barf bags in their carry-on luggage.

His brothers reached the same understanding when the Camaro zipped out of the parking lot at warp speed, Jesse hooting from the passenger seat. In the back, Namgyu had his arms up like a rider anticipating the first impossibly steep drop on a rollercoaster.

Kazu seized Eunjae's arm. "You just saved my life, man."

"Same," said Max, latching on to his other arm. "Let us pay you back." And then he joined forces with Kazu to whisk Eunjae into Jiyeon's car, going so far as to prevent escape by shutting the door and leaning their combined weight against it.

"Guys, no. You're going to get me killed."

"By who? Her dad? Please, he loves you. 'Liiioooon-niiiiimmmm!'"

Eunjae tried again. "Seriously, let me out before Denny sees."

"Heard him say something about too many brothers. Oh, and calling for a police escort. Is he a cop? FBI? What's the deal there?"

"He has resources." That was Jiyeon, hopping in next to Eunjae and starting the car. "Please don't ask me what that means. Are you two riding with us? There's room."

"Nope," answered Kazu, a borderline demonic grin on his face. "Wouldn't dream of it." He yanked Max away and left Eunjae to his doom. "Have fun, kids!"

Cheering erupted from all three rows of Denny's SUV, part of it contributed by a confused but very excited Mr. Han. Nicky popped up through the open moon roof and shouted, "Good luck, my son!"

And then, much to Eunjae's horror, Max broke away from Kazu at the last second. He threw his head back, and belted out a very familiar chorus. "Cause you should be my laaaayyydaaayyy —"

After gesturing forcefully for Denny to stop glowering and start driving, Jiyeon handed back Eunjae's phone. "Do I know that song?"

"*Wedding Dress* by Taeyang," he choked out, having reached peak mortification. It was the song he performed at his audition for Emerald, and then again on *King of Mask Singer* in the iconic lion costume he had yet to live down. As Max's warbling continued to echo after them down the street, Eunjae fastened his seatbelt and willed himself to spontaneously combust. *Should've shoved him into the Camaro,* whispered the voice of Invisible Jaehwan. He wasn't wrong. Too many brothers, indeed.

The closer they came to Wanna Waffle, the more abysmal the traffic became. At a red light, Jiyeon took the opportunity to pull her hair back into a ponytail. She had an olive green cargo jacket thrown across her lap: Eunjae's, which she must have retrieved from her room before they left the apartment. Jiyeon offered it to him as soon as she finished with her hair.

"Didn't want you to forget," she explained. "Sounds like there's some pages folded up in the pocket."

"Oh, my notes." He took these out, then tossed the jacket into the back seat. Definitely still no need for that. "Were you off today?" Time to talk about literally anything other than songs about wedding dresses.

"Can you tell? Olivia would never let me within three feet of the salon dressed like this. She wants us to look a certain way. 'On brand' and all that." She fished a bobby pin out of the cup holder and pinned a loose strand in place, then pulled on a baseball cap that cast part of her face in shadow. "I love to dress up, don't get me wrong. Nice to get a break from that on my days off, though. I was on brand for years, right? The brand *was* me."

Eunjae had yet to be there for one of her days off. He'd only seen Jiyeon in the bright colors and patterns of her workday clothes, with flowers and ribbons in her hair. It was like getting another glimpse at who she was, the truth that defined her. Glancing over while she was preoccupied with driving, he knew that he wanted to be around for the next day off, and the next, and the next.

He wanted to be part of the story on all the days in between, however that story might go. Eunjae kept this to himself, though. Who was he to reach for anything like that? Besides, it was impossible for him to ignore what it would mean for Jiyeon to be tied to him in any way. He wasn't just Eunjae, some guy from Brisbane. He was also Ari. Considering what he'd learned about her that evening, this only further complicated everything.

Who could say what his future held? It all depended on what happened here, tonight.

The boulevard leading to Wanna Waffle had been decked out in Emerald Entertainment's green and lavender pennants, the palm trees adorned with long strings of lights. It was impossible to even see the sidewalk thanks to the sheer number of pedestrians thronged along the street.

Eunjae sank down lower, wary of being spotted. Fortunately, visibility was low. Par for the course at an Apollo event, the air bristled with homemade signs that said things like 'SHINE BRIGHT 4 APOLLO' and 'PRINCE KAZU WILL U MARRY ME'. Jesse fans murmured to one another over armfuls of sunflowers. Eunjae spotted a troupe of Jungwoo devotees clustered in a knot, arms linked, each carrying a single red rose. From the car, it was difficult to tell whether they were laughing or crying.

He desperately wanted to cover Jiyeon's eyes before she could get a good look at any of the Sunshines bearing lion plushies or the ones in custom jean jackets bedazzled with ARI IS MY ANGEL. Unfortunately, she was driving and that would be dangerous.

The car crept forward inch by inch through an atmosphere that seemed strangely somber. These people must be so tired. He had to wonder how many hours some of them had been waiting. A few times, Eunjae thought he saw the flash of a tear-stained face, a fevered glint in someone's eyes.

"They're not just waiting in line," Jiyeon observed with growing concern. "Over there, next to those teenagers with the inflatable hammers — that looks like a ticket booth. And the line is moving. Slowly, but it's moving. Eunjae... I think this event is starting *tonight*."

Blurred asphalt is the only thing we see in the first thirty seconds of the video, along with glimpses of Freddie's white sneakers as she runs with the phone pointed at the ground. She slows down significantly upon reaching the crowded intersection where a horde of Apollo fans has congregated. The camera swings upward and captures a fleeting view of palm trees wrapped in string lights. Pennants snap in the strong breeze.

Freddie lifts the phone, focusing on a lanky figure wading his way through the masses: her co-host, Jooney Chun. The back of his highlighter yellow shirt is printed with the *Omma Gosh!* podcast logo. She catches up to him, swearing softly under her breath as someone nearly brains her with an officially licensed Apollo light stick.

"What do you see?" she yells at him, fighting to be heard over the din.

Jooney holds his own phone aloft, recording the scene from

as high over his head as possible. His response is initially too muddled to decipher. Freddie endeavors to push and shove her way a little closer in an effort to get better audio.

"Nothing," Jooney yells back at her. He's forgotten to remove his sunglasses. Freddie snatches them off his face with the hand that isn't gripping the phone.

"Has anything happened? Have you been paying attention? What is the point of you being taller than me, what a waste!"

"Some agency people were walking around. I think they're having technical issues."

"Huh. Here, get online and do some digging. I saw news vans around the corner. Maybe they've got something."

"Right. We need intel." Jooney dutifully begins searching on his phone. Meanwhile, Freddie tows him along beside her, steadily getting closer to the stage through an effective mix of pointy elbows and shouting, "Look! It's Jaehwan from Apollo!" at the top of her lungs. The latter method never fails to get people moving.

Freddie's slash and burn strategy wins them a spot with a downright decent view. "Much better," she says. "Okay, Chun. It's tea time."

The footage goes black, then cuts to Jooney facing the camera. His khakis are hopelessly wrinkled and the sunglasses have relocated to the top of his head. He waits for Freddie's signal, clears his throat, and then begins.

"Folks, we're here at the Apollo event that's blowing up the Internet and possibly half the universe. As you're probably aware — because how could you miss it? — posts about a surprise event in LA started going up on the group's socials not too long ago. Barely any details, of course, except for the address to a noraebang in the shopping center behind me."

Jooney points to the karaoke bar's neon sign. "I'm glad we decided not to bring Ma 'cause this place is insane right now. The Apollo members themselves posted a video where they said a lot of things that I just *really* want to dig into. Now, I know tons of people online are already saying Apollo might disband —"

"They're not disbanding!" a woman shouts at him. Freddie tells her in no uncertain terms to back off and quit obstructing quality journalism.

Jooney continues. "I definitely don't have the whole story at this point in time, but my interpretation of their livestream was that they want to clear things up with fans, make sure people are aware of some shady things happening behind the scenes at Emerald Entertainment. So I wouldn't panic just yet and start freaking out about a disbandment —"

The woman from earlier squawks at him again. "Apollo hasn't disbanded!"

"And I just said to back off, Sharon!"

"Hold on, is her name really Sharon...?"

"The rest of it, Jooney," Freddie redirects him urgently.

"Oh!" He produces his phone. The screen is already unlocked, and when Freddie zooms in, we can see that Jooney has pulled up an Instagram account. Almost tripping over his own words, he says, "Aside from what is apparently a fight between Apollo and their agency, we've got another twist to this story. It's the fact that the group posted from the account of Emma Han — yes, *that* Emma Han, the hairstylist, content creator, and influencer — initially as a livestream and then reposted as a recording with all of Apollo's socials tagged."

"You know who we're talking about," Freddie puts in, breathless with excitement. "We had her on the show last year when we went to Seoul Fashion Week. She's @jiye_unnie on all her social media channels. You've probably seen her super popular haircut videos and K-beauty recommendations. A ton of them went viral. And if you missed those, here's a reminder that Emma Han had some pretty big names as clients. We're talking A-listers like Chloe Janssen and Riley Mendoza, just to name two."

"I'll have to watch all of this again before we talk about it on tomorrow's bonus episode, but here's the gist: this is going down as one of the biggest, most dramatic events in K-pop. Like, never mind that the group is openly facing off against the agency that houses them, that's crazy enough. But why are they posting from someone else's account? Where did they post this from? Looks like someone's house? What's the story here?"

"We did notice that all of the members' personal accounts are currently featuring the same graphic. You've gotta wonder if the agency took over."

"It's a plausible theory. Anyway, according to a tweet from some very detail-oriented individual out there, Emma had 1.3 million followers on the platform at the time this video streamed from her account. As of right now, that number has blown up to around two million and still counting. Before this, she hadn't posted in well over six months."

Freddie sighs. "Unnie, if you're watching, I've missed you. Come back and tell me which lipstick to buy. I need so much guidance. I'm an only child! You were the only big sister I ever had!"

"Are you processing this?" Jooney exclaims, pocketing his phone. "I have so many questions. I won't be the only one, not by a long shot. How is Apollo linked to Emma Han? Could she potentially tell us anything about what went down between the group and Emerald Entertainment? And why did she choose to come back to social media now after writing in her last post that she was done with it forever?"

He points at the camera. "Don't worry, folks. We'll find out."

42

Eunjae had no idea how Jiyeon contrived to find parking, but she did. They got out and navigated the rest of the way on foot, weaving through the crowd at a jog whenever possible.

"Where are the others?" Jiyeon called to him.

"Not sure. I got Max for a minute but then the signal cut out."

"Let's just keep going. I have a key, maybe the back door? We can take this street all the way there. Then you could just cut through the shop."

It was worth a try. They certainly wouldn't make much headway from any other direction. Wanna Waffle's front door was beyond their reach, cordoned off behind a veritable wall of Emerald Entertainment security guards, barriers, and bright green tape.

In the shopping center parking lot, Eunjae sighted a temporary stage that had been built for the event. This, too, was on the other side of the barrier. Apollo songs thumped from the speakers: *Blame it on Me, Win/Win, Trickster*. The first wave of fans had been rewarded for showing up so early. Their prize was being allowed to vie for space in the audience, standing room only. Strangely, there wasn't much of a festive air to the proceedings. If anything, there was an air of confusion. *Did you see it? The boys posted a video. Do you think they'll really show up?* And then: *Do you think they've been kidnapped???*

Even from one street removed, Eunjae knew it when the event began in earnest. There was a perceptible shift in energy, an electric thrill that seemed to brighten the night by degrees. Namgyu's verse in *Never Too Late* faded out midway through, ceding the airwaves to a song that didn't belong to Apollo. Eunjae recognized it as *Secret Garden* — a song by Jewell.

So the founders were here, then. Once again, they'd come to deal with Eunjae in person.

Jiyeon grabbed his arm as a golf cart came screeching to a halt alongside them. He expected to find an Emerald staffer at the wheel, maybe even one of Apollo's managers. Instead, it was Denny.

"Finally!" he bellowed at them, somehow looking just like the Emerald security guards in his appropriated green polo and black slacks. He even had an earpiece to go with the radio at his hip. A very official looking name badge dangled from the lanyard around his neck.

As they climbed into the golf cart at Denny's express urging, Jiyeon hissed, "Where did you get that uniform? And don't you dare use the word 'resources' or I'll teach Eunjae how to make the secret waffle batter. I'll give him a written copy and everything."

"You wouldn't!" Denny hissed back. "Stop distracting me from the mission!" He maneuvered around a small horde of Sunshines clad in oversized t-shirts screen-printed with Nick's face. All of them were crying. They scurried out of the way as Denny honked the horn to oblivion. "You and your brothers," Denny ranted at Eunjae, "should be classified as a natural disaster. This area is a wreck. The blast radius is at least two miles out in all directions."

"Do you know where they are?"

"Waiting for you. Don't worry, I handled it. We're going there right now." He then turned his attention back to Jiyeon. "And you! Why are you here? Your follower count's gone past two mil, thanks to the Apollo posts. If anyone sees you here, that's it."

Jiyeon flinched at the news. "That was fast."

"I told you this was gonna happen. You should've dropped Ryan off and gone back home."

"I couldn't do that." Poking her brother between the shoulder blades, Jiyeon said, "Molly Merriweather would tell me to see it through to the end."

"Molly Merriweather would tell you that wearing a hat doesn't count as a disguise," Denny replied tersely. "Switch me when we get to the back lot. I'll go with him from there."

Scattered applause reached them on the breeze. Denny powered up a ramp and onto the sidewalk, then tore right across a patch of grass to reach the parking area behind Wanna Waffle. This was blocked off as well, but instead of Emerald security guards, three police cruisers barred access, lights strobing red and blue. This was the only reason why the crowd had failed to invade the space.

"You really did get a police escort," marveled Eunjae. He could see figures inside each SUV, some maniacally waving at him. This solved the mystery of where Denny had stashed the other members of Apollo.

"We cater the precinct's annual holiday breakfast. Waffles are the currency of power." Denny pointed at his sister. "Get going. I promise I'll get them out after."

From inside one of the police cruisers, an excited voice could be heard asking, "Does anyone else feel like they're in a Tom Cruise movie?"

Jiyeon came around to assume Denny's place at the wheel. "I thought golf carts couldn't go any faster than twenty miles per hour," she remarked. "Didn't this move super fast, to you?"

"Custom job, I bet. I'm sure Denny knows a guy."

"I'm sure he does, too." She climbed in again, eyeing the gas pedal warily. "Don't tell him that I'm coming back."

"Hey, no. Don't do that."

They'd both heard the chatter as they pushed their way through the crowd, certain words repeated and amplified. The people were talking about Apollo, of course, but the conversations also bubbled over with speculation about her.

Maybe it was just his own hunger to know more, but every mention of her seemed to stand out clearer, reach him sooner. *Emma, Emma, Emma,* Eunjae had picked up again and again. *The one with the cute hair videos. I didn't know she was a fan. Pretty unnie who does the breakup haircuts, you remember her. Didn't she work with a bunch of actresses? Where's she been all this time? How does she know the boys? Probably an attention grab. I hope she posts again and tells us what's going on.*

He worried that this was already starting to get to her. She'd grown subdued after that update on her exploding follower count. But just for a moment, Jiyeon reached over to give his hand a squeeze. Eunjae could almost pretend that nothing had changed.

"I'll be there," she said to him. "I'm seeing this through to the end."

"I owe you a fourth song, then."

Jiyeon just smiled at him from beneath the brim of her baseball cap. Then she was off, and the others spilled out of the cruisers to congregate at the shop's back door.

Eunjae hurried to catch up. Denny had just finished lecturing the members of Apollo against foolishly touching the gong on the counter, as there would be dire consequences. "Sorry I couldn't buy you more time," he said to Eunjae, letting him into the shop, "but I did sabotage the audio equipment. Had some help from that guy over there. The one who came to get you last time. How many freaking brothers do you have?"

It was the equivalent of a dunk in frigid sea water. "Eight," answered Eunjae, already dashing for the adjacent room. Three steps ahead of him, Max launched himself at Jungwoo and had to be restrained by both Namgyu and Nick.

"You! It was you who told them we'd be here! That's why they started it early! What the fuck is wrong with you? You said that you wouldn't help them!"

"Max, let him go. MAX!"

Jungwoo rubbed at the spot on his jaw where Max had managed to land a punch. He locked eyes with Eunjae. "I did tell them. I said you'd probably come here and you wouldn't wait until morning once you saw what they'd done. Thankfully I guessed right. We have to end this tonight, Ari. We needed to end it an hour ago but I couldn't reach any of you. Haewon had my phone taken away as soon as I got back to Seoul. I had to just hope that you'd realize what was going on."

He hauled Eunjae over to the window. Through the barest gap in the blinds, Eunjae saw a sea of grief-stricken faces. The oddness he'd noticed all night suddenly made terrible sense — the crowd being so subdued, all those groups of Sunshines crying with their arms around each other. He'd pushed his suspicions aside because half the audience always seemed to be in tears at Apollo events. Tears of happiness, tears brought on by euphoria. Eunjae hadn't even considered that the fans might be crying out of sorrow.

"They've disbanded us," said Jungwoo, his voice ringing hollow in

Eunjae's ears. "Haewon and Soyeon were going to announce it on stage, but the microphones weren't working. My guess is that it rolled out on social media while the crew was trying to figure out the audio issues. All that's left is to march everyone out there and make us say goodbye."

"But they can't do that!" Eunjae felt like he'd taken the punch instead of Jungwoo. "I didn't break my contract. I told them I was staying."

"Ari, they're furious with you. You've run away twice now."

"That doesn't matter. I could run away again and Emerald still wouldn't retain the right to just disband us out of the blue. I've read that contract a thousand times. They can only do that under the penalty clause, and the only way for us to trigger the penalty clause is for someone to break contract."

Kazu spoke up from the other side of the room. "Then maybe they haven't disbanded us. You don't know that for sure, right? Whatever they planned to say up there, they haven't gotten to say it yet."

"It's a disbandment. Why else would the fans be that upset? Look at them."

"A good guess, Jungwoo, but not exactly right."

Haewon came through the orange door with Soyeon close behind her. They were dressed for their stage appearance in coordinating outfits of brilliant, blazing white. Emeralds glittered at their wrists and throats. Soyeon's necklace was studded with gems so large and so close together that the piece brought to mind a jeweled collar. Armor, Eunjae thought. And here he'd shown up as his plain, vulnerable self.

"We haven't disbanded Apollo," Soyeon said dully. "Your fans have simply assumed that a disbandment is forthcoming."

They were treated to Haewon's frosty smile. "What else can they expect? It's only logical now that Ari's contract has been terminated."

8/12/2008

Dear Jewelbox, our beloved fans,

The first time I appeared before you as Jewell's Haewon, I was only 17 years old. Back then, I felt all the time that I was lacking. I knew I could work harder and become a better Haewon who would make you proud. With all of my heart, I thank you for the ten years you've spent watching over me. Jewell was able to shine so bright because of our fans who believed in us no matter what. Someday when I look back on my youth, I know I won't regret that I gave those precious years to you. We belong to you, our fans. That will always be true.

The title of our final album was Emerald Green. I've read that emeralds are a symbol of rebirth. I didn't choose this name for the album, but it seems meaningful, doesn't it? That's what I want to believe.

To sing and dance for you, and to be with my sisters, has been the great joy of my life. Even now as I write you this letter, my eyes are filled with tears and it's so difficult to see the page. The only thing that helps is the knowledge that we will meet again soon. Keep watching over me. I won't let you down!

Shine forever,

Jewell's Haewon

12 August 2008

Dear Jewelbox,

We always began and ended our shows with these words: shine forever. Isn't forever a long time? It's such a long time that I can't imagine it.

I know that when you hear the news today, you'll feel so many things at once: sadness, confusion, maybe anger. It might feel like the end. I understand. But I also hope you'll feel pride in what we've become together: Jewell and our Jewelbox, always shining side by side. It might be the end… but it doesn't mean that we need to say goodbye.

There have been so many days when I've felt too tired or too imperfect to keep following this path. On those days, I've thought of my sisters, and I've also thought of you. It's when I think of your smiling faces that I know for sure: we can shine forever, after all.

Soyeon

43

"Terminated," murmured Eunjae. They'd fired him. That was the big news.

Haewon had a leather folio tucked under her arm. She produced a crisp sheaf of documents and fanned them out on a nearby table, pushing the napkin holder aside with a manicured hand. She said, "The termination can be revoked. It's not too late to fix what you've done, even after that outrageous video you posted. We have new paperwork right here."

"For fuck's sake," raged Max.

His outburst garnered no reaction. "Instead of saying goodbye to all those sad people out there, you can simply tell them what happened. The official story, that is."

"The official story." A storm roiled beneath Kazu's glacial demeanor. His hands had clenched into fists.

Bitterly, Nicky asked, "Is it the one where you put that penalty in our contracts because it's supposed to save us from ourselves?"

"Oh, there will be no mention of that. If you want Apollo to continue, if you want to heal your fans' poor little broken hearts, no one can go off script. You'll stand on that stage together and explain to the audience that Ari wanted to quit. He begged us to end his contract because he just couldn't take it anymore."

Haewon looked to Jungwoo. "Isn't that what you told me, the night you found him here? You were so worried. *He isn't strong enough for the long game*, you said."

Jungwoo hung his head in shame. "Leave him alone," Eunjae cut in.

"Is this why they love you, Ari? Did they follow you down this road because you forgive them even when they turn on you?"

"He didn't turn on me." Jungwoo was only human. He was allowed to be afraid, to make mistakes.

"It's nice to hear you taking his side, now. I'd like to think we can still make you see reason." She motioned at the dining area's dim interior. "He was right to be concerned for you. How is this anything to aspire to? And do you really think these people, this life, would satisfy you for very long?"

"Don't talk to hyung that way," Jesse cried out.

Soyeon dropped into a chair. "Haewon-ah," she murmured. "Remember why we're here. Don't get carried away." Her gaze seemed a little less distant, although Eunjae could've been imagining it. He could hardly think straight thanks to the pain. He could barely stop himself from shouting everything in his heart.

How is this anything to aspire to?

But it was everything to aspire to. He knew that now.

Haewon dropped her line of questioning, although the clipped tone suggested that she chafed under her sister's warning. She went back to addressing the group as a whole. "Anyway, since you all love your brother so much, you decided that it was better to disband rather than limp along for another few years, one member short. Then it will be Ari's turn in the spotlight.

"I don't know how much of an actor you are, but you'll need to do your best. Confess that the guilt is too much to bear. Tell your fans that you can't allow the group to fall apart just because of your selfishness. Tell them you'll stay. As brothers, they were prepared to go down with you, but you won't let it happen. You'll dig deep and get over yourself. All for one, one for all." She clapped. "Done! No more disbandment. No more termination."

Haewon straightened the printed pages on the table. "The rules will be stricter and the penalties a little higher, but let's be fair — you deserve it. Then the fans go away feeling oh, so relieved and the drama makes you more popular than ever. Perhaps we should be thanking you for this catastrophe, after all."

"Why did you bother with all of this?" Kei spoke up, visibly trembling. "You brought the fans out here, you set up this whole charade — for what? So we can help you tell your lies?"

"See, I knew you would react this way. I understand because I lived it too. The fans are the ones who brought you here, when we really think about it. It's their love that sustains you. But they're fickle, too. They can love you, and they can ruin you. None of you can stand to see them hurt, can you? Even though you hate them sometimes, I'm sure. That's why I knew you would come if I brought them here."

"It should've been enough that you bullied Ari into staying," said Namgyu. "You didn't need to punish us, or Sunshines, or anybody. How could you do this? After Polaris refused to credit you for your work, you still wrote that clause into our contracts. You made it so we could lose our music." He swiped at tears with the sleeve of his sweater. "Like we weren't going to lose enough."

"I did nothing to deserve what Polaris did to me," Haewon

volleyed back. "I tried to fight for myself and my work, but I never took it this far. I never ran away. I put up with the schedule, I showed up even when I was sick and had barely slept for days. None of what they did to me was fair, but I tried to be fair for you."

"So if one of us tries to leave the group, losing all our work is only right. That's what you think is fair."

She smirked at Eunjae. "You think you shouldn't be punished. Even after everything you've done, and everything we've given you. I can see it in your eyes."

"Everything you've *given* me?" He tried to keep controlling his temper but didn't fully succeed. "I wasn't given any of this. Forced into it, yeah. I auditioned because I was a kid who felt like I had no other choice. But everything after that? I earned it."

Eunjae came forward, then, heart slamming in his chest. "If I do what you want — if I go out there and tell these lies for you — will you remove the penalty clause from our contracts?"

Haewon only regarded him coldly. "No."

"Because it saved you from disbandment. Without the clause, Jewell would've fallen apart when Soyeon tried to leave. That's what you said, but I don't think it's true."

He approached Soyeon. "Noona," said Eunjae, addressing her as an elder sister just as she'd once asked all Emerald Entertainment artists to do, in happier and easier times. "When Polaris threatened you with the musketeer clause, you felt too guilty to go through with quitting. After that, how did you feel?"

"How dare you force her to remember that?" Haewon launched into him immediately. "She hates to think about it. You're out of line."

But now Soyeon let out a sob, and Eunjae knew that he'd asked the right question. "Noona, you wanted to quit because you weren't happy anymore. Leaving was what you needed to do for yourself. Then you saw that doing this for yourself would make your sisters suffer, so you gave up. The penalty clause kept Jewell together. Did it really save you, though? I don't think it did. And you know it wouldn't have saved us, either."

"Stop it!" Haewon shrilled. She moved as though to shield Soyeon from Eunjae. He stood his ground. Although Soyeon was upset, she hadn't contradicted him.

"I'm sorry to make you cry," Eunjae said to her. "I'm sorry to remind you of something so painful. But the pain you went through then and the pain you're going through now, you allowed it to happen to me, to everyone in this group. Even though it's too late to change that now, you could change it for the ones who come after us. Soyeon-noona, please. Remove that clause from all Emerald contracts going forward. Make it so no other group has to go through this."

Haewon was now incandescent with fury. "Don't talk like this is over. I won't say it all again, Ari. Go out there, stick to the script, and fix what you've broken. Or would you rather change the termination to a resignation? That clause isn't going anywhere. You know what will happen if you insist on quitting."

"I'm not quitting. You fired me. You said it yourself when you came in."

He'd given it one last try, but now this had to end. Eunjae held up his phone. "Is it okay if I record the rest of this conversation? Based on the terms I signed at renewal two years ago, I have the right to request a recording or transmission of any meeting that pertains to my contract. And I think you should have a record of it, too."

44

The room was so quiet that Eunjae's heartbeat seemed twice as loud in his ears. At first he thought his request would be denied, but Soyeon brought out her own phone and set it on the table. "Go ahead," she said, much to Haewon's alarm.

Eunjae thanked her, then opened the right app and pressed record. He took out the pages he'd been keeping in his jacket pocket and smoothed out the creases.

"To summarize, Emerald Entertainment terminated my exclusive contract for multiple violations.

"First, failing to comply with the group's promotional schedule. Because I ran away, our fanmeeting was canceled and the unit project was postponed.

"Second, failing to cooperate with agency staff. I refused to accompany my managers to the airport. I'm sure Doyoung will confirm it for you in a statement. Nami will, too. I made that call. Running away was my idea.

"Third, abuse of power. I persuaded the other members to leave the country with me, including younger members, which can be argued as misuse of authority."

"Where are you going with this?" demanded Haewon, seething.

"I'm making sure you got it all," Eunjae answered. "The contract states that terminating an agreement between the agency and the artist requires ample proof of just cause or misconduct."

It caused Eunjae no small measure of disquiet, that the conflict had come down to this. Knowingly provoking Emerald was a huge risk. What he'd wanted most was to settle this amicably. The hope for a bloodless resolution had remained at the forefront of his thoughts, and sometimes this made Eunjae feel more than a little absurd. But if he stopped believing that it might work out in a way that was kinder to all of them, then the situation felt that much harder to bear.

He shuffled the back pages to the front, pushing these forward for the founders to review. "I also signed a separate contract for employment without prior permission from Emerald Entertainment. I work here." He gestured at the dining area Haewon had disparaged earlier. "You can look through the documents — they're all valid. I'm allowed to live and work in the United States because I have dual Australian and American citizenship. Something to thank Leila for, I guess."

"This is ridiculous."

"It's not. I'm helping you. Acquiring additional employment can be argued as a conflict of interest. There's a whole section on that. Also, any earnings made while under contract with Emerald are supposed to be reported so that the agency can take its cut. Those are both described as grounds for termination in my contract. Make sure you present it all to the board."

Eunjae didn't dare to stop, not even to take a breath. Not now.

"Fire me," he said. "To trigger the penalty clause, I would have to quit. And because I'm not quitting — because you've decided to fire me — the clause doesn't apply. You can't disband Apollo even after I leave.

You can't keep the rights to our music, either. That only happens if I try to terminate the contract myself. Your legal team didn't cover for that while they were writing this."

"Let me just send an email about it right now," sniped Haewon.

"Maybe you should fire them, too," someone sniped back at her.

Jaehwan's voice, Eunjae realized with a start. It wasn't an imaginary, sibilant whisper in his mind, this time. Max had his phone out. The actual Jaehwan was there on the line.

"Finish it, Ari," he said. "We're with you. No matter what happens next, we're here."

Everyone had moved to stand near him and Eunjae never noticed because he was so busy talking. He had a brother to the left and to the right, brothers at his back with their hands on his shoulders. His throat ached and his eyes burned as he delivered his final argument. He worded it exactly as Arthur had advised a few days before.

"I, Ari Goldsmith-Song, accept the termination of my exclusive contract with Emerald Entertainment."

He bowed to Haewon and Soyeon. "Thank you for the twelve years I lived under your roof. I'm grateful for what you taught me. I'm glad I was part of what you built, and that you saw something special about me, something worth caring for and protecting."

The walls shook with his brothers' cheering and applause even as Haewon's mouth shaped a rebuke, or perhaps a refusal. Eunjae couldn't hear her over the tumult of voices raised in victory, in praise, in pride. He wasn't done yet, though.

"The remaining members won't be forced to disband, but I can't leave them with you. If you won't remove the penalty clause, then I'm petitioning the board to have the rest of Apollo placed under disciplinary review. Section 6 of the contract says that participating in misconduct as an accomplice is grounds for termination. They were all my accomplices. End their contracts, too."

"No. They stay until their contracts expire. If they want to be terminated, they'll have to file injunctions individually." Haewon shook her head, dry-eyed, arms wrapped tightly around herself as though she might shatter at any minute. "You wouldn't even be brothers, without us. We're the ones who brought you together."

"We're brothers because we chose to be," Kazu contradicted her. "That won't change. And if we have to take legal action, we will."

"Tell yourselves whatever you want," she said. Especially for Eunjae, she added, "Soon enough, you'll see: you've thrown it all away, and for what?"

"This isn't everything I am," Eunjae replied, "and this isn't the end, either."

"You're right. It's not the end at all. This fight isn't over until I say it is."

Haewon was poised to say something further, but she fell silent when Soyeon rose from her chair. "That's enough." She turned to face her sister, the tracks of tears still gleaming on her face. "Ari fought well. He's won, fair and square. Let him go."

"I can't believe this. You're giving up again."

"Haewon-ah. Do you remember how it all started? The dream we had and the company we wanted to build? Because it isn't this. Who we've become, it's not anything like who we wanted to be."

Her gaze fell upon Eunjae and each of his brothers, one by one. The noise died down instantly, save for Haewon's sharp intake of breath as Soyeon said, "As the majority shareholder of Emerald Entertainment, I approve the termination of Ari Goldsmith-Song. He is free to seek representation by an agency of his choice, and I wish him a long and successful career. Any career he might want to pursue."

Eunjae could hardly process it. He bowed again. He bowed as low as he could, and all around him, his brothers bowed as well.

"I'm a majority shareholder too," Haewon interjected. "You can't authorize that on your own. Not without the full board behind you."

"I own more shares than anyone with a stake in Emerald, including you. Did you forget that, too? You insisted." Soyeon's voice was gentle, but weighted down with sadness. "Because I'm older, and because I was leader. Not that I've acted like much of a leader, these past few years."

"You're still not leading. You're being a coward. We could fight this, fight them together, but you won't. It's like you don't care what this will do to us. I feel like we've gone back in time." Bitterly, Haewon added, "Why should they have it all when we never could?"

She left the room, then. Soyeon didn't turn to watch her go.

"Furthermore," she went on, a slight tremor in her voice, "I find the remaining members of Apollo to be in violation of company policy as willing accomplices to Ari. All members assisted Ari in failing to meet contractual obligations. I hereby terminate their contracts as well."

Soyeon plucked a sheet of paper from the table, then flipped it over. "Who has a pen? Jungwoo, I know you always carry one around."

With a trembling hand, Jungwoo drew a pen out of the front pocket of his shirt. He gave it to Soyeon, who wrote several lines in clean, steady script across the blank page. At the bottom, she signed it with her name.

"Here," she said to Eunjae. "Now you have it in writing. It's good enough for the time being." And then she bowed to them, too. Careful to speak loudly enough for both phones to record, Soyeon added one more statement.

"As per the contract terms cited by Ari, the members of Apollo retain the rights to their music, all related royalties, and the trademark to their name. No penalties are invoked."

Soyeon reached out to clasp Eunjae's hand. He pulled her into a hug, rendered speechless, and she let go of a sob she must have been holding in the whole time. Seven more pairs of arms wrapped around them both.

"You're free," she said, and Eunjae found his voice again at last.

"Thank you."

The members of Apollo run onto the stage carrying Ari on their shoulders. They're all either cheering, grinning like idiots, or both.

Vanessa - (*smacking her friend in the arm*) They're here!!!! THEY'RE HERE!!!!!! OMG!!!!!!!!!!! OMG LOOK AT MY PRINCE!!!!!! LOOK AT HIM!!!!!!!!

Kazu - Sunshines, it's a nice night! (*waits for other members to join him, then counts to three in Korean*) Hana, dul, set.

All Members - Shine bright, it's Apollo!

Vanessa - (*incoherent shrieking*)

Jesse - You guys are up past your bedtime.

Kei, in Japanese - Says the baby who's up past his bedtime.

Jesse - (*pointing at him*) You're a baby too! I know how old you are!

Nicky - SUNSHINES I LOVE YOUUUUUU!

Crowd - (*applause, yelling, screaming, crying*)

Some Girl Nearby - OPPA SARANGHAE!

Kazu - (*gesturing at Ari*) Okay, okay. Put the kid down, let's roll.

Vanessa - (*more incoherent shrieking*)

Jungwoo - First, we need to thank you. You've been out here all night, waiting for us. And we know you've been confused, scared, everything. But you waited for us like you always do.

Vanessa - (*only filming Kazu while other members are talking*) How long have we been here, do you know?

Vanessa's Friend, off screen - Our whole lives.

Jesse - You've probably noticed we're having some audio issues. We'll talk as loud as we can, but if you could please help us out —

Crowd - (*yelling, crying*)

Kei - Still too loud! Try again! (*brandishes cardboard cutout of Jaehwan at the audience*)

Namgyu - Yes! Let's be quiet! Haha!

We switch to Jenna's video briefly because Vanessa refuses to film anyone other than Kazu.

Jenna - Hey, can you get your sign out of my face, please? Seriously?

Jenna's Boyfriend, off screen - Get your sign out of her face! She can't see!

Jenna - I hope they explain what's going on.

Jenna's Dad, off screen - I'm sure they will. Come on, drink some water.

Jenna - Thanks, Dad. Wait, what is Jesse wearing?

Are those silk pajamas?

Jenna's Boyfriend - Damn, I want some.

Jesse - Sunshines are so patient. And they're so pretty. Look at them! LOVE YOU GUYS.

Crowd - (*incoherent shrieking*)

Max - We took forever to get out here cause we were busy getting fired.

Crowd - (*collective gasp*)

Jenna - What?

Kazu - It was more complicated than that actually, but thank you Max.

Kei - And we did get fired.

Crowd - (*still gasping*)

> *Vanessa has finally zoomed out a little because she wants to record an interaction between Kazu and Ari which is happening off to the side. Kazu has his hand on Ari's shoulder and appears to be offering some kind of pep talk. Ari is shaking his head, but laughing.*

Vanessa - (*utterly scandalized*) — and what I'm saying is, like, I'm still processing that? They *fired* my husband?

Max - *(pointing to a doubter in the crowd)* What? You don't believe we could get fired? Well, we did.

Vanessa - So they're not with Emerald anymore? Or what?

Vanessa's Friend - I haven't had enough coffee to deal with this. Or wine. I'd take some wine right now.

Jenna has a better view of the next part; she's positioned almost right in front of center stage.

Max - Since we've been fired, we can do whatever we want. (*looking right at Jungwoo*) Check the tabloids in a few hours and you'll see what I mean.

Jungwoo, in Korean - What? What are you talking about?

Ari - (*steps between Max and Jungwoo, murmuring something that makes them both scoff*)

Kazu - (*clears throat*) Thank you again, Max. We can't actually do whatever we want, but I'll tell Hwannie how... helpful you've been.

Jesse - (*snatches Jaehwan cutout out of Kei's grasp and waves it in Max's face*)

Max - Wait, don't —

Crowd - (*laughing*)

Jenna - The tabloids? What did he do now? Dad, high alert.

Jenna's Dad - On it. This is exciting!

Jenna's Boyfriend - There's nothing on Facebook yet.

Jenna - Ian, a bunch of randos on Facebook never counts as a credible news source. Try the *Omma Gosh* people.

Jenna's Boyfriend, apparently named Ian - Shit, I forgot about them!

A posterboard sign blocks Jenna's view. The video cuts out abruptly; when it resumes, Jenna is filming from a much higher vantage point because she's sitting on Ian's shoulders.

Ian, in the background - This is important to her! Your sign is ugly anyway!

Nicky - We know you're all asking the same question: is Apollo disbanding? The answer is no.

Namgyu - Apollo is forever! Apollo and Sunshines ALWAYS!

Kei - Namgyu is right sometimes!

Crowd - *(switches to ecstatic cheering, weeping, etc)*

Jenna, Ian, and Dad - Oh, thank god!

Jungwoo - We're lucky to have fans all over the world, and we want all Sunshines to hear this from us directly.

Here, the members take turns translating in different languages. Meanwhile, Vanessa is openly weeping in the background. Her friend has taken the phone and is recording for her. She's a good friend so she zooms in on Kazu every time he speaks.

Kazu - We've had a crazy few days. We want to tell you everything, but there's not enough time tonight. You'll be hearing more about it soon. And by the way, Ari's the reason we made it through.

Namgyu - (*in Korean*) He talked so much again, haha! Need to find a charging cable! (*in English*) Our brother is very tired!

Ari Fan - OPPA YOU CAN COME SLEEP AT MY HOUSE!

Ari - (*nervous laughter*) Ah, man. I don't even know where to start with this. Thank you to everyone who caught our video and listened to what we had to say. All of it was true.

Additional Ari Fan - Ari! Why was it posted by Emma Han?

Crowd - *(general chatter because they just remembered the livestream came from Emma's account)*

Vanessa - *(sniffling)* Okay I have swerved into Ari's lane like twice in my life and I do want to know the answer to that question.

Vanessa's Friend - It was that damn *Trickster* MV.

Vanessa - Doesn't her family have a restaurant here? I thought I heard that somewhere.

Vanessa's Friend - Maybe? *(sighs)* When Trevor broke up with me, I *so* wanted to have Emma chop off all my hair.

Vanessa - Same. Except there was no way I'd ever be able to afford a haircut at that fancy salon where she used to work. She was at Isabeau LA, right?

Vanessa's Friend - Yeah, that's it. She did Tessa Fong's hair for the *Kill Me Twice* premiere, remember? That movie sucked but Tessa's hair was amazing.

Vanessa and her friend end up chatting for the next few minutes, making it difficult to hear what Ari is saying. Jenna's video is clearer.

Ari - Everything we said on that video is true and, as of tonight, Apollo is no longer represented by Emerald Entertainment.

Crowd - (*VERY LOUD GASP HEARD ALL THE WAY IN ANTARCTICA*)

Kazu - I think PR would say that we've 'amicably parted ways'.

Max - What the hell was amicable about that?

Ari - We don't know what's next for us yet, but the

most important thing is that we're here together. And we're staying together, no matter what. All of us as brothers, but also Apollo and our fans.

Jesse - We don't need a piece of paper to tell us we're brothers! That's a Jaehwan original, and there *will* be shirts!

Ari - We'll keep going. Thank you for trusting in us. Thank you for your time and your love.

All Members Except Max - WE BELONG TO OUR FANS!

Max - WE'RE FUCKING FREE!

Crowd - (*thunderous applause, cheering, crying*)

Ari - Our, um, substitute manager found us a guitar. How about a song?

EPILOGUE

Two Nights Later

Jiyeon waits with her brother in a plain black van. Compared to the motley assortment parked in this beachside lot, their vehicle is like a hole in the universe, a patch of night sliced out of the sky and outfitted with wheels. Its windows are lightless voids. Through the tinted glass, she watches an endless succession of waves come rolling to shore.

She's taken the middle row. Her legs are tucked beneath her, a paper cup cradled in one hand. Hot chocolate has been acquired from a cart over by the pier, along with churros that she and Denny have long since devoured. "Do I want to know where you got this thing?" Jiyeon asks him now, drumming her fingers on the center console.

From the driver's seat, Denny gives a noncommittal grunt in response. "Pulled a few strings."

"Only a few strings, because mysterious black vans are a dime a dozen, I guess."

"Hey, I only needed two. Believe me, it was a lot easier than convincing Mom that all ten Ryans were not, in fact, gonna fit in our apartment." He pauses. "Eleven Ryans. Whatever. Too many brothers."

"Seven brothers in LA," amends Jiyeon. "One brother in Seoul, and just one Ryan." *Eunjae.* It takes effort to call him by any other name, now.

"And that one Ryan will be more than enough trouble for you all by himself," Denny shoots back. He glares at her in the rearview mirror. "I just can't believe you did that, Yeonnie. This is a mess."

She sighs. "I had to do it. If we switched places, if it had been your call, you would've done the same thing."

"First of all, I wouldn't have adopted a random pop star on a random Wednesday night!"

"So you wish we'd never met him?"

"No!" Denny drags a hand down his face. "You should've just stuck with the shop account. That plan was fine."

"A couple thousand followers wasn't enough. That video needed to be seen by as many people as possible."

They've been over this already, but he has yet to be convinced that her logic was sound. As usual with Denny, the righteous indignation might just burn eternal.

"What if you're wrong? What if it doesn't die down?"

"It will. Right now everyone wants to know why the livestream was posted from my account, but soon enough they'll stop asking. I just have to wait it out. Disappear again."

"That won't work a second time!"

But it might. All she has to do is stay resolutely out of the picture. The world wants Apollo, not Emma Han, for all the intrigue she's stirred up. The resurrection of her dead social media platform is only fascinating because it's linked to the boys.

"Plus," Denny continues, warming up to a full blown monologue, "it's not just about you anymore. Even if you never touch Instagram again, you've gotten yourself caught up in all this nonsense. Apollo's so famous that it's stupid. Their fans are freaking manic, okay? I've done the research and I need you to understand how bad this could get. It's potentially very, very, very, very bad. Ten times worse than how it was before. Especially if you keep doing stuff like coming back into the madhouse after I tried to send you out of it."

Jiyeon has no regrets about turning back instead of heading home. She hadn't dared to come close enough for a view of the stage, but she could hear Eunjae's voice when he spoke to the crowd, and she'd known from his voice that he'd won.

Denny shifts in his seat, arms crossed, staring straight ahead. "I never want to see you go through that again. I thought you were done with it."

"I am," Jiyeon insists. "This doesn't mean I'm going back to that life. It was just... something I had to do. I had to help, Den."

His shoulders go slack, the tension giving way to empathy. "Yeah, Yeonnie. I know."

"It's already been reported that my family owns a restaurant in the same shopping center where the event was held," she reminds him. "No one wants to believe this was just a coincidence, but they'll have to accept it eventually."

"Why accept it when they could just keep digging?"

Jiyeon sets her drink down in the cup holder. There is movement up ahead, figures progressing from the resort in the distance and down the deserted beach at a leisurely pace. Voices drift on the sea breeze, punctuated by laughter and raucous cheering.

"They can dig if they want to, then," she says. "There won't be anything for them to find."

"You only need to be caught with Ryan one time —"

"Caught doing what? We can't be caught if we stay away from each other from now on."

"You're gonna stay away from him."

"Yeah."

"And he's gonna stay away from you."

"Uh-huh."

Denny's laughter thunders through the van's interior like the first rumbles of an impending rockslide. He checks his watch, then pulls the key out of the ignition. "That," he declares, swiveling around to face her, "is complete horsefeathers."

"Horsefeathers?"

"You know what I mean!"

"I really don't!"

Shaking with mirth, Denny says, "Oh, man. Jesus, noona. Good luck." Then he tosses her the keys, still chuckling darkly, and climbs out of the van. "Drive it back to the pier when you're done. I'll meet you there. Ryan Kim can walk back to the hotel with his eight million brothers."

Directives issued, Denny departs from the scene. Jiyeon blinks and her brother has disappeared among the dunes. Not even a full five minutes later, Eunjae takes his place.

They move quickly. He goes for the final row, easing himself into the shadows while Jiyeon slides the door shut in his wake. The parking lot remains as it was, this end of the beach still devoid of the usual evening crowd. She feels certain no one has seen. Even so, the pair of them sit in silence for a while, half expecting to be chased out of the vehicle at any second.

Nothing happens. No cameras flash and no wild-eyed Apollo fans come crawling out of the clumps of swaying seagrass to challenge Jiyeon to a duel. She exhales the breath she's been holding and says, "Well. That was more stressful than I thought it would be."

"I think we're good. None of my brothers followed me here."

"That's your number one concern?"

He laughs a little. "Yes." But the amusement is short-lived. "I still wish you hadn't posted for us."

"But it's a good thing I did. It worked."

Somberly, Eunjae says, "Denny told me you aren't working for Olivia anymore."

"Our Woosung," sighs Jiyeon. "He always was a tattletale."

"Just worried about you. I know how that is."

She shrugs. "It's almost funny. Olivia was thrilled with me for the first time in a long, long time. So many people suddenly wanted a haircut. I had to leave before she started displaying me in the window like a zoo animal."

She doesn't want to talk about her past: the follower count and celebrity clients, the sponsorship deals, the interminable, tortured calculus of views and likes, saves and shares. The emotions retain their potency, but the memories themselves are blurred, no longer rendered in crisp technicolor. It's as if those days were lived by another person, a separate entity dwelling blithely in a parallel universe.

It was a nightmare, but she could make it look so pretty. Even better, she had a knack for making it look like it was true.

The last thing she posted as Emma was a video of the sea on a night much colder than this one. In the caption, she'd tried to explain why she was leaving. She'd promised that she was fine, she was safe, but she was never coming back. This, at long last, was supposed to be the truth.

Eunjae doesn't push her for the details. Maybe he's already scrolled through the posts in her profile, now a virtual monument to who she used to be. If she closes her eyes, Jiyeon can see that grid of photos and videos, impeccably styled, curated with such care. Here is Emma Han twisting her hair into seemingly effortless milkmaid braids. Here is Emma Han peddling $50 shampoo she doesn't even like, for a sponsorship deal that puts money into her savings account. The dream, the dream. What wouldn't she do, for the dream?

Eunjae leans forward. He tugs on her sleeve. "Thank you."

She turns around to face him, very much against her better judgment. But Eunjae is here with her, now. She hasn't seen him since that night when there was suddenly no choice but to confront the truth. How many more times will they be able to talk like this? And then she thinks, *it would always have to be like this*. Meeting in secret, dodging millions of watchful eyes.

Jiyeon rests her head in the crook of one arm, the leather upholstery grown warm against her skin. She looks up at Eunjae in the dark. "We shouldn't meet up again," she tells him. The words are also for herself.

"I know."

"This has to be the last time."

He's quiet for a while. "Do you want it to be the last time?"

Jiyeon closes her eyes. "No."

"So we have the same problem." And his relief is so palpable that she almost can't bear to try again, but she does. This is not a choice to make lightly. They can't go running headlong into it.

"I saw the video where you said you don't want to date in secret. And I understand, okay? After everything I've seen and read, I just... I know that things were already hard for you, before. Trying to make this work could make it so much worse."

His head snaps up. "Me? Never mind about me." Eunjae rakes a hand through his hair, easily the most agitated she's ever seen him. "Things were hard for you, too. You got out. You started over. I feel like I've already ruined that for you."

"You didn't ruin anything," she protests, stunned that he could even come to this conclusion.

"You've had to quit your job. The shop's been closed for two days because the fans won't stop coming. Reporters keep trying to follow you guys home."

"It won't be that way forever. We're so boring that they'll lose interest soon. When you go home —" But Jiyeon can't bring herself to finish the sentence.

"This feels like home, to me," Eunjae says. "Maybe that sounds crazy. It's true, though. And it's like... what have I done?"

Jiyeon decides that she just can't stand it anymore. She scoots close enough to poke him in the arm. "Here's what you've done. Are you listening? You pretended to have amnesia. You got yourself a new job. You washed *a lot* of dishes. You sat for hours and watched a Korean drama with terrible writing, never complaining, just because my parents love it."

The flicker of a smile flashes across his face. Jiyeon keeps going.

"You read the entire *Molly Merriweather* series in two days. You saw that Denny had secretly always wanted a brother and that's what you gave him. I told you about maybe opening some small place of my own one day, so you spent your lunch break finding me one. Other people might have looked for a busy cross street or the cheapest rent. You decided to filter by sunset views and nearby florists. Really, you're something else."

This is not what she's supposed to be doing. She was supposed to let him go and say goodbye. But how can she?

"You've done so much, Eunjae. It was magic. We're out of time now and I wish…"

"I wish we had more of it," he finishes for her.

Headlights flash around a bend, speeding towards the boardwalk, the live band, the Ferris wheel. Eunjae angles himself in her direction, and although he comes no closer, she feels as though he has.

"Yeon-ah," he says softly, reaching for her. "Let's just run away."

Jiyeon ends up laughing in spite of it all. "Oh, sure. Something we're both good at." But she slips her hand into his, and everything is so clear, everything makes perfect sense.

The breeze picks up outside the van, whistling through the seagrass, tossing the echoes of his brothers' voices like skipped rocks across the waves. Eunjae's gaze never wavers. "When I think about what I'd be putting you through, I know I shouldn't ask you to give me a chance. I know it, but I still want a chance."

"Just the one?" she asks, suddenly feeling a little lightheaded. More and more lately, his presence is like a change in altitude. Denny can never find out about this.

"I'll get it right the first time."

"And when they catch us? Because you know they will."

"We'll deny it."

"Sounds so simple," she murmurs.

"That's just how it goes. Deny for years, then turn around and announce your wedding is in three days. Everybody does it." Eunjae pauses, then adds in a hurry, "Not that we need to talk about weddings right now."

But Jiyeon just blinks at him. "You'd be willing to keep this secret…

for *years*?"

"So long as it's you. For however long you'll have me."

And how exactly was she ever supposed to argue with that?

When Jiyeon lets go of Eunjae's hand, it's only so she can climb over the seat and into his arms instead.

AUTHOR'S NOTE

Everything in the story has been written based on personal experience as a fan, with so much love but also a fair amount of research. Sometimes research meant a LOT of reading about topics such as the Hallyu wave and idol contracts. At other times, research meant scrolling through every K-pop post I've ever saved on Instagram. (Regardless, it was all very scholarly in nature.) Apollo is not based on any real K-pop groups, past or present. The members do not have equivalents in real life because I made them up, along with all their chaotic antics, and the same can be said for every other character in the book. Additionally, no idols or industry experts were involved in the writing of *This Place is Magic*.

Becoming a successful K-pop idol demands talent, endurance, dedication, and sacrifice. Idols give up their youth to the industry and to their fans in exchange for fame and fortune. They also surrender a number of other intangibles: privacy, independence, romance. Eunjae's struggles are drawn directly from reality.

Recruited at a very young age, idols begin their journey by moving to Seoul, away from their families, to train under entertainment companies which still hold a tremendous amount of power over artists today. The 'musketeer clause' written into Apollo's contracts is purely fictional. However, its stipulations are drawn from similar penalty clauses found in idol contracts past and present. It is absolutely true that aspiring idols once signed contracts spanning as long as ten years. Breaking these contracts could lead to financial ruin. While the legal arrangements between idols and their agencies have improved in many aspects, these agreements were once known as 'slave contracts' due to their intensely restrictive nature.

Artists' rights have become more central to the conversation in recent years. Groundbreaking litigation such as the contract dispute from girl group SES in 2001 and the pivotal lawsuit filed by boy group TVXQ in 2009 resulted in intervention from South Korea's Fair Trade Commission. More recently, the girl group Loona managed to emancipate themselves from their agency, Blockberry Creative, through publicized and controversial legal proceedings that lasted several years. For an example of a group leaving their agency without requiring litigation, Got7 chose to leave industry behemoth JYP Entertainment when their contracts were up for renewal in 2021. All seven members signed with seven different agencies. They refused to disband, even coordinating a group comeback in 2022 despite the many different directions they've taken in life. I suspect that K-pop contract terms will continue to evolve, face challenges, and generate news headlines.

Whether you're a fan of K-pop or not, I think it's vital to recognize that the industry can be brutal, and that idols are humans too. Personally, I love my K-pop groups and wish them well. I hope they get enough sleep, enough to eat, and the chance to actually live the romances they sing about so often. That's part of why I wanted to write about an idol in the first place — I wanted to give him a warm home, a loving family, time to rest. I wish I could give the same to all my favorite idols out there.

Lastly, I want to talk about Eunjae's beloved Miss Vivi. My

family immigrated to the United States from the Philippines when I was four years old, seeking a better life, and we know many relatives and friends who have done the same. It's very common for the breadwinner in a Filipino family to travel overseas, find a job, and send money to family back home. Often, they don't return to their loved ones in the Philippines for years and years at a stretch. My own mom left in order to find work and file with immigration to bring her family from Davao City, Philippines to San Diego, California.

It was important for me to include Miss Vivi, who poured all her love into Eunjae and was unable to do that in person for her own children. The immigrant experience looms large in my life and I seek to shed light on it wherever I can. My people's diaspora continues; it is not a set period in time. In my work as a writer, I hope to continue bringing my heritage into focus, not just for others, but also for myself.

ACKNOWLEDGMENTS

This Place is Magic became a serious project in June 2023. By serious, I mean that I decided I was going to write an entire three act storyline based on an Instagram photo of a K-pop idol wandering a random street on a summer evening. (As one does.) I wrote this story to prove to myself that I could write something again — write it all the way through, from beginning to end, even though my whole world had changed since the days when I last took a project to completion. Did I still have the magic, or had it run dry? I wasn't sure, but every night at midnight I would come sit with Eunjae, and it was proof that writing doesn't have to be agony. It was proof that writing is still magic. So I guess what I'm weirdly saying is, I would like to thank *This Place is Magic* for being magic, for me.

There are too many K-pop idols to thank for providing the soundtrack to my life since I was a teenager buying BoA albums at the Korean stationery shop in 2004. Please get lots of sleep! I care about you!

Stakeholders! With all my heart, thank you Aly, Anne, Ayana, Carrie, and Charlene for being the earliest supporters of *This Place is Magic*. You have tolerated my endless babbling about this book for months now and I have no idea why you haven't hit the Unsubscribe button on my lunacy. Some of you even read it at work and got tissue stuck to your eye. Others read 200 pages straight and tanked their iPad battery. I'm not naming names but I love you.

I'm grateful to my fake brother for all the informal Korean

lessons and waffle wisdom. Harabeoji, daebak!

Carrie read this manuscript almost as many times as I did (A LOT) and I couldn't ask for a better editor or a better friend. Additionally, the cover is a dream come true thanks to Erion (@erion.makuo) — bro, you can always find me in the Drift. And huge thanks to my actual sister for the interior artwork! WGPG!

My husband deserves a great deal of gratitude for being the reason why I can authentically write the kind of love that is comfortable and warm, funny and absurd, and why I think love is so easy. And without my four-year-old, I'd never have guessed that I could write a book to the tune of Mario brawling with Donkey Kong while a preschooler banged on a xylophone at the same time. I'd be lost without you guys.

Ayana, I wish every writer could have such an unfailing, unflagging, unstoppable one-woman cheering squad for their work. Unfortunately, I won't share. I'm bratty and insufferable. Without you, there would be no Eunjae, no Apollo, and no Han family. Once upon a time, you were a wee sixteen-year-old baby who messaged me on Tumblr that my silly story had kept you up 'til 2am. I had never received such a compliment before. You changed my life and I spade you with all my heart.

To the original Ivy Lane Apartments, painted forest green and surrounded by flowering trees — you were my first home in America. I don't know if you're still around, but I'll always remember you.

Last but not least, thank you to every single reader who gives this book a chance. I hope you know that you're magic for me, too.

DRAMATIS PERSONAE

Apollo

- **Jaehwan (Jeon Jaehwan)** - Apollo's leader and exasperated mother. Serving in the army.

- **Kazu (Ueda Kazuhiko)** - Cheapskate eldest member of Apollo; allergic to clothes.

- **Nicky (Kim Ahnjong)** - Apollo's choreographer and professional pot-stirrer.

- **Namgyu (Hong Namgyu)** - The main vocalist. His head is empty and full of sunshine!

- **Jungwoo (Park Jungwoo)** - Songwriter, composer, producer, playboy...??

- **Ari (Ari Goldsmith-Song / Song Eunjae)** - Our protagonist and head dishwasher.

- **Max (Max Lee)** - Rapper and PR nightmare. Needs to wash his mouth out with soap.

- **Kei (Moriyama Keiichi)** - Rapper who dreams of singing ballads. Craves structure.

- **Jesse (Ahn Ji-woon)** - The youngest member; career crybaby.

Wanna Waffle

- **Joey Han (Han Jin-cheol)** - Drama enthusiast, retired security officer, original gong breaker.

- **Lizzie Han (Han Bo-yeon)** - Wanna Waffle's official owner. Austen fan. Secret F1 driver??

- **Han Jiyeon (Emma Han)** - A hairstylist who adopts random K-pop idols on random Wednesday nights.

- **Denny Han (Han Woosung)** - Alas, you lack the security clearance for this information...

- **Janie Han Cortez (née Han Jihae)** - The eldest Han sibling. Lives in Spain with her husband, Sam.

- **Jeannie Vho** - Part time Wanna Waffle employee. Don't make her do things, she's a baby.

- **Evan Bautista** - Part time Wanna Waffle employee, full-time octopus expert.

Emerald Entertainment

- **Sun Soyeon** - Co-founder and majority shareholder of Emerald Entertainment.

- **Choi Haewon** - Co-founder of Emerald Entertainment. Talented but often uncredited songwriter.

- **Yoon Hyunseok** - CEO of Emerald Entertainment. *("We don't like him." - Kei)*

- **Seo Nami** - Apollo manager who's lasted the longest; she's probably *so* tired.

- **Ji Doyoung** - Apollo's least favorite manager. *("Collective groaning" - Apollo members)*

Friends & Family

- **Hazel Lim** - An actress who co-starred in Apollo's music video for *Trickster*.

- **Arthur Hong** - An estate lawyer. Jiyeon's ex-boyfriend. Eunjae's email buddy.

- **Simon Song** - Eunjae's dad. A commercial airline pilot for Qantas.

- **Leila Goldsmith-Song** - *("I have nothing to say about that woman." - Jaehwan)*

- **Ezra Goldsmith-Song** - Eunjae's little brother. Attends a fancy boarding school in Singapore.

- **Vivian Romero** - Eunjae's beloved nanny.

Yet More People!

- **Jooney Chun** - Co-host of the weekly K-pop news podcast *Omma Gosh!*

- **Frederica "Freddie" Dang** - Co-host and producer for *Omma Gosh!*

- **Maisie Chun** - *Omma Gosh!* co-host and titular mom. Specifically, Jooney's mom.

- **Sunshines** - The official name used for Apollo's fans.

ABOUT THE AUTHOR

Irene Te is a veteran K-pop fan and critically acclaimed author of cozy contemporary stories full of humor and heart. Her debut novel, *This Place is Magic*, was chosen by librarians as the best entry in contemporary fiction for the 2024 Indie Author Project and received the Grand Prize at the 32nd Annual *Writer's Digest* Self-Published Book Awards. When she's not writing, Irene works as a freelance curriculum and instructional designer. She lives in Houston, Texas with her husband and son. Generally, she loves anything ending in -cake.

You can visit Irene at **www.irenete.com** or connect with her on Instagram (**@irenewritesthings**).

THANKS
for reading!

LET'S CONNECT!

🌐 irenete.com

 @irenewritesthings

P.S. Subscribe to my **monthly email** for the latest updates and exclusive **bonus content**, including 2 extra chapters for *This Place is Magic*!

irenewritesthings.substack.com